We hope you enjoy this copy of

WHEN GOD
WAS A RABBIT

Bring this voucher into WHSmith
between 18th June and 2nd July 2015 and
get **60% OFF** Sarah Winman's new novel
A YEAR OF MARVELLOUS WAYS

Only **£6.79** RRP £16.99

**60%
OFF**
with this
voucher

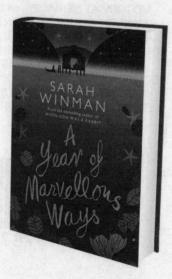

3787 6135

'Perfectly captures the hazy, magical nature of youth and all its mysteries, against a backdrop of real-life events' *Elle*

'At times laugh-out-loud funny, at others gut-wrenchingly sad, the book is peppered with unique and complex characters who are so original, well-observed and believable that you'll be completely absorbed into their world' *Easy Living*

'The characters' personal stories; those of Elly's brother, his friend Charlie, and her correspondence with her long-lost childhood playmate, Jenny Penny, are compelling throughout' *Observer*

'Gloriously offbeat . . . Winman's narrative voice is beautifully true, with a child's unsentimental clarity . . . A superb debut' *The Times*

'In the way that David Nicholls' *One Day* follows two people through their lives, this traces a family story over four decades in the most unexpected way' *Red*

'Savour the fragile beauty of the writing. Another Mark Haddon in the making? We reckon so' *Irish Times*

'It's rare to find a novel you're recommending to friends, family and colleagues by page sixty but *When God was a Rabbit* is just that kind of book . . . it's funny, recognizably true and heartbreaking in equal measure . . . A truly great book to lose yourself in' *Stylist*

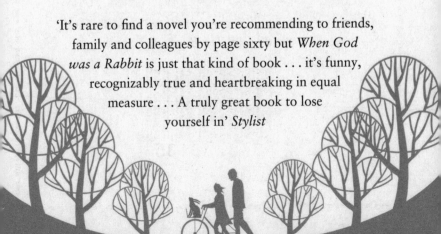

'A genuinely captivating read' *Glamour*

'Winman's characterisation is exemplary and her prose is smart and sassy, with a crisp, easygoing style similar to that of Kate Atkinson or Patrick Gale' *Waterstone's Books Quarterly*

'There are books that tug on the heartstrings, and then there are full-on tractor pulls. *When God Was a Rabbit* falls into the latter category . . . [Winman's] prose has an elegiac, simple beauty, which she uses to nimbly guide her characters through thirty-odd eventful years of history' *Globe and Mail*

'Winman pulls a good number of rabbits from her hat in a picaresque coming-of-age tale . . . [An] affecting and original debut' *Library Journal*

'A heartbreaking story of the secrets and hopes of a sister and brother who share an unshakable bond. Winman shows impressive range and vision' *Publishers Weekly*

'A story of siblings, friendship, secrets and love, told with sadness and humour' *Marie Claire*

'An exciting debut . . . a fabulously quirky novel' *Woman & Home*

'Utterly charming . . . A page-turner with a gritty plot, gently told' *The Bookseller*

'No bare-bones plot summary can do justice to this wonderfully wise and compellingly readable tale of love and friendship in all their forms, of family uncircumscribed by biological bonds, and of loss worse than death. A remarkable first novel, worth savoring' *Booklist*

'Every once in a while a book comes along that makes you grateful you can read . . . this book pulls you in and makes you want to devour it in one go' *Heat*

'A wonderful coming-of-age story . . . each character is created with a sense of depth and feeling that draws you in whole-heartedly. A cliché, but this book will have you howling with laughter one minute and reaching for the tissues the next . . . A great debut that cements Winman as an exciting new writer' *Red*

'Winman's fiction debut, spanning the late 1960s and early 2000s, boasts one of the more endearingly unconventional families in a while' *Kirkus*

'[A] dark comic tale of the push-me-pull-you of the ties that bind between two siblings, Elly and her brother Joe' *Vogue Australia*

'Tantalisingly imaginitive' *Metro*

Sarah Winman grew up in Essex. She attended the Webber Douglas Academy of Dramatic Art and went on to act in theatre, film and television. *When God was a Rabbit* is her first novel. She lives in London.

SARAH WINMAN

When God Was a Rabbit

R
headline
review

First published in 2011 by HEADLINE REVIEW
An imprint of HEADLINE PUBLISHING GROUP

First published in paperback in 2011 by HEADLINE REVIEW
An imprint of HEADLINE PUBLISHING GROUP

3

Cataloguing in Publication Data is available from the British Library

ISBN 978 0 7553 7930 9 (B format)

Typeset in Sabon by Avon DataSet Ltd, Bidford-on-Avon, Warwickshire

Printed and bound in Great Britain by Clays Ltd, St Ives plc

Headline's policy is to use papers that are natural, renewable and recyclable
products and made from wood grown in well-managed forests and other
controlled sources. The logging and manufacturing processes are expected
to conform to the environmental regulations of the country of origin.

HEADLINE PUBLISHING GROUP
An Hachette UK Company
Carmelite House
50 Victoria Embankment
London EC4Y 0DZ

www.headline.co.uk
www.hachette.co.uk

to Dad

I DIVIDE MY LIFE INTO TWO PARTS. NOT REALLY A BEFORE and After, more as if they are bookends, holding together flaccid years of empty musings, years of the late adolescent or the twentysomething whose coat of adulthood simply does not fit. Wandering years I waste no time in recalling.

I look at photographs from those years and my presence is there, in front of the Eiffel Tower maybe, or the Statue of Liberty, or knee-deep in sea water, waving and smiling; but these experiences, I now know, were greeted with the dull tint of disinterest that made even rainbows appear grey.

She featured not at all during this period and I realise she was the colour that was missing. She clasped the years either side of this waiting and held them up as beacons, and when she arrived in class that dull January morning it was as if she herself was the New Year; the thing that offered me the promise of beyond. But only I could see that. Others, bound by convention, found her at best laughable, and at worst someone to mock. She was of another world; different. But by then, secretly, so was I. She was my missing piece; my complement in play.

One day she turned to me and said, 'Watch this,' and pulled from her forearm a new fifty-pence piece. I saw the flattened edge peeking out of her skin like a staple. She didn't produce it from the air or from her sleeve – I'd seen all that before – no, she pulled it from her actual skin and left a bloody scar. Two days later the scar was gone; the fifty pence, though, still in her pocket. Now this is the part where nobody ever believes me. The date on the coin was odd. It was nineteen years hence: it was 1995.

I cannot explain the magic trick just as I cannot explain her sudden expertise in the piano that strange morning in church. She had no tutelage in these pastimes. It was as if she could will her mind into talent and, through the willing, achieve a sudden and fleeting competency. I saw it all and marvelled. But these moments were for my eyes only: proof of some sorts, that I might believe her when the time was necessary.

Part One

1968

I DECIDED TO ENTER THIS WORLD JUST AS MY MOTHER GOT off the bus after an unproductive shopping trip to Ilford. She'd gone to change a pair of trousers and, distracted by my shifting position, found it impossible to choose between patched denims or velvet flares, and fearful that my place of birth would be a department store, she made a staggered journey back to the safe confines of her postcode, where her waters broke just as the heavens opened. And during the seventy-yard walk back down to our house, her amniotic fluid mixed with the December rain and spiralled down the gutter until the cycle of life was momentously and, one might say, poetically complete.

I was delivered by an off-duty nurse in my parents' bedroom on an eiderdown that had been won in a raffle, and after a swift labour of twenty-two minutes my head appeared and the nurse shouted *Push!* and my father shouted *Push!* and my mother pushed, and I slipped out effortlessly into that fabled year. The year Paris took to the streets. The year of the Tet offensive. The year Martin Luther King lost his life for a dream.

For months I lived in a quiet world of fulfilled need. Cherished and doted on. Until the day, that is, my mother's milk dried up to make way for the flood of grief that suddenly engulfed her when she learnt her parents had died on a walking holiday in Austria.

It was in all the papers. The freak accident that took the life of twenty-seven tourists. A grainy photograph of a mangled coach lodged between two pine trees like a hammock.

There was only one survivor of the crash, the German tour guide, who had been trying on a new ski helmet at the time – the thing that had obviously saved his life – and from his hospital bed in Vienna, he looked into the television camera as another dose of morphine was administered, and said that although it was a tragic accident, they had just eaten so they died happy. Obviously the trauma of plummeting down the rocky crevasse had obliterated his memory. Or maybe a full stomach of dumplings and strudel *had* softened the blow; that is something we would never know. But the television camera stayed on his bruised face, hoping for a moment of sensitive lucidity for the heartbroken families back home, but it never came. My mother remained grief-stricken for the whole of my second year and well into my third. She had no stories to recall, no walking stories or funny first words, those events that give clues to the child that might become. The everyday was a blur; a foggy window she had no interest in wiping clear.

'What's Going On' sang Marvin Gaye, but no one had an answer.

And yet that was the moment my brother took my hand. Took me protectively into his world.

He had skirted the periphery of my early life like an orbiting moon, held between the alternate pull of curiosity and indifference, and probably would have remained that way, had Destiny not collided with a Tyrolean coach that tragic, pivotal afternoon.

He was five years older than I was, and had blond curly hair that was as unfamiliar to our family as the brand-new car my father would one day buy. He was different from other boys his age; an exotic creature who secretly wore our mother's lipstick at night and patterned my face with kisses that mimicked impetigo. It was his outlet against a conservative world. The quiet rebellion of a rank outsider.

I blossomed into an inquisitive and capable child; one who could read and spell by the age of four and have conversations usually reserved for eight year olds. It wasn't precocity or genius that had become my bedfellow, simply the influence of this older brother, who was by then hooked on the verse of Noël Coward and the songs of Kander and Ebb. He presented a colourful alternative to our mapped-out lives. And every day as I awaited his return from school, my longing became taut, became physical. I never felt complete without him. In truth, I never would.

'DOES GOD LOVE EVERYONE?' I ASKED MY MOTHER AS I reached across a bowl of celery to take the last teacake. My father looked up from his papers. He always looked up when someone mentioned God. It was a reflex, as if he were about to be hit.

'Of course he does,' my mother replied, pausing in her ironing.

'Does God love murderers?' I continued.

'Yes,' she said. My father looked at her and tutted loudly.

'Robbers?' I asked.

'Yes.'

'Poo?' I asked.

'Poo's not a living thing, darling,' she said seriously.

'But if it was, would God love it?'

'Yes, I expect he would.'

This was not helping. God loved everything, it seemed, except me. I peeled off the last curve of chocolate, exposing the white marshmallow mound and the heart of jam.

'Are you all right?' asked my mother.

'I'm not going back to Sunday school,' I said.

'Hallelujah!' said my father. 'I'm glad about that.'

'But I thought you liked it?' said my mother.

'Not any more,' I said. 'I only really liked the singing bit.'

'You can sing here,' said my father, looking back down at his papers. 'Everyone can sing here.'

'Any reason?' my mother asked, sensing my withholding.

'Nope,' I said.

'Do you want to talk about anything?' she asked quietly, reaching for my hand. (She had started to read a book on child psychology from America. It encouraged us to talk about our feelings. It made us want to clam up.)

'Nope,' I said again through a small mouth.

It had been a simple misunderstanding. All I had suggested was that Jesus Christ had been a mistake, that was all; an unplanned pregnancy.

'Unplanned indeed!' screamed the vicar. 'And where did you get such blasphemous filth, you ungodly child?'

'I don't know,' I said, 'just an idea.'

'Just an *idea*?' he repeated. 'Do you honestly think God loves those who question his Divine Plan? Well, I'll tell you, missy, he does not,' and his arm shot out and pointed towards my banishment. 'Corner,' he said, and I wandered over to the chair facing the damp, crumbling green wall.

I sat there thinking about the night my parents had crept into my room and said, 'We want to talk to you about something. Something your brother keeps saying to you. About you being a mistake.'

9

'Oh, that,' I said.

'Well, you weren't a mistake,' said my mother, 'just un-planned. We weren't really expecting you. To turn up, that is.'

'Like Mr Harris?' I said (a man who always seemed to know when we were about to sit down and eat).

'Sort of,' said my father.

'Like Jesus?'

'Exactly,' said my mother carelessly. 'Exactly like Jesus. It was like a miracle when you arrived; the best miracle ever.'

My father put his papers back into his battered briefcase and sat next to me.

'You don't have to go to Sunday school or church for God to love you,' he said. 'Or for *anyone* to love you. You know that, don't you?'

'Yes,' I said, not believing him.

'You'll understand that more as you get older,' he added. But I couldn't wait that long. I'd already resolved that if this God couldn't love me, then it was clear I'd need to find another one that could.

'WHAT WE NEED IS ANOTHER WAR,' SAID MR ABRAHAM
Golan, my new next-door neighbour. 'Men need wars.'

'Men need brains,' said his sister, Esther, winking at me as
she hoovered around his feet and sucked up a loose shoelace,
which broke the fan belt and made the room smell of burnt
rubber. I liked the smell of burnt rubber. And I liked Mr Golan.
I liked the fact that he lived with a sister in his old age and not a
wife, and hoped my brother might make the same choice when
that far-off time came.

Mr Golan and his sister had come to our street in September
and by December had illuminated every window with candles,
announcing their faith in a display of light. My brother and I
leant against our wall and watched the blue Pickford van turn
up one mild weekend. We watched crates and furniture carried
carelessly from the truck by men with cigarettes in their mouths

and newspapers in their back pockets.

'Looks like something died in that chair,' said my brother as it went past.

'How do you know?' I asked.

'Just know,' he said, tapping his nose, making out he had a sixth sense, even though the other five had proven many times to be shaky and unreliable.

A black Zephyr pulled up and parked badly on the pavement in front, and an old man got out, a man older than any man I'd ever seen before. He had goose-white hair and wore a cream corduroy jacket that hung off his frame like loose skin. He looked up and down the road before heading towards his front door. He stopped as he passed us and said, 'Good morning.' He had a strange accent – Hungarian, we later learnt.

'You're old,' I said. (I'd meant to say 'Hello'.)

'I'm as old as time,' he said, and laughed. 'What's your name?'

I told him and he held out his hand and I shook it very firmly. I was four years, nine months and four days old. He was eighty. And yet the age gap between us dissolved as seamlessly as aspirin in water.

I quickly shunned the norm of our street, swapping it instead for Mr Golan's illicit world of candles and prayers. Everything was a secret and I guarded each one like a brittle egg. He told me that nothing could be used on Saturdays except television, and when he returned from *shul* we ate exotic foods – foods I'd never tasted before – foods like matzo bread and chopped liver and herring and gefilte fish balls, foods that 'evoked memories of the old country', he said.

'Ah, Cricklewood,' he'd say, wiping a tear from his blue, rheumy eyes, and it was only later at night that my father would sit on my bed and inform me that Cricklewood bordered neither Syria nor Jordan, and it certainly didn't have an army of its own.

'I am a Jew,' Mr Golan said to me one day, 'but a man above all else,' and I nodded as if I knew what that meant. As the weeks went by I listened to his prayers, to the *Shema Yisrael*, and believed that no God could fail to answer such beautiful sounds, and often he would pick up his violin and let the notes transport the words to the heart of the Divine.

'You hear how it weeps?' he said to me as the bow glided across the strings.

'I do, I do,' I said.

I would sit there for hours listening to the saddest music ears could bear, and would often return home unable to eat, unable even to talk, with a heavy pallor descending across my young cheeks. My mother would sit next to me on my bed and place her cool hand on my forehead and say, 'What is it? Do you feel ill?' But what could a child say who has started to understand the pain of another?

'Maybe she shouldn't spend so much time with Old Abraham,' I heard my father say outside my door. 'She needs friends her own age.' But I had no friends my own age. And I simply couldn't keep away.

'The first thing we need to find,' said Mr Golan, 'is a reason to live,' and he looked at the little coloured pills rolling around in his palm and quickly swallowed them. He began to laugh.

'OK,' I said, and laughed too, although the ache in my stomach would years later be identified by a psychologist as nerves.

He then opened the book he always carried and said, 'Without a reason, why bother? Existence needs purpose: to be able to endure the pain of life with dignity; to give us a reason to continue. The meaning must enter our hearts, not our heads. We must understand the meaning of our suffering.'

I looked at his old hands, as dry as the pages he turned. He wasn't looking at me but at the ceiling, as if his ideals were already heaven-bound. I had nothing to say and felt compelled to remain quiet, trapped by thoughts so hard to understand. My leg, however, soon started to itch; a small band of psoriasis, which had taken refuge under my sock, was becoming heated and raised, and I urgently needed to scratch it – slowly to start with – but then with a voracious vigour that dispelled the magic in the room.

Mr Golan looked at me, a little confused.

'Where was I?' he said.

I hesitated for a moment.

'Suffering,' I said quietly.

'Don't you see?' I said later that evening, as my parents' guests huddled silently around the fondue burner. The room fell silent, just the gentle gurgling of the Gruyère and Emmental mix and its fetid smell.

'He who has a *why* to live for, can bear almost any *how*,' I said solemnly. 'That's *Nietzsche*,' I continued with emphasis.

'You should be in bed, not wondering about death,' said Mr Harris, who lived in number thirty-seven. He'd been in a bad mood since his wife left him the previous year, after her brief affair with (whispered) 'another woman'.

'I'd like to be Jewish,' I pronounced, as Mr Harris dipped a large hunk of bread into the bubbling cheese.

'We'll talk about it in the morning,' said my father, topping up the wine glasses.

My mother lay down with me on my bed, her perfume tumbling over my face like breath, her words smelling of Dubonnet and lemonade.

'You said I could be anything I wanted when I was older,' I said.

She smiled and said, 'And you can be. But it's not very easy to become Jewish.'

'I know,' I said forlornly. 'I need a number.'

And she suddenly stopped smiling.

It had been a fine spring day, the day I actually asked him. I'd noticed it before, of course, because children would. We were in the garden and he rolled up his shirtsleeves and there it was.

'What's that?' I said, pointing to the number on the thin translucent skin of his underarm.

'That was once my identity,' he said. 'During the war. In a camp.'

'What kind of camp?' I asked.

'Like a prison,' he said.

'Did you do something wrong?' I said.

'No, no,' he said.

'Why were you there, then?' I asked.

'Ahh,' he said, raising his index finger in front of himself. 'The big question. Why were we there? Why were we there indeed?'

I looked at him, waiting for the answer; but he gave none. And then I looked back at the number: six digits, standing out harsh and dark as if they had been written yesterday.

'There's only one story that comes out of a place like that,' Mr Golan said quietly. 'Horror and suffering. Not for your young ears.'

'I'd like to know, though,' I said. 'I'd like to know about horror. And suffering.'

And Mr Golan closed his eyes and rested his hand on the numbers on his arm, as if they were the numbers to a safe and one he rarely opened.

'Then I will tell you,' he said. 'Come closer. Sit here.'

My parents were in the garden fixing a birdhouse to the sturdy lower branch of the apple tree. I listened to their laughter, to their shrieks of command, to the 'Higher' 'No, lower' of clashing perspectives. Normally I would have been outside with them. It was a task that would have thrilled me once, the day being so fine. But I'd become quieter those last couple of weeks, gripped by an introversion that steered me towards books. I was on the sofa reading when my brother opened the door and leant awkwardly in the doorframe. He looked troubled; I could always tell because his silence was flimsy and craved the dislocation of noise.

'What?' I said, lowering my book.

'Nothing,' he said.

I picked up my book again and as soon as I did he said, 'They're going to cut my knob off, you know. Or part of it. It's called a circumcision. That's why I went to the hospital yesterday.'

'What part?' I asked.

'Top bit,' he said.

'Will it hurt?'

'Yeah, probably.'

'Why are they going to do that, then?'

'The skin's too tight.'

'Oh,' I said, and must have looked confused.

'Look,' he said, a little more helpfully. 'You know that blue

16

roll-neck jumper you've got? The one that's too small?'

'Yes.'

'Well, you know when you tried to put your head through and you couldn't and it got stuck?'

'Yes.'

'Well, your head's like my knob. They've got to cut off the skin – the roll-neck part – so the head can be free.'

'And make a round neck?' I said, sounding much clearer.

'Sort of,' he said.

He hobbled around for days, swearing and fiddling with the front of his trousers like the madman who lived in the park; the man we were told never to go near, but always did. He recoiled at my questions and my request for a viewing, but then one evening about ten days later, when the swelling had subsided and we were playing in my bedroom, I asked him what it was like.

'Happy with it?' I said, finishing the last of my Jaffa cake.

'I think so,' he said, trying to suppress a smile. 'I look like Howard now. I have a Jewish penis.'

'Just like Mr Golan's penis,' I said, lying back onto my pillow, unaware of the silence that had immediately filled the room.

'How do you know about Mr Golan's penis?'

A pale sheen now formed across his face. I heard him swallow. I sat up. Silence. The faint sound of a dog barking outside.

Silence.

'How do you know?' he asked again. 'Tell me.'

My head pounded. I started to shake.

'You mustn't tell anyone,' I said.

He stumbled out of my room and took with him a burden that,

in reality, he was far too young to carry. But he took it nevertheless and told no one, as he had promised. And I would never know what actually happened when he left my room that night, not even later; he wouldn't tell me. I just never saw Mr Golan again. Well, not alive, anyhow.

He found me under the covers, breathing in my nervous, cloying stench. I was fallen, confused, and I whispered, 'He was my friend,' but I couldn't be sure if it was my voice any more, not now that I was different.

'I'll get you a proper friend,' was all he said as he held me in the darkness, as defiant as granite. And lying there coiled, we pretended that life was the same as before. When we were both still children, and when trust, like time, was constant. And, of course, always there.

MY PARENTS WERE IN THE KITCHEN, BASTING THE TURKEY. The meaty roast smells permeated the house and made both my brother and I nauseous, as we attempted to finish off the last two chocolates from a box of Cadbury's Milk Tray. We were standing in front of the Christmas tree, the lights dangerously flickering and buzzing due to a faulty connection somewhere near the star (something my mother had already warned me not to touch with wet hands). We were frustrated, looking at the piles of unopened presents scattered about underneath, presents we weren't allowed to touch until after lunch.

'Only another hour to go,' said my father as he skipped into the living room dressed as an elf. His youthful features stood out from under his hat, and it struck me that he looked more like Peter Pan than an elf: eternal boy rather than spiteful sprite.

My father was into dressing up. He took it seriously. As seriously as his job as a lawyer. And every year he liked to surprise us with a new festive character, and one that would remain with us throughout the Christmas period. It was like having an unwanted guest forcibly placed amidst our lives.

'Did you hear me?' my father said. 'Only another hour till lunch.'

'We're going outside,' said my brother sullenly.

We were bored. Everyone else on our street had already opened their gifts and were parading the Useful and the Useless in front of our envious eyes. We sat dejectedly on the damp front wall. Mr Harris ran past, showing off his new tracksuit, a tracksuit that unfortunately showed off too many parts of him.

'It's from my sister Wendy,' he said before unnecessarily sprinting down the road, arms splayed out wide towards an imaginary finishing post.

My brother looked at me. 'He hates his sister Wendy.'

I thought she couldn't much like him, as I watched the purple, orange and green flash disappear round the corner, narrowly missing Olive Binsbury and her crutch.

'Lunch!' shouted my father at three minutes to two.

'Come on then,' said my brother. 'Once more unto the breach.'

'Once more where?' I said, as he led me towards the dining room and the scent of my parents' selfless and enthusiastic offerings.

It was the box I saw first; an old cardboard television box that obscured my brother's head and made his feet tap out their way like white sticks.

'Am I nearly there yet?' he said, heading towards the table.

'Nearly,' I said.

He placed the box down on the table. I could smell the fecund dampness of straw. The box moved jerkily, but I wasn't scared. My brother opened the flaps and pulled out the biggest rabbit I'd ever seen.

'I said I'd get you a proper friend.'

'It's a rabbit!' I said with piercing delight.

'A Belgian hare, actually,' he said, rather brotherly.

'A Belgian hare,' I repeated quietly, as if I'd just said words that were the equivalent to *love*.

'What do you want to call it?' he asked.

'Eleanor Maud,' I said.

'You can't name it after you,' my brother laughed.

'Why not?' I said, a little deflated.

'Because it's a boy,' he said.

'Oh,' I said, and I looked at its chestnut-brown fur and its white tail and the two little droppings that had fallen from his arse, and thought that he did indeed look like a boy.

'What do you think I should call him then?' I asked.

'*God*,' said my brother grandly.

'Smile!' said my father, pointing his new Polaroid camera in front of my face. FLASH! The rabbit struggled in my arms as temporarily I went blind.

'You OK?' asked my father as he excitedly placed the film under his arm.

'Think so,' I said, walking into the table.

'Come on, everyone! Come and watch this,' he shouted, and we huddled around the developing image, saying, 'Ooh' and 'Ahh' and 'Here she comes', as I watched my blurred face sharpen into focus. I thought the new, short haircut that I'd pleaded for looked odd.

'You look beautiful,' said my mother.

'Doesn't she?' said my father.

But all I could see was a boy, where once I would have been.

JANUARY 1975 WAS SNOWLESS AND MILD. A DRAB, uninspiring month that left sledges unused and resolutions unsaid. I tried most things to delay my imminent return to school, but eventually I passed through those heavy, grey doors with the sullen weight of Christmas Past pressed firmly on my chest. This would be a *dull* term, I concluded, as I dodged airless pools of malignant torpor. Colourless and *dull*. Until I turned the corner, that is, and there she was; standing outside my classroom.

It was her hair I noticed first, wild and dark and woolly, and breaking free from the ineffectual Alice band that had slipped down onto her shiny forehead. Her cardigan was too long – handmade and handwashed – stretched at the last wringing out, and it hung down by her knees and was only a little shorter than the grey school skirt we were all forced to wear. She didn't notice me as I walked past her, even when

I coughed. She was staring at her finger. I looked back; she'd drawn an eye on the skin at the tip. Practising hypnosis, she would later say.

I held up the final picture of my rabbit to the bewildered faces of my classmates.

'. . . And so at Christmas, god finally came to live with me,' I ended triumphantly.

I paused, big smile, waiting for my applause. None came and the room fell silent, unexpectedly went dark; the overhead lights useless and straining and yellow against the storm clouds gathering outside. All of a sudden, the new girl, Jenny Penny, started to clap and cheer.

'Shut up!' shouted my teacher, Miss Grogney, her lips disappearing into a line of non-secular hatred. Unknown to me, she was the product of missionaries who had spent a lifetime preaching the Lord's work in an inhospitable part of Africa, only to have found that the Muslims had got there first.

I started to move towards my desk.

'Stay there,' said Miss Grogney firmly, and I did, and felt a warm pressure build in my bladder.

'Do you think it's right to call a hare—' Miss Grogney started.

'It's a rabbit, actually,' interrupted Jenny Penny. 'It's just called a Belgian—'

'Do you think it's right to call a rabbit *god*?' Miss Grogney went on with emphasis.

I felt this was a trick question.

'Do you think it's right to say, "I took *god* out on a lead to the *shops*"?'

'But I did,' I said.

'Do you know what the word "blasphemy" means?' she asked.

I looked puzzled. It was that word again. Jenny Penny's hand shot up.

'Yes?' said Miss Grogney.

'Blasphemy means stupid,' said Jenny Penny.

'Blasphemy does not mean *stupid*.'

'What about rude, then?' she said.

'It *means*,' said Miss Grogney loudly, 'insulting God or something *sacred*. Did you hear that, Eleanor Maud? Something *sacred*. You could have been stoned if you'd said that in another country.'

And I shivered, knowing full well who'd have been there to cast the first one.

Jenny Penny was waiting at the school gates, hopping from one foot to another, playing in her own spectacular world. It was a strange world, one that had already provoked the cruelty of whispers by morning's end, and yet it was a world that intrigued me and crushed my sense of normality with the decisiveness of a fatal blow. I watched her wrap a see-through plastic rain bonnet around the mass of frizzy curls that framed her face. I thought she was waiting for the rain to stop, but actually she was waiting for me.

'I've been waiting for you,' she said.

I blushed.

'Thanks for clapping,' I said.

'It was really good,' she said, hardly able to open her mouth due to the tightness of her bow. 'Better than everyone else's.'

I unfolded my pink umbrella.

'That's nice,' she said. 'My mum's boyfriend's going to buy me one of them. Or a ladybird one. If I'm good, that is.'

But I wasn't that interested in umbrellas any more, not now

that she'd mentioned a different word.

'Why's your mum got a boyfriend?' I said.

'Because I don't have a dad. He ran away before I was born.'

'Gosh,' I said.

'I call him "my uncle", though. I call all my mum's boyfriends my uncles.'

'Why?'

'Easier. Mum says people judge her. Call her names.'

'Like what?'

'Slag.'

'What's a slag?'

'A woman who has a lot of boyfriends,' she said, taking off her rain bonnet and inching under my umbrella. I shuffled over and made room for her. She smelt of chips.

'Fancy a Bazooka?' I asked, holding the gum out in my palm.

'No,' she said. 'I almost choked last time I had one. Almost died, my mum said.'

'Oh,' I said, and put the gum back in my pocket, wishing I'd bought something less violent instead.

'I'd really like to see your rabbit, though,' Jenny Penny said. 'Take it out for a walk. Or a hop,' she added, doubling over with laughter.

'All right,' I said, watching her. 'Where do you live?'

'In your street. We moved there two days ago.'

I quickly remembered the yellow car everyone was talking about, the one that arrived in the middle of the night pulling a dented trailer.

'My brother will be here in a minute,' I said. 'You can walk home with us, if you like.'

'All right,' she said, a slight smile forming on her lips. 'Better than walking home by myself. What's your brother like?'

'Different,' I said, unable to find a more precise word.

'Good,' she said, and started once again to hop from one foot to the glorious other.

'What are you doing?' I said.

'Pretending I'm walking on glass.'

'Is it fun?'

'Try it if you like.'

'OK,' I said, and I did. And it strangely was.

WE WERE WATCHING *THE GENERATION GAME*, SHOUTING, 'Cuddly toy, cuddly toy,' when the doorbell rang. My mother got up and was gone for quite a while. She missed most of the conveyor belt bit, the good bit, and when she came in she ignored us and went over to my father and whispered in his ear. He stood up quickly and said, 'Joe, look after your sister. We're going next door. We won't be long.'

'OK,' my brother said, and we waited for the front door to slam before he looked at me and said, 'Come on.'

The night was cold and urging frost, and much too harsh for slippered feet. And we crept nimbly in the shadow of the hedge until we reached Mr Golan's front door, thankfully still on the latch. I paused in the doorway – three months since I'd last crossed it; since I began to avoid my parents' questions and his pleading, rheumy eyes – my brother offered his hand, and together we passed through the hallway, with its smell of old coats and stale meals, and headed towards the kitchen where the sound of subdued voices lured us like flickering bait.

My brother squeezed my hand. 'All right?' he whispered.

The door was ajar. Esther was seated on a chair and my mother was talking on the telephone. My father had his back to us. No one noticed our entrance.

'We think he took his own life,' we heard our mother say. 'Yes. There are tablets everywhere. I'm a neighbour. No, you were talking to his sister before. Yes, we'll be here. Of course.'

I looked at my brother. He turned away. My father moved towards the window, and it was then that I saw Mr Golan again. But this time he was lying on the floor; legs together, one arm out straight, the other bent across his chest as if he'd died practising the tango. My brother tried to hold me back, but I escaped his hand and crept closer.

'Where's his number?' I said loudly.

They all turned to look at me. My mother put down the receiver.

'Come away, Elly,' my father said, reaching towards me.

'No!' I said, pulling away. 'Where's his number? The one on his arm? Where is it?'

Esther looked at my mother. My mother turned away. Esther opened her arms, 'Come here, Elly.'

I went to her. Stood in front of her. She smelt of sweets. Turkish delight, I think.

'He never had a number,' she said softly.

'He did. I saw it.'

'He never had a number,' she repeated quietly. 'He used to draw the numbers on himself, whenever he felt sad.'

And it was then that I learnt that the numbers, which looked as if they had been drawn on yesterday, probably had been.

'I don't understand,' I said.

'Nor should you,' said my father angrily.

'But what about the horror camps?' I asked.

Esther placed her hands on my shoulders. 'Oh, those camps were real and the horror was real, and we must never forget.'

She pulled me towards her; her voice faltered a little. 'But Abraham was never there,' she said, shaking her head. 'Never there. He was mentally disturbed,' she added, as casually as if she'd been talking about a new hair colour. 'He came to this country in 1927 and he had a happy life. Some may say a selfish life. He travelled a lot with his music and had great success. If he kept taking his tablets, then he was my old Abe. But if he stopped – well, he became a problem; to himself, to others . . .'

'Then why did he tell me all those things?' I said, tears streaming down my cheeks. 'Why did he *lie* to me?'

She was about to say something when she suddenly stopped and stared at me. And I believe now that what she saw in my eyes, what I saw in hers – the *fear* – was the realisation that she knew what had happened to me. And so I offered my hand, to her the lifeline.

She turned away.

'Why did he lie to you?' she said hastily. 'Guilt, that's all. Sometimes life gives you too much good. You feel unworthy.'

Esther Golan let me drown.

MY MOTHER BLAMED IT ON SHOCK, A DELAYED REACTION to the sudden loss of her parents. That was how her lump had started, she said, as she placed the Bakewell tart onto the kitchen table and handed us the plates. The trigger of unnatural energy, she said, that whirls and gathers momentum until one day, when you are drying after a bath, you feel it sitting there within your breast and you know it shouldn't be there but you ignore it until months go by and the fear adds to its size and then you sit in front of a doctor and say, 'I've found a lump,' as you start to unbutton your cardigan.

My father believed it was a cancerous lump, not because my mother was genetically prone to such a thing, but because he was looking out for the saboteur of his wonderful life. He'd started to believe that goodness was finite and even a glass that was once half full, could suddenly become half empty. It was strange to watch his idealism turn so rapidly to slush.

My mother wouldn't be away for long, a few days at most, for the biopsy and the assessment, and she packed with a calm assurance as if she was going away on holiday. Only her best clothes went with her, perfume too, even a novel – one she would describe as a good read. Shirts were folded with a small sachet of lavender pressed between the cotton and the tissue paper, and doctors would soon exclaim, 'You smell lovely. It's lavender, isn't it?' And she would nod to the medical students crowded around her bed, as one by one they offered their diagnosis of the growth that had taken illicit refuge.

She placed a pair of new pyjamas into her tartan overnight bag. I ran my hand over the fabric.

'It's silk,' my mother said. 'A present from Nancy.'

'Nancy buys you nice presents, doesn't she?' I said.

'She's coming to stay, you know.'

'I know,' I said.

'To help Daddy look after you.'

'I know.'

'That's good, isn't it?' she said.

(It was that book again; the chapter called: 'Hard Things to Tell Small Children'.)

'Yes,' I said quietly.

It was strange, her going away. Her presence in our young lives had been unequivocal, unfailing. Always there. We were her career, and long ago had she given up that other world, choosing instead to watch over us night and day in constant vigilance – her shield, she would one day tell us, against a policeman at the door, a stranger on the telephone, a sombre voice announcing that life had once again been torn apart: that unmendable rip that starts at the heart.

I sat on the bed, noting her qualities in a way most people would have reserved for an epitaph. My fear was as silent as her multiplying cells. My mother was beautiful. She had lovely hands that lifted the conversation when she spoke, and had she been deaf, her signing would have been as elegant as a poet speaking verse. I looked at her eyes: blue, blue, blue; same as mine. I sang the colour in my head until it swamped my essence like sea water.

My mother stopped and stretched and gently placed her hand on her breast; maybe she was saying goodbye to the lump, or imagining the cut. Maybe she was imagining the hand reaching in. Maybe I was.

I shuddered and said, 'I've got a lump too.'

'Where?' she asked.

And I pointed to my throat, and she pulled me to her and held me, and I smelt the lavender that had escaped her shirts.

'Are you going to die?' I asked, and she laughed as if I'd told her a joke, and that laughter meant more to me than any *No*.

Aunt Nancy didn't have any children. She liked children, or at least she said she liked us, and I often heard my mother say there was really no room in Nancy's life for children, which I found quite odd, especially since she lived alone in quite a large flat in London. Nancy was a film star; not a massive one, by today's standards, but a film star none the less. She was also a lesbian, and was defined as much by that as she was by her talent.

Nancy was my father's younger sister, and she always said that he got the brains *and* the looks and she got whatever was left over, but we all knew that was a lie. When she flashed her film-star smile I could see why people were in love with her, because we all were actually, just a bit.

She was mercurial; her visits often fleeting. She'd simply turn up – sometimes out of nowhere – a fairy godmother whose sole purpose was to make things right. She used to share my bedroom when she stayed over and I thought life was brighter with her around. She made up for the blackouts the country was suffering from. She was generous, kind, and always smelt divine. I never knew the scent; it was just her. People said I looked like her and although I never said it, I loved the fact that I did. One day my father said that Nancy had grown up too quickly. 'How can you grow up too quickly?' I'd asked. He told me to forget it but I never did.

At the age of seventeen Nancy joined a radical theatre group and travelled around the country in an old van, performing improvised plays in pubs and clubs. Theatre was her first love, she used to say on chat shows, and we would huddle round the television and burst into laughter and shout, 'Liar!' because we all knew that it was Katherine Hepburn who was really her first love. Not *the* Katharine Hepburn, but a world-weary heavy-set stage manager who declared unencumbered love to her after a performance of their unpromising two-act play, *To Hell and Back and That's OK*.

They were in a small village just outside Nantwich and their first encounter took place down the back alley of the Hen and Squirrel; it was a place usually reserved for urination but on that night, Nancy said, there was only the smell of romance in the air. They were walking side by side, carrying props back to the van when Katherine Hepburn suddenly pushed Nancy into the pebble-dashed wall and kissed her, tongues and all, and Nancy dropped her box of machetes and gasped at the speed of this feminine assault. Describing it afterwards, she said, 'It felt so natural and sexy. Just like kissing myself' – the ultimate accolade for an award-winning actress.

My father had never met a lesbian before, and it was unfortunate that K. H. should be his first, because his liberal

34

cloak was pulled away to reveal an armoury of caricatured prejudice. He could never understand what Nancy saw in her, and all she ever said was that K. H. had amazing inner beauty, which my father said must be extremely hidden, since an archaeological dig working round the clock would probably have found it hard to discover. And he was right. She *was* hidden; hidden behind a birth certificate that said Carole Benchley. She was a self-confessed cinephile whose knowledge of films was surpassed only by her knowledge of mental health care within the NHS; a woman who frequently tiptoed across the celluloid line that kept Dorothy on the Yellow Brick Road and the rest of us tucked up safely in bed.

'Sorry I'm late!' shouted Nancy one day, as she rushed into a café to meet her.

'Frankly, my dear, I don't give a damn,' said K. H.

'That's all right then,' said Nancy, sitting down.

Then looking round, and with raised voice, K. H. said, 'Of all the gin joints in all the towns, in all the world, she walks into mine.'

Nancy noticed the people in the café staring at them.

'Fancy a sandwich?' she said quietly.

'If I have to lie, steal, cheat or kill, as God is my witness, I'll never be hungry again.'

'I'll take that as a yes then,' said Nancy, picking up a menu.

Most people would have instantly recognised the joyous pact that had been made with lunacy, but not Nancy. She was young and ever the adventurer, and went with the excitement of her first stirrings of lesbian love.

'She was a great lover, though,' my aunt used to say, at which point either my mother or father would stand up and say, 'Anyway . . .' and my brother and I would wait for the rest, but there never was any more, not until we were older, *anyway . . .*

I'd never known my father to cry before, and the night after my mother left would be his first. I sat at the bottom of the stairs eavesdropping on the conversation, and I heard his tears stutter between his words.

'But what if she dies?' he said.

My brother crept down the stairs and sat next to me, wrapping us both in a blanket still warm from his bed.

'She's not going to die,' Nancy said commandingly.

My brother and I looked at each other. I felt his heart beat faster, but he said nothing; held me tighter.

'Look at me, Alfie. She's not going to die. Some things I know. You have to trust. This is not her time.'

'Oh God, I'll do anything,' my father said, '*anything*. I'll be anything, *do* anything, if only she'll be all right.'

And it was then that I witnessed my father's first bargain with a God he never believed in. The second would come nearly thirty years later.

My mother didn't die and five days later she returned to us looking better than we'd seen her in years. The biopsy had been a success and the benign lump quickly removed. I asked to see it – I'd imagined it black like coal – but my brother told me to shut up, said I was being weird. Nancy cried the moment my mother walked through the door. She cried at odd times and that was what made her a good actress. But in his room later that night, my brother told me it was because she had been secretly in love with my mother since the first time they had met.

He told me that she had gone to Bristol to spend the weekend with her brother (our father, of course) who was in his last year at university there. They had gone walking along the Mendip

Hills, and when the numbing cold had entered their bones, they in turn entered a pub and sat, dazed, in front of a roaring hearth.

Nancy was at the bar ordering a beer and a lemonade when a young woman, soaked to the skin, barrelled through the door, and headed over to where she was standing. Nancy was transfixed. She watched the young woman order a Scotch, watched her down it in one. Watched her light a cigarette. Smile.

They were soon in conversation. Nancy learnt that the woman's name was Kate, and her pulse flared at the solid sound of her name. She was in her second year, studying English, and had just finished with a boyfriend the previous week – bit of a dullard, she said – and she laughed and threw her head back, revealing the soft down of her neck. Nancy gripped the bar and blushed as the sudden weakness in her legs moved north. And that was the exact moment she decided that if she couldn't have this woman, then her brother should.

'Alfie!' she screamed. 'Come here and meet someone really nice!'

And so it was Nancy who did the courting for my father during his final break from university. It was Nancy who delivered the flowers to my mother, Nancy who made the phone calls and Nancy who made the reservations for the clandestine dinners. And finally it was Nancy who wrote the poems that my father never knew about, the ones that made my mother fall in love with him and 'reveal' the hidden depths to his oft stagnant emotions. By the time the new term started, my father and mother were head over heels in love, and Nancy was a confused fifteen year old limping away on the uneven surface of a bruised heart.

'Is she still in love with her?' I asked.

My brother sighed. 'Who knows?'

'GOOD MORNING,' SAID NANCY, OPENING HER EYES TO THE dull November morn.

'Hello,' I said.

'What's up?' she said, rolling over and meeting my face.

'It's the auditions today,' I said to her quietly, placing my red and blue school tie over my head.

'What auditions?' she said, quickly sitting up.

'For the Nativity play,' I said.

'I didn't know you were interested in that.'

'I wasn't, but Jenny Penny persuaded me.'

'What part are you going up for?' Nancy asked.

'Mary, Joseph, the usual,' I said. 'The *lead*.' (Omitting baby Jesus since it was a nonspeaking part and also I didn't know if I'd been forgiven for saying he was a mistake.)

'What do you have to do in the audition?' she asked.

'Just stand there,' I said.

'Nothing more?'

'Nope,' I said.

'You sure?'

'Yes, Jenny Penny said so,' I said. 'She said they can tell star quality just by that. She said it's in my jeans.'

'OK then. Well, good luck, angel,' she said, leant across to her bedside table and opened the drawer.

'Take these,' she said. 'For luck. They exude star quality and always work for me.'

I'd never heard her use the word *exude* before. I would use it later that day.

I walked briskly to the end of the road where a large privet hedge had made its home. It was where I always met Jenny Penny to walk to school; we never met at her house because it was difficult at her house, something to do with her mum's new boyfriend. She got on OK with him, she said, when her mum was there. But her mum wasn't always there, you see; she was often at funerals now, a new hobby that she had recently embraced. I guessed her mum simply liked to cry.

'Laughing? Crying? It's all the same really, isn't it?' said Jenny Penny.

I didn't think it was but I didn't say anything. Even then I knew her world was different from mine.

I looked up the road and saw Jenny Penny running towards me with a shimmering line of moisture hanging off her plump upper lip.

'Sorry I'm late,' she said.

She was always late because she had unmanageable hair.

'That's all right,' I said.

'They're nice glasses,' she said. 'Did you get them from Nancy?'

'I did,' I said proudly. 'She wears them at premieres.'

'I thought so,' said Jenny.

'They don't look too big?' I ventured.

'No, they don't,' she said. 'But they're really dark. Can you see all right?'

'Of course I can,' I said, lying, having just missed a lamppost but not unfortunately the curl of dog turd that was positioned at its base. It coated the underside of my shoe like grease and its sour smell lounged around in my nostrils.

'What's that smell?' asked Jenny, looking around.

'Winter drawing in,' I said with a heavy sigh, and I grabbed her arm and we marched towards the safety of the black iron gates.

In hindsight, I probably should have taken the glasses off for my audition, because I stumbled towards the school assembly hall like an old seer.

'Sure you're OK?' said the prefect, leading me by the arm.

'Yes, I'm fine,' I said as I tripped over his shoe. The large doors opened and Jenny Penny ran out.

'How'd it go?' I asked eagerly.

'Great,' she said, giving me the thumbs up.

'What part did they give you?' I whispered.

'The octopus. Nonspeaking,' she said. 'What I wanted.'

'I didn't know there was an octopus,' I said.

'There's not,' she said. 'They asked me to be a camel. But with all the animals marching in two by two, there must have been an octopus.'

'That's Noah's Ark,' I said.

'Same thing. Still the Bible,' she said. 'They'll never know the difference.'

'Probably not,' I said, trying to be supportive.

'I'm making the costume myself,' she said, and I suddenly felt nervous.

40

As I walked into the great hall, I could barely make out the five faces seated behind the desk; but there was one face that cut through the blackness like the all-seeing eye of Horus: my old teacher, Miss Grogney. The Nativity play was her 'baby' and she boasted that she had written it all by herself; strangely omitting any mention of either Matthew or Luke.

'Eleanor Maud?' said a man's voice.

'Yes,' I said.

'Are you OK?' he asked.

'Yes,' I said.

'Are your eyes OK?' he asked.

'Yes,' I said, nervously adjusting the frames on my face.

'Don't fidget,' shouted Miss Grogney, and I waited for her to add, *You blasphemer*.

'What do you have for us?' asked the man.

'What?' I said.

'Your audition piece,' said Miss Grogney.

Panic gripped my unprepared being.

'Well?' said Miss Grogney. 'Hurry up.'

I moved slowly to the front of the stage, words floating in and out of my mind, some lucid, many random, until a group huddled together and I recognised the coherent rhythmic pattern. I couldn't remember it all, but it was one of Nancy's favourite speeches and I'd heard her practise it as religiously as a scale. I didn't understand it all, but maybe they would and I coughed and said, 'It's from the film *The Covenant** and I'm the character Jackie and I'm ready.'

* The Covenant was released earlier that year, 1975, and enjoyed a cult following due to a fetishistic sex scene in a crypt. It was directed by B. B. Barole, a young man tipped for stardom, until he was tipped over the edge by acid.

'Go ahead,' said Miss Grogney.

I took a deep breath and opened my arms.

'I know you won't pay for the shoes or even the dress. But what about the abortion, godammit! At least give me money for a bottle of gin.'

'That's enough!' screamed Miss Grogney, and she pointed her finger at me. 'You. *Wait.*'

I stood in my self-imposed darkness and watched them huddle together and whisper. I heard them say, '*Interesting*'. I heard them say, '*Great idea*'. But what I didn't hear them say was *Mary* or *Joseph*.

That night, my mother carried in her favourite casserole dish and placed it, steaming, onto the table. The kitchen was dark and candles flickered on every surface.

My mother lifted the lid. Rich dark smells of meat and onion and wine.

'I wish we could dine like this every night,' my brother said.

Dine was his new word. *Fine dining* would come next.

'Maybe we could have a séance later?' said Nancy, and my mother quickly looked at her – a look I'd seen so often – a look that said, *Bad idea, Nancy, and you'd know that if you had children.*

'You're quiet, Elly. Everything OK?' asked my mother.

I nodded. If I spoke I felt tears would tumble out onto the backs of my words. I stood up instead, mumbled something about 'forgetting to feed him' and went towards the back door. My brother handed me a torch, and with two carrots in my pocket I slipped out into the cold night.

It felt late but it wasn't; the darkness of our house made it feel late. The climbing frame cut a weird skeleton in the dusk like a spine bending backwards. It would be demolished the coming spring and used for firewood. I walked down the path towards the hutch. God was already straining at the wire; his nose was twitching, picking up the scent of my sadness as determinedly as a dog. I flicked the catch and he bundled towards me. Wisps of blue and green fur stood out in the torchlight; a good idea left over from a bored weekend when Nancy and my brother dyed his pelt and took pictures of him balanced on their heads. God loved performing as much as Nancy. I pulled him onto my lap. He felt good, he felt warm. I bent down and kissed him.

'Don't worry,' he said, in his strangled little voice. 'It'll all come good in the end. Always does.'

'OK,' I said calmly; unperturbed that it was actually the first time I'd ever heard him speak.

I saw the long striding shape of Nancy come down the path towards me. She had a cup in her hand, steam spiralling into the chill November sky.

'So tell me,' said Nancy, crouching down, 'how did it go?'

My mouth made a kind of shape, but I was too distraught to speak, so I had to whisper it instead.

'What?' she said, leaning towards me.

I cupped my hand around her ear and whispered it again.

'The innkeeper?' she said. 'The bloody innkeeper?'

I shook my head, convulsions racking my body. I looked up at her and said, 'The *blind* innkeeper.'

IT WAS THE DAY OF THE PERFORMANCE, AND SHE CREPT OUT of the backstage shadows like a giant tarantula rather than the octopus she was supposed to be, and when Miss Grogney saw her, she screamed as if her throat had been cut by the devil himself. There was no time to get Jenny Penny out of that costume and into the camel one, and so Miss Grogney told her to remain in the darkest, furthermost reach of the stage, and should she even see the flicker of a tentacle, she would suffocate her with a large plastic bag. Baby Jesus started to cry. Miss Grogney told him to shut up and called him a wet blanket.

I quickly peaked through the curtain and scanned the audience to see if my mother and Nancy were there. It was a good turnout, almost full; better than the harvest festival that had clashed so disastrously with a local football fixture, when only twenty people turned up to give thanks for what they were about to receive, which at the time ran to two dozen cans of baked beans, ten loaves and a box of windfall apples.

Nancy saw me and winked, just before Miss Grogney's firm hand landed on my shoulder and pulled me back into Christian times.

'You'll spoil the magic if you keep looking out,' she said to me.

I thought, I'm going to spoil it anyway, and my stomach knotted.

'Where are the camels?' Miss Grogney shouted.

'They've got the hump with you,' said Mr Gulliver, the new teacher, and we all laughed.

'Not funny, Mr Gulliver,' she said as she wandered off the stage and caught her toe on a sandbag.

'Good luck,' I whispered to Jenny Penny as she waddled over to the manger, casting an eerie shadow on the back wall. She turned round and gave me a huge smile. She'd even blacked out a couple of her teeth.

The lights dimmed. I felt sick. Music crackled into the auditorium. I wiped my hands on my red tunic and they left a sweaty smear. I put on my sunglasses. In the darkness I was blind. I poked one of the sheep up the arse with my white stick and he started to cry. I apologised to Miss Grogney and said I couldn't see what I was doing and she said, 'God fortunately wasn't so blind,' and I felt a shiver run down my back.

The straw in the manger smelt strong. I'd brought it from home and even though it wasn't clean, it was authentic. Michael Jacobs, who was playing Baby Jesus, had been scratching himself ever since he'd been placed in the oversized manger, and under the lighting his heavy-set features, together with a smudge of dirt, made him look as if he had a full beard. I tapped my stick and felt my way into position.

The scene with the Angel Gabriel seemed to go well and I

45

heard the audience exclaim and clap when Maria Disponera, a new Greek girl, forgot her lines and simply said, 'You there, Mary. You having baby. Go to Bef-lem.' She'd got such an important part because her parents owned a Greek restaurant and Miss Grogney was allowed to visit as much as she wanted, until she smashed plates one night when no one else was smashing plates.

The shepherds were a dozy lot and pointed in the opposite direction to the star, and as they wandered off, they appeared truculent and bored as if it was a ferret that was entering the world and not the Son of God. It looked more hopeful when the Three Kings entered, until, that is, one of them dropped his box of frankincense, which was actually a porcelain tea caddy with earl grey inside. A gasp rose up from the auditorium as his mother reached for a handkerchief and silently wept at the loss of a treasured family heirloom. He hadn't told her he was taking it. Like he didn't tell her he smoked her cigarettes. And in between her quiet sobs, a lone sheep, slow to leave the stage, emitted a sudden scream and collapsed onto its stomach as a sharp piece of broken china embedded itself into its bony knee. The Three Kings stepped over him to exit. Only Miss Grogney had the foresight to creep onto the stage in the scene change and drag the child off like some cumbersome, skinned pelt.

I was in position behind my fake door. Suddenly, I heard a knock.

'Yeees?' I said, the way Nancy had told me to say it and I opened the door and quickly stepped forward into Mary's light. The audience gasped. Nancy said I looked like a cross between Roy Orbison and the dwarf in *Don't Look Now*. I knew who neither was.

'I am Mary and this is Joseph. We have nowhere to stay. Do

46

you have room in your inn?'

My heart thumped; my tongue felt thick and heavy. *Say it, go on, say it.*

'You need a room?' I said, suddenly veering away from the script.

I saw Mary and Joseph look at each other. Miss Grogney peered from the wings at me, holding up her script and pointing to it.

'Let me think,' I said.

The silence in the theatre was thick, clawing with anticipation. My heart was beating hard, my throat tight. *Say it*, I said to myself, *say it*. And then I did.

'Yes,' I said, 'I have a room, with a lovely view at an excellent rate. Come this way, please,' and with my white stick tapping ahead, two thousand years of Christianity was instantly challenged as I led Mary (now crying) and Joseph towards a double en-suite with TV and mini bar.

And as the curtain closed for an early interval, the bearded Jesus was left forgotten in the large bassinet in the corner of the stage, looking around at all that could have been. Suddenly panicked by Jenny Penny's arachnid shadow creeping towards him, he attempted to climb from the manger, but caught his foot in his swaddling clothes and unfortunately fell forwards onto a papier-mâché rock, that Miss Grogney later told the police 'had set much harder than anyone could have imagined'.

His screams sent shudders around the auditorium, and as Jenny Penny tried to lead the audience in the opening verse of 'Joy to the World!' the first of the ambulance and police sirens could just be heard above the chords.

BABY JESUS IN COMA

That was the early headline. There was no picture of Michael Jacobs, only a picture of a weeping king, who wasn't weeping because of the accident but because his mother was telling him off for stealing. One witness commented that it was the end of Christmas for the community, but my brother said we shouldn't go that far and that Jesus would rise again. Not until Easter, said Jenny Penny, crying into a pillow.

Of course it was Miss Grogney who blamed both Jenny and me for the whole tragedy, and told the police as much, but they were having none of it. It was a Safety Issue, and as she was supervising the whole *palaver* (they actually used that word), the blame should lay fairly and squarely on her round shoulders. She would resign before the inquest, treating the whole incident as a question of faith. She'd renounce modern life and do good deeds. She'd move to Blackpool.

My mother had tried to contact Mrs Penny throughout the day and eventually *she* contacted my mother and said that she was in Southend-on-Sea eating cockles, and could my mother look after Jenny for the night. Of course, my mother said, and promptly told her all that had happened.

'I'll be there as soon as I can,' said Mrs Penny. 'Tomorrow OK?' And then like a dingo scenting blood, she added a little too eagerly, 'When's the funeral?'

'He's not dead yet,' said my mother sharply, albeit a little carelessly.

BABY JESUS DEAD

That was the late headline. My father's *Evening News* was handed around in a quiet daze. All vital signs were missing and so his atheist family had agreed to turn off the life-support machine.

'Christ, that was quick,' said Nancy. 'What were they doing? Saving electricity?'

'Not funny, Nancy,' said my mother, hiding her face. 'Not funny at all.'

But even I saw my father laugh, and my brother, and Jenny Penny swore that she saw my mother laugh as she looked up from her hot chocolate. She loved moments like that. The inclusiveness of family. I guess because she had none.

JENNY PENNY'S MOTHER WAS AS DIFFERENT FROM MINE AS any mother could be; a woman who was in fact a child herself, in constant need of the gilded approbation of a peer group, no matter how young it happened to be. 'How do I look, girls?' 'Do my hair, girls.' 'Am I pretty, girls?'

It was fun at first – like having a rather large doll to play with – but then her expectations and demands would override all, and her fierce resentment would hang in the room like a gaudy light fitting, exposing the youth she no longer had.

'"Mrs Penny" sounds so old, Elly. We're friends. Call me Hayley. Or Hayles.'

'OK, Mrs Penny, I will next time,' I said. But I couldn't.

Her everyday existence was secretive. She didn't have a job but was rarely at home, and Jenny Penny had few clues to her mother's lifestyle, except that she loved having boyfriends and loved developing various hobbies that were conducive to her lifestyle as a 'gypsy'.

'What's a gypsy?' I asked.

'People who travel from place to place,' said Jenny Penny.

'Have you done that a lot?'

'Quite a lot,' she said.

'Is it fun?' I asked.

'Not always,' she said.

'Why?'

'Because people chase us.'

'Who?'

'Women.'

They lived in a temporary world of temporary men; a world that could be broken up and reassembled as easily and as quickly as Lego. Fabric hung from most walls in staggered strips, and around the doorframe was a pattern of flowered handprints in pinks and reds, which in the dingy light looked like the bloodied hands of a crime scene searching for an exit. Rugs were strewn around the floor and in the corner perched on a Book of Nudes was a lamp with a shade made of magenta silk. It threw a brothel-like hue into the room – not that I knew about brothels at that time – but it was red and eerie and suffocating, and made me feel ashamed.

I rarely went upstairs because the current boyfriend would so often be asleep, having in common with all the others a nocturnal existence of late shifts and even later drinking. But I used to hear the footsteps above, the toilet flush, the worried look on Jenny's face.

'Shh,' she said. 'We have to be quiet.'

And it was because of this restriction that we seldom played in her room – not that there was much to play with – but she had a hammock that caught my eye, which was suspended above a flattened poster of a calm, blue sea.

'I look down, rock and dream,' she said to me proudly. 'The Lost City of Atlantis is somewhere below me. An adventure waiting for me.'

'Have you ever seen the sea before?' I asked.

'Not really,' she said, turning away, wiping off a small handprint that had smeared the centre of a mirror.

'Not even at Southend?' I said.

'Tide was out,' she said.

'It comes back, you know.'

'My mum was too bored to wait for it to come back. I could smell it, though. I think I'd like the sea, Elly. Know I would.'

Only once did I see a boyfriend. I'd gone upstairs to use the toilet and, being alone and inquisitive, I crept into Mrs Penny's room, which was warm and musty with a large mirror at the foot of the bed. I saw his back only. A naked lump of a back that was as uncouth in sleep as it probably was in wakefulness. Even the mirror didn't reveal his face, it only revealed mine as I stood hypnotised by the wall to my left, where Mrs Penny had written in lipstick 'I am me' over and over again, until the multi-coloured cursive shapes merged into a tangled mess of expression that hauntingly said, 'Am I me'.

I was transfixed by the possibility of imagination within this home, no matter how strange it appeared to be. This wasn't the quiet symmetry of *my* everyday: the rows of terraced houses with their rectangular gardens and the routines as reliable as sturdy chairs. This wasn't the world in which things matched, or even went with. This was a world devoid of harmony. This was a world of drama, where comedy and tragedy fought for space.

'There are givers and takers,' said Mrs Penny as we sat down to sweets and squash. 'I'm a giver. What are you, Elly?'

'She's a giver, Mum,' said Jenny Penny protectively.

'Women are givers, men are takers.' So said the oracle.

'My dad gives a lot,' I said. 'Gives all the time, in fact.'

'Then he's a rare bird,' she said, and quickly changed the subject to something that no one could contradict. When Jenny Penny left the room her mother reached for my hand and asked if I'd ever had my palm read. She was highly skilled at reading palms, she said, tarot cards and tea leaves too. She could read anything; it was her gypsy blood.

'Books?' I asked naïvely.

And she blushed and laughed, and her laugh sounded angry.

'Come on, girls,' she said as Jenny reappeared. 'I've had enough of your boring games, I'm taking you out.'

'Where to?' asked Jenny Penny.

'Surprise,' her mother said, in that awful singsong way of hers. 'You like surprises, don't you, Elly?'

'Um,' I said, not really sure that in her hands I did.

'Here – coats!' she said, and threw ours at us as she stormed towards the front door.

She drove badly and erratically, and used her horn as a battering ram to push in and around wherever it was necessary. The dented trailer clattered behind us and swung dangerously around corners, riding up on the pavement, missing pedestrians' feet by inches.

'Why don't we take it off?' I'd suggested at the start.

'Can't,' she said, revving into first. 'It's attached. Soldered on. Where I go, it goes. Like my girl,' and she laughed loudly.

Jenny Penny looked down at her shoes. I looked down at mine too. I saw a floor cluttered with Coca-Cola cans and tissues and sweet wrappers and something odd that looked like a flaccid balloon.

We saw the church up ahead and, without signalling, turned sharply into the car park. Horns blared. Fists were threatening.

'Fuck off!' shouted Mrs Penny as she parked badly behind the hearse: a gaudy expression of life, mocking the transport of the departed. She was asked to move. She did it begrudgingly.

'House of God,' she said. 'What does He care?'

'He doesn't,' said the funeral director. 'But we can't get the coffin out.'

We walked into church, Mrs Penny between us, holding our hands, her body bent forwards in an embodiment of sadness. She ushered us into the pew and handed round tissues. Looked up and smiled gently at the truly bereaved. She marked down the corners of the hymn book in preparation for song and threw down the hassock, on which she knelt in prayer. Her actions were fluid and graceful – professional, even? – and from her mouth came a strange whispered reverie, unstoppable even on the intake of breath, and for the first time since I'd known her, she looked as if she truly belonged.

As the church slowly filled up, Jenny Penny pulled me towards her and motioned me to follow. We slipped out and crept along the side wall until we came to a heavy wooden door that said: *Choir Room*. We entered. It was empty and felt airtight. Uncomfortable.

'Have you done this before?' I asked. 'Been to a funeral, I mean?'

'Once,' she said, not that interested. 'Look!' She wandered over to the piano.

'Have you seen a dead body before?'

'Yep,' she said. 'In a coffin. The lid was off. They made me kiss it.'

'Why?'

'God knows.'

'What did it feel like?'

'Kissing a fridge.'

She pressed a key and a clear mid-range note rang out.

'Maybe you shouldn't touch anything,' I said.

'It's all right, no one can hear,' she said, and pressed the note again. Bing, bing, bing. She closed her eyes. Breathed intently for a moment. Then brought her hands up in front of her chest and blindly laid them on the black and white keys in front.

'Do you know how to play?' I whispered.

'No,' she said, 'but I'm trying something,' and as she pressed down on the notes, I was ambushed by the most beautiful music I'd ever heard. I watched her sway, overcome. The rapture across her brow, the luminescence. I watched her *be* someone in that moment; free of the shunting, and the making-do, and the calamitous criticism that forged her way and always would. She was whole. And when she opened her eyes, I think she knew it too.

'Again,' I said.

'Don't think I can,' she said sadly.

All of a sudden organ music boomed around the church. The music was dulled by the stone walls of the room, but the heavy bass notes reverberated throughout my body, ricocheting against my ribs before barrelling into the cavern that was my pelvis.

'That'll be the coffin,' said Jenny Penny. 'Come on, let's have a look, it's really cool.' She opened the door and we caught its slow procession as it passed.

*

We sat on the wall outside and waited. The clouds were quite low, arm's length from the steeple, falling, falling. We listened to the singing. Two songs, joyous songs, hopeful songs. We knew them but didn't join in. We kicked our legs and had nothing to say. Jenny Penny reached across and held my hand. Her palm was slippery. I couldn't look at her. Our guilt and our tears were not for each other. They were for someone else that day.

'You two are *so* boring,' said Mrs Penny, as we sat in the Wimpy Bar, trying to eat lunch.

She looked refreshed and invigorated, with no sign of the morning's events clinging to her once mournful face. Normally I'd have been ecstatic eating food I rarely ate, but I couldn't even finish my beefburger or my portion of chips or the tumbler of Coca-Cola that was as big as a boot. My appetite, along with the one for life, had momentarily disappeared.

'I'm out tonight, Jenpen,' said Mrs Penny. 'Gary said he'll look after you.'

Jenny Penny looked up and nodded.

'I'm gonna have fun! Fun! Fun!' said Mrs Penny as her mouth gorged a quarter of the bun, leaving a smear of lipstick to compete with the ketchup. 'Bet you girls can't wait to grow up, eh?'

I looked at Jenny Penny. Looked at the circle of gherkin on the side of my plate. Looked at the wipe-down table. Looked at everything except *her*.

All through the evening, the visions of the tiny white coffin, not even two feet long, stayed with me. It was bedecked with pink roses and a teddy; carried in protective arms like a newborn. I never told my mother where I'd been that day, nor my father; only my brother learnt of that strange day, the day when I discovered that even babies could die.

Why were we there? Why was Mrs Penny there? Something unnatural held their world together and it was a feeling that, at that age, I couldn't yet put a word to. My brother said it was probably the braided twine of heartbreak. Of disappointment. Of regret. I was too young to disagree. Or to fully understand.

THERE HAD BEEN A BOMB BLAST ON A TUBE TRAIN LEAVING West Ham station. My father had left his meeting early and was on that train when the blast occurred. That's what he told us during the brief phone call to say he was *fine*, to say he *really* was all right and *not* to worry. And when he walked through the door that Monday evening in March, with flowers for his wife and early Easter eggs for his kids, his suit was still coated with dust and the last tread from the carriage floor. A strange smell hung about his ears – a smell that alternated between burnt matches and singed hair – and a patch of dried blood had pooled at the corner of his mouth. He'd bitten his tongue in shock, and after checking that it was miraculously still intact, he'd calmly picked himself up and wandered silently with the other passengers towards the exit doors and the fresh air beyond.

He laughed and played football in the garden with my brother. He dived to save goals and muddied his knees. He did everything to show us how far away he'd been from death. And it was only when we went to bed and decamped back down to the middle stair, that we heard the house groan, quite literally, with the deflation of his spirit.

'It's getting closer,' he said.

'Don't talk such rot,' said my mother.

'Last year, and now this. It's hunting me down.'

The previous September, he'd travelled to the Park Lane Hilton to witness passport forms for an important client, and was about to leave when a bomb tore through the foyer, killing two people and injuring countless others. And had it not been for a desperate last-minute piss he'd needed to take, he too might have been added to the casualty list that mournful week. Instead, a weak bladder had saved his life.

But as the weeks proceeded, instead of accepting that both brushes with death were in fact miracles of survival, my father convinced himself that the vengeful shadow of Justice was looming ever closer. He believed it was simply a matter of time before its jaws would shut and he would find himself a prisoner behind those gated slabs of bloody teeth, realising that all had passed. That life had, in fact, gone.

The football pools rapidly became my father's lifeline – or obsession – and a win had become so necessary to his existence that some mornings he convinced himself it had happened already. He'd sit at the breakfast table and point to a magazine and say, What house shall we buy today? This one or this one? And I'd look at this deluded man masquerading as my father and quietly reach for the toast. He'd never been bothered by money before and probably wasn't then, but the winning had become a test of faith. He simply needed proof that he was still a lucky man.

*

I chose the same numbers every week: my birthday, Jenny Penny's birthday and Christmas Day – days that were important to me. My brother never went for numbers, rather closed his eyes and allowed his pencil to hover over the grid and to move across the teams like a cup in a séance. He believed he was touched by the god of fortune or some other such notary, and that was what made him different. I said what made him different were 'those shoes' he secretly wore at night.

My mother on the other hand, chose anything. 'Let me have a look,' she used to say and I would sigh because she didn't have a method and when she said, 'Let me have a look,' I knew she was being random, and such randomness annoyed me; it was like someone carelessly colouring in an orange using only a blue pen. I was convinced that's why we never won and never would win, but my father still ticked the box that said *No publicity*, and placed it on the mantelpiece with the exact change to await its midweek collection. And as he did he left with it his pledge: Come Saturday our life will change.

That Saturday we waited for our life to change on the touchline of a rugby pitch, which seemed as good a place to be as any. It happened to be my brother's first rugby match, this boy whose idea of a contact sport had previously only been conkers, and yet here he was jumping up and down, eagerly awaiting the second half of the match like any normal boy; and normal I wasn't used to. He'd started secondary school the year before, a private school my father was paying an arm and a leg for (leaving the remaining two for my own education, he'd said) and one in which he'd reinvented himself as someone completely different from the one before. I liked them both, worrying only that the new one, with his new *normal* interests, might not like me. My feet felt the earth as fragile as eggshells.

A player ran over to my brother and whispered to him. 'Tactics,' my father said. My brother nodded and then bent down and rubbed dirt into his hands; I gasped. It was an act so unnatural and queer that I froze in anticipation of the repercussions. And yet once again there were *none*.

A piercing chill had settled on our side of the pitch, and the listless sun, which had graced us earlier, was now playing hide-and-seek behind the tall towers of council flats that dominated the sports field, and left us shivering in shadow. I tried to clap my hands together but I could hardly move. I was wedged into a coat that Mr Harris had bought for me the week before – a totally erroneous purchase that gave benefit to no one except the shop. It was the first time I'd ever worn it, and when I'd finally squeezed into it and gasped at the true horror of its visual impact, there wasn't enough time to get back out of it *and* into the car, without one of my parents purposefully breaking my arms to do so.

Mr Harris had seen it in a sale and instead of thinking: would Eleanor Maud like this coat? Would this suit Eleanor Maud? He must have thought: that ugly thing is nearly her size and won't she look stupid in it? It was white with black arms and a black back, and as tight as a knee support but less useful, and although it was keeping the cold at bay, I felt it was simply because the cold stopped as it approached me and burst into laughter, rather than by any practical means. My parents were too polite (weak) to say I didn't have to wear it. All they could say was the gesture was kind and better weather would be here soon. I said I could be dead by then.

The whistle blew and the ball was kicked into the air. My brother ran towards it, head high, never taking his eye off it as it descended; watching, instinctively veering around obstacle players, surprisingly fast, and then the jump. He hovered as he gathered the ball and then offset it with a simple flick of his wrists to the man inside. My brother had my mother's hands: he made that ball talk. I cheered and thought I'd raised my arms in the air but I hadn't, they were still stiffly by my side; ghost arms of a paralysed person.

'Come on, the blues,' shouted my mother.

'Come on, blues!' I screamed, making her jump, making her say, 'Shh.'

My brother raced down the line, ball tucked neatly under his arm. Thirty yards, twenty yards, dummy to his left.

'Come on, Joe!' I screamed. 'Go, Joe! Go, Joe!'

A tap to his ankle, he didn't fall, no one with him still; fifteen yards and he's looking around for support, the goal line in sight; and then out of nowhere, rearing from the mud, a five-headed human wall. He hit it at speed, and bone and gristle and teeth collided and bedded down with him into the blood and mud. Bodies fell on top of him, toppling from both sides until the supporters and the pitch fell silent.

The sun slowly reappeared from behind the tower and illuminated the sculpture of human rubble, under which my brother lay. I looked up at my parents; my mother had turned round unable to watch, her hands shaking, covering her mouth. My father clapped and shouted loudly, 'Well done, boy! Well done!' – an unusual response to a possible broken neck. It was obvious I was the only one to sense any danger, and so I dashed onto the pitch. I had only got halfway towards him when someone shouted, 'P-p-p pick up a Penguin!'

I stopped and looked around. People were laughing at me. Even my parents were laughing at me.

The referee peeled off the battered players, until there,

crumpled at the bottom, lay my brother, motionless, half embedded in the mud. I tried to bend towards him but was hindered by my strait-jacket, and in one momentous effort, I lost my balance and fell onto him and winded him, the force of which propelled him into a sitting position.

'Hello,' I said. 'Are you all right?'

He looked at me strangely, not recognising me.

'It's me. *Elly*,' I said, waving my hand in front of his face. 'Joe?' I said again, and instinctively slapped him across his cheek.

'Ow,' he said. 'What did you do that for?'

'I saw someone do it on the telly.'

'Why are you dressed as a penguin?' he said.

'To make you laugh,' I said.

And he laughed.

'Where's your tooth?' I said.

'I think I swallowed it,' he said.

We were the last to leave the ground, and the car was slowly heating up by the time they clambered into the back.

'Have you got enough room?' my mother asked from the front.

'Oh, yes, plenty of room, Mrs P,' said Charlie Hunter, my brother's best friend, and of course he had plenty of room because my mother had pulled her seat so far forward that her face was pressed against the windscreen like a splattered fly.

Charlie had played scrum half in the match (so I was told), and I thought it the most important position because he decided where the ball should go, and in the car on the way home I said, 'If Joe's your best friend why didn't you give him the ball more?' And laughter and a vigorous rub of my head came as my reply.

I liked Charlie. He smelt of Palmolive soap and peppermints, and looked like my brother, but just a darker version of him. It was this darkness that made him seem older than his thirteen years and a little wiser. He bit his nails like my brother, though, and as I sat between them, I watched them gnaw at their fingers like rodents.

Mum and Dad liked Charlie and always gave him a lift home after matches because his parents never came to watch him play and they thought that was sad. I thought that was lucky. His father worked for an oil company and had shunted his family back and forth from oil-rich country to oil-rich country until the natural resources of both were exhausted. His parents divorced – which I found extremely exciting – and Charlie opted to live with his father and a latchkey existence, rather than with his mother, who had recently married a hairdresser called Ian. Charlie cooked his own meals and had a television in his room. He was wild and self-sufficient, and my brother and I both agreed that should we ever be shipwrecked, it would be better if we were shipwrecked with Charlie. Around corners I leant unnecessarily in to him to see if he'd nudge me away, but he never did. And as the heat finally reached the back seats, the red in my cheeks masked the blushes I felt as I looked from Charlie to my brother and back again.

Charlie's street was the show street of an affluent suburb not far from us. Gardens were landscaped, dogs clipped and cars valeted. It was a way of life that seemed to drink the remaining dregs of my father's half-empty glass and left him wilting in the weekend traffic.

'What a lovely house,' said my mother, with not a jealous thought coursing through her mind.

She was always like that: grateful for life itself. Her glass was not only half full, it was gold plated with a permanent refill.

'Thanks for the lift,' said Charlie, opening the door.

'Any time, Charlie,' said my father.

'Bye, Charlie,' said my mother, her hand already on the seat lever, and Charlie leant across to Joe and said quietly that they'd talk later. I leant in and said I would too, but he'd already got out of the car.

That evening, the sound of football results droned in from the living room; a distant update like a shipping forecast, but not as important and certainly not as interesting. We often left the television on in the living room when we went into the kitchen to eat. It was for company, I think, as if our family had been destined to be bigger and the disconnected voice made us feel complete.

The kitchen was warm and smelt of crumpets, and the darkness from the garden strained at the window like a hungry guest. The plane tree was still bare; a system of nerves and veins stretching out into the blue-black sky. *French navy*, my mum called it; a *French-navy sky*. She turned the radio on. The Carpenters, 'Yesterday Once More'. She looked wistful, sad even. My father had been called away at the last moment, offering support and options to a rogue many would say was undeserving. My mother started to sing. She placed the celery and winkles onto the table, the boiled eggs too – my favourite – which had cracked and spewed their viscous fluids into patterns of white trailing innards around the pan.

My brother came in from his bath and sat next to me, shiny and pink from the steaming water. I looked at him and said, 'Smile,' and as if on cue he smiled, and there in the middle of his mouth was the dark hole. I fed a winkle through it.

'Stop it, Elly!' my mother snapped, and turned off the radio.

'And *you*,' she said pointing to my brother, 'don't encourage her.'

I watched my brother lean over and catch his reflection in the back door. These new wounds went with the new him; there

65

was something noble about the landscape that now inhabited his face and he liked it; he gently touched the swelling around his eye. My mother slammed a mug of tea in front of him and said nothing; an action purely to interrupt his brooding pride. I reached for another winkle; hooked it with the end of my safety pin and tried to pull its uncoiling body away from the shell, but it wouldn't come. Instead it clung on hard, which was odd; for even in death it said, 'I won't let go.' *Won't let go.*

'How are you feeling?' my mother said.

'Not too bad,' I said.

'Not *you*, Elly.'

'I'm fine,' my brother said.

'Not nauseous?'

'No.'

'Dizzy?'

'No.'

'You wouldn't tell me, though, would you?' she said.

'No,' he said, and laughed.

'I don't want you to play rugby any more,' my mother said curtly.

And he calmly looked at her and said, 'I don't care what you want, I'm playing,' and he picked up his tea and drank three large gulps, which must have burnt his throat, but he never let on.

'It's too dangerous,' she said.

'Life's dangerous,' he said.

'I can't bear to watch.'

'Then don't,' he said. 'But I'm still playing because I've never felt more alive, or more myself. I've never felt so happy,' and he got up and left the table.

My mother turned towards the sink and wiped her cheek. A tear maybe? I realised it was because my brother had never equated himself with the word *happy* before.

*

I put god to bed with his usual late-night snack. His hutch was on the patio now, shielded from the wind by the new fence the neighbours had put up, the neighbours we didn't know too well, who had moved in after Mr Golan. Sometimes I thought I could still see his old face peering through the fence slats, the pale eyes that had the translucency of the blind.

I sat down on the cold patio slabs and watched god's movement under the newspaper. I pulled the blanket around my shoulders. The sky was dark and vast and empty and not even a plane disturbed that sullen stillness, not even a star. The emptiness above was now mine within. It was a part of me, like a freckle, like a bruise. Like a middle name no one acknowledged.

I poked my finger through the wire and found his nose. His breath was slight, warm. His tongue insistent.

'Things pass,' he said quietly.

'Are you hungry?'

'A bit,' he said, and I pushed a carrot baton through the wire.

'Thanks,' he said. 'Much better.'

I thought it was a fox at first, the snuffling, the sound of dislodged leaves and I reached for an old cricket bat that had been left out since the previous summer. I made my way towards the sound, and as I got near to the back fence I saw her body fall from the shadows, a pink furry heap now prostrate on a bale of straw. She looked up at me, her face smudged with dirt.

'Are you all right?' I asked.

'Yes,' she said as I helped her up and brushed the leaves and twigs from her favourite dressing gown.

'I had to get out, they're arguing again,' she said. 'They're really loud, and Mum threw a lamp at the wall.'

I took her hand and led her back up the path towards the house.

'Can I stay over tonight?' she asked.

'I'll ask my mum,' I said. 'I'm sure she'll say yes.' My mother always said yes. We sat down next to the hutch and huddled against the cold.

'Who were you talking to out here?' Jenny Penny asked.

'My rabbit. It speaks, you know. Sounds like Harold Wilson,' I said.

'Really? Do you think he'll talk to me?'

'Dunno. Try,' I said.

'Hey, rabbity rabbit,' she said, as she prodded him in the stomach with her chunky finger. 'Say something.'

'Ouch, you little shit,' said god. 'That hurt.'

Jenny Penny waited quietly for a moment. Then looked at me. Waited a moment more.

'Can't hear anything,' she finally said.

'Maybe he's just tired.'

'I had a rabbit once,' she said. 'When I was really little, when we lived in a caravan.'

'What happened to it?' I asked, already sensing the strange inevitability of it all.

'They ate it,' she said, and a lone tear tracked down her muddy cheek to the side of her mouth. 'They said it had run away, but I knew the truth. Not everything tastes like chicken,' and she'd hardly finished the sentence before the white skin of her knee was exposed to the cold night air and she ran it viciously across the rough edge of the paving slab. Blood appeared instantly; ran down her plump shin to her ragged ankle sock. I stared at her, both attracted and repulsed by the suddenness of her violence, by the calm now sweeping across her face. The back door opened and my brother walked out.

68

'Christ, it's freezing out here! What are you two doing?'

And before we could answer he looked down at Jenny's leg and said, 'Shit.'

'She tripped,' I said, not looking at her.

My brother bent down and held her leg up to the shaft of light emanating from the kitchen.

'Let's see what you've done,' he said. 'God, that's messy. Does it hurt?' he asked.

'Not any more,' she said, stuffing her hands into her overly large pockets.

'You'll need a plaster,' he said.

'Probably,' she said. 'Maybe two.'

'Come on then,' he said, and he lifted her up and held her against his chest.

I'd never thought of her as young before. There was something ageing about her nocturnal existence, about her self-sufficiency enforced by neglect. But that night, nestled against him, she looked small and vulnerable; and wanting. Her face rested peacefully against his neck; her eyes closed to the sensation of his care as he carried her inside. I didn't follow them straight away. I let her have her moment. That uninterrupted moment when she could dream and believe that all I had was hers.

A FEW DAYS LATER MY BROTHER AND I AWOKE TO SHOUTS
and terrifying screams. We converged on the landing holding
an array of makeshift weapons – I, a dripping toilet brush;
he, a long, wooden shoehorn – until my father raced up the
stairs followed by my mother. He looked pale and gaunt, as
if, in the hours between asleep and awake, he'd lost a stone
in weight.

'I said it, didn't I?' he told us, the fog of madness obscuring
the familiarity of his features.

My brother and I looked at each other.

'I said we'd win, didn't I? I *am* a lucky man. A blessed
man, a *chosen* man,' and he sat down on the top stair and
wept.

Heaving sobs tore at his shoulders, loosening years of
torment, and momentarily his esteem seemed buoyed by the
magic of that slip of grid paper held between his thumb and

forefinger. My mother caressed his head and left him, foetus-like, on the stairs. She led us into their bedroom, which still smelt of sleep. The curtains were drawn, the bed scruffy and cold. We were both strangely nervous.

'Sit down,' she said.

We did. I sat on her hot-water bottle and felt its lingering warmth.

'We've won the football pools,' she said matter-of-factly.

'Blimey,' said my brother.

'What's wrong with Dad then?' I said.

My mother sat down on the bed and smoothed the sheets.

'He's traumatised,' she said, not hiding the fact that he clearly was.

'What does that mean?' I said.

'Mental,' whispered my brother.

'You know what your father thinks about God and stuff like that, don't you?' she said, still looking down at the area of sheet that had hypnotised her hand into slow circular movements.

'Yes,' my brother said. 'He doesn't believe in one.'

'Yes, well, now it's complicated; he's prayed for this and he's been answered and a door has opened for your father, and to walk through that door he knows he'll have to give something up.'

'What will he have to give up?' I asked, wondering if it might be us.

'The image of himself as a bad man,' said my mother.

The football pools win was to remain a secret to everyone outside of the family, except Nancy, of course. She was on holiday at the time in Florence with a new lover, an American actress call Eva. I wasn't even allowed to tell Jenny Penny, and when I kept drawing piles of coins just to give her a clue, she took it as a coded message to steal money from her mother's purse, which she duly did, and exchanged for sherbet dabs.

Excluded from talking about our win to the world outside, we stopped talking about the win to our world inside, and it soon became something that had momentarily happened to us, rather than the life-changing event most normal people would have allowed it to be. My mother still looked for bargains in the shops and her frugality became compulsive. She darned our socks, patched our jeans, and even the tooth fairy refused to reimburse me for a particularly painful molar, even when I left it a note saying that every additional day accrued interest.

One day in June, about two months after 'the win', my father pulled up in a brand-new silver Mercedes with blacked-out windows, the type usually reserved for diplomats. The whole street came out to witness the brutality of such ostentation. When the door opened and my father stepped out, the street echoed with the sound of broken teeth as jaws dropped to the floor. My father tried to smile and said something wan, something about a 'bonus', but unknown to him he had inadvertently climbed onto that ladder reserved for the élite, and was already looking down on the kind familiar faces he'd shared years of his life with. I felt embarrassed and went inside.

We ate dinner in silence that evening. The subject on everyone's lips was 'that car', and it soured the taste of every morsel that passed it. Finally, my mother could stand it no more and calmly asked, '*Why?*' as she got up to get another glass of water.

'I don't know,' said my father. 'I could, so I did.'

My brother and I looked to my mother.

'It's not us. That car is not us. It stands for everything ugly in this world,' she said.

We turned to my father.

'I've never bought a new car before,' he said.

'It's not the newness of the car, for God's sake! That car's a bloody down payment on a house for most people. That car says we are something that we're not. That car is not a car, it's a bloody statement of all that's wrong in this country. I shall never ride in it. Either it goes or I shall.'

'So be it,' said my father, and he got up and left the table.

Awaiting my father's choice of Wife or Wheels, my mother disappeared, leaving only a note that said: *Don't worry about me.* (We hadn't been, but it suddenly made us.) *I shall miss you, my two precious children* – the bold omission of my father hovering in the air like the smell of last Christmas's festering Stilton.

During this period of trial separation, my father drove to his Legal Aid position undaunted by his sudden singleness, and brought an unquestioning glamour to the potholed car park his offices shared with a greasy spoon. Criminals would enter and openly ask for the lawyer 'who's got them wheels outside'. They saw it as a badge of success, not knowing that the only person wearing it had never felt more of a failure.

One night he stopped me in the kitchen and asked me about the car.

'You like it, don't you, Elly?'

'Not really,' I said.

'But it's a beautiful car.'

'But no one else has got one,' I said.

'That's a good thing, isn't it? To stand apart and be different?' he said.

'I'm not sure,' I said, quite aware of my own muted need to fit in, somehow simply to hide. 'I don't want people to know I'm different.'

And I looked up and saw my brother standing in the doorway.

AS MY FAMILY FELL APART, SO DID MY SCHOOL LIFE. I happily abstained from reading and writing projects by wilfully letting the teacher know that there were domestic problems in our household, and I took every opportunity to embrace the possibility that I too might come from a broken home. I told Jenny Penny that my parents were probably divorcing.

'How long for?' she asked.

'As long as it takes,' I said, repeating my mother's dramatic, final words; the words I'd overheard her say, as she closed the front door defiantly in my father's face.

I was quite happy in this new life, just Jenny Penny and me, and we would go and sit in the bottom shed, a welcome quiet away from the chaos and unhappiness that being rich had somehow instilled. My brother had made it comfortable inside, and there was a small electric heater that god always liked to sit in front of whilst his fur cooked and gave off a sour smell. I sat on the fraying armchair that used to be in our lounge, and offered Jenny Penny the old wooden wine crate. I pretended to order vodka martinis from our invisible waiter: the drink of the rich, my brother used to say, the drink of the sophisticate. The drink that would one day mark the start of my eighteenth birthday celebrations.

'Cheers!' I said and took a sip.

'Cheers,' she said.

'What's the matter?'

'Nothing,' she said.

'You can tell me anything, you know,' I said.

'I know,' she said, and pretended to finish off her martini.

'What is it?' I asked her again.

She looked more pensive than usual.

'What'll happen to me if your mum and dad split up for good? Who will I go with?' she asked.

What could I say? I hadn't even made the choice myself. There were pros and cons to both my parents and my list was far from complete. I handed her god instead, who was starting to give off his rather pungent scent. He comforted her instantly, and tolerated the harsh, abrasive groping of her chubby fingers, as tufts of his fur fell carelessly to the ground.

'Ouch,' he said, 'not a-bloody-gain. Arse. Ouch.'

I bent down to pick up my glass and as I did, I noticed a magazine part hidden under the chair. I knew what it was before I opened it – could tell by the cover – but I opened it nevertheless, and ran my eyes over an assorted display of nude bodies doing various things with their private parts. I didn't know vaginas and penises were used in those ways, but by that age, I'd understood that people had a fondness for touching them.

'Look at that,' I said to Jenny Penny as I held the picture in front of her face. But she didn't look. Or laugh. Or say anything actually. She did something quite unexpected. She burst into tears and ran.

I found her huddled in the shadow of the almond tree, halfway down the alley where we'd once found a dead cat, poisoned probably. She looked scrappy and orphaned in the twilight, surrounded by the scent of urine and shit as it conspired with the warm breeze. Everyone used the alleyway as a toilet or a dumping ground for the no-longer-useful. I sat down beside her and moved her hair away from her mouth, away from her pale brow.

'I'm going to run away,' she said.

'Where to?'

'Atlantis,' she said.

'Where's that?'

'No one really knows where it is,' she said, 'but I'll find it and then I'll go and then they'll worry,' and she looked at me and her dark eyes melted into the deep, shadowed sockets.

'Come with me,' she pleaded.

'OK, but not before next week,' I said (knowing that I had a dental appointment), and she agreed, and we leant our backs against the fence and inhaled the smell of its recent creosote coating. Jenny Penny looked calmer.

'Atlantis is special, Elly. I heard about it recently. It was sunk by a huge tidal wave quite a few years ago and it's a magic place with magic people. A lost civilisation probably still alive,' she said. I sat transfixed by the surety in her voice; it was hypnotic; otherworldly even. Made everything possible.

'There are lovely gardens and libraries and universities, and everyone is clever and beautiful, and they are peaceful and help each other and they have special powers and know the mysteries of the Cosmos. We can do anything there, be anything, Elly. It's our city and we'll be really happy.'

'And all we have to do is find it?' I said.

'That's all,' she said, as if it were the easiest thing in the world to do. And I must have looked doubtful because it was at that moment that she suddenly said, 'Watch this!' and performed the magic trick of pulling the fifty-pence piece out of her plump arm.

'Here,' she said, handing me the coin.

I held it in my hand. It was bloody and warm, as if of her essence, and I half expected it to disappear, to simply melt into the weirdness of the night.

'Now you can trust me,' she said.

And I said I did, as I looked down at the strange coin with the even stranger date.

My mother returned eight days later, more refreshed than when she'd had her lump removed. Nancy had taken her to Paris, where they'd stayed in St-Germain and met Gérard Dépardieu. She arrived with bags and clothes and new make-up, and looked ten years younger, and when she stood in front of my father and said, 'Well?' we knew immediately that he'd lost. He said nothing, and after that afternoon we never saw the car again. In fact, we were never allowed to talk about the car again without my father falling into an abyss of shame and a sudden self-induced amnesia.

My parents were writing Christmas cards together in the dining room and, bored by my own company and lack of my brother's, I decided to go to the shed instead and look at the remaining pages of the magazine I'd carefully put back for another day.

The garden was dark and shadows of trees bent towards me in the breeze. There were bright hard berries on the holly and everyone said it would snow soon. The anticipation of snow was as good as the reality at that age. My father had made me a new sledge in preparation and I could see it propped up by the side of the shed, its metal runners waxed and shining ready for the glide. As I passed by the shed window, I saw flickering torchlight within. I picked up a stray cricket stump and slowly made my way to the door. It was hard to open the door quietly because it stuck halfway on the concrete step, and so instead I pulled the door quickly towards me and saw the fractured image of Charlie on his knees in front of my shivering, naked brother. My brother's hand caressing his hair.

I ran. Not because I was scared, not at all – I'd seen that interaction in the magazine; a woman was doing it that time and maybe someone was watching, though I couldn't be sure – but I ran because I'd trespassed on their clandestine world, and I ran because I realised it was a world that no longer held a place for me.

I sat in my room and watched the clock rotate a slow languid hour as the carols from downstairs grew loud. My mother was singing along as if she was in a choir; being rich made her sing more confidently. I was asleep when they came in. My brother woke me up; he only did that when it was important. Budge up, they said, and they both squeezed into my bed, bringing the cold from outside.

'You can't tell anyone,' they said.

'I won't,' I said.

'Promise?'

'Promise,' I said, and I told my brother I'd seen it all before anyway, in the magazines in the shed. He said they weren't his and together we said, 'Oh,' as the awful realisation dawned on us that they were probably the quiet consolation of our father.

Or our mother. Or maybe both. Maybe the shed had been the scene of the amorous lead-up to my conception, and I suddenly felt guilty about the uncontrollable urges that hid in the tree of my genealogy.

'I want to go to sleep now,' I said, and they kissed me good night and crept away.

In the darkness I thought about the images, and about Mr Golan, and I felt old. Maybe this was what my father meant when he said that Nancy had grown up too quickly; I suddenly started to understand.

THE BUNTING WAS UP AND THE MERCURY SLOWLY RISING, and capes made from Union Jacks rose and fell against the contours of our young backs. It was the last weekend in May. 1977. Our Queen had never been so popular.

The Sex Pistols blared out from the record player that Mrs Penny had held hostage ever since her dramatic arrival at the street party, half an hour before.

She'd cut a towering figure as she'd tottered up the road in an unbuttoned silk shirt that reminded our neighbour Miss Gobb 'of a pair of jammed curtains. And no one needs to see what's going on in *her* living room'.

Mrs Penny stopped at the first trestle table and handed over the box she was carrying.

'Made it myself,' she said.

'You didn't?' asked Olive Binsbury nervously.

'No, I nicked it.'

Silence.

'Joke. *Joke*,' said Mrs Penny. 'It's a Victoria sponge – after the old Queen,' and everyone laughed. Too loudly. As if they were scared.

She pogoed and spat and flexed her studded fist, and came close to electrocution when her four-inch stiletto heel got caught in the precariously long extension lead that had started to fray at the edge of a mossy wall. Only the quick thinking and even quicker reflexes of my father prevented her cindered demise, when he shoved her gently onto a pile of beanbags and sent the remaining two inches of her skirt up to her exposed waist.

'Oh, Alfie, you are naughty!' she shouted as she rolled laughing into the gutter, and as my father tried to help her up, she pulled him down on top of her ripped fishnets and tiny leather skirt, which, Miss Gobb also noted, would have been more useful as a purse. My father stood up and brushed himself down. Tried to rid himself of her perfume, which clung like tired fingers to a cliff face.

'Let's try again, shall we?' he said, as he lifted her to her feet.

'My hero,' she said, licking her purple pouting lips.

My father laughed nervously. 'Didn't have you down as a royalist, Hayley.'

'Still waters, Alfie,' she said, reaching for my father's arse and finding my mother's hand instead.

'Kate, didn't see you there, love,' said Mrs Penny.

'Can you give Greg Harris a hand with traffic patrol?'

'I'll give him a hand with something,' she said, and teetered off to our makeshift barricade that hadn't as yet got the required police approval, as it temporarily blocked off our road from Woodford Avenue.

Jenny Penny and I were on trestle-table duty, covering them in Union Jack paper tablecloths and placing paper cups and plastic cutlery at 'sensible' intervals along the edge. We laid out plates of jam tarts and chocolate rolls and Wagon Wheels, that immediately started to glisten in the rare, balmy sunshine.

'I wrote to the Queen once,' said Jenny Penny.

'What did you write?'

'Asked if I could live with her.'

'What did she say?'

'Said she'd think about it.'

'Do you think she will?'

'Can't see why not.'

A car beeped angrily behind us. We heard Jenny Penny's mother shout, 'Oh, fuck off. No I'm not. Go on, back up. You're not coming through.'

Beep! Beep! Beep!

Jenny Penny looked pale. Someone turned the music up – my mother probably – to drown out the louder expletives.

'Oh, listen,' I said, raising my finger heavenwards. 'This is my favourite.'

Jenny Penny listened. She smiled. 'Mine too. I know *all* the words. I'll start. "I see a little silhouetto of a man. Scary mush, Scary mush, will you do the fandango?"'

'You're not coming through!' screamed Mrs Penny.

' "Thunderbolt and lightning, very very frightening. MEEE!"' I sang.

Mr Harris ran towards us. 'Where's your dad, Elly?'

' "Galileo, Galileo, Galileo."'

' "Fig Roll!"' screamed Jenny Penny.

'Your father, Elly? Where is he? This is serious. I think there's going to be a fight.'

' "I'm just a poor boy, nobody loves me,"' I sang.

'Oh, fuckit,' said Mr Harris, walking off.

'And that's what I think of your cousin in the police!' shouted

83

Mrs Penny as she exposed her jiggling breasts.

'Yikes,' said my father, running past us, rolling up his sleeves. 'Trou-ble,' he said in that broken-up, annoying way of his.

' "Let him go!" ' sang Jenny Penny.

' "I will not let you go," ' I sang.

'It's just a simple misunderstanding,' said my father.

'Let me go!' shouted Mrs Penny.

'We can sort this out over a cup of tea,' said my father calmly.

' "I will not let you go!" '

' "Let him—" '

'WILL YOU TWO SHUT THE HELL UP NOW!' screamed Mr Harris, pulling the plug from the record player. He led us by the arm to the dappled shade of the large plane tree.

'Now sit down and don't move until I say so,' he said, wiping away the sweat that had formed under his nose. Jenny Penny moved.

'Don't you dare,' he said before unscrewing his pewter hip flask and downing at least half of its contents. 'Some of us have duties to perform. *Important* duties.'

Mr Harris officially opened the party at two o'clock that afternoon, heavily aided by the remaining contents of his hip flask and his sailing horn. He made a rousing speech about the importance of monarchy and how it separates us from the uncivilised world. Especially the Americans. My parents looked down at their feet and said something uncharacteristically rude. He said that queens are necessary to the heritage of our country, which made my brother and Charlie laugh, and said that should the monarchy ever fall, he would hang himself and finish what his first wife had promised.

'To His Majesty,' he said, raising his glass and sounding his hooter.

Nancy turned up dressed as Elizabeth the First. She was in disguise because she'd just had a film out and wanted to avoid a photographer who was keen to catch her in a compromising position.

'Hey, beautiful!' she said when she saw me.

'Nancy,' said Jenny Penny, barging her way through, 'can I ask you a question?'

'Course you can, darling.'

'Is Shirley Bassey a lesbian?'

'I don't think so,' said Nancy, laughing. 'Why?'

'Alice Cooper?'

'No. Definitely not.'

'What about Vanessa Redgrave?'

'No.'

'What about Abba?'

'Which one?'

'All of them.'

'Don't think so.'

'So none of them are?'

'No. Why do you want to know, sugar?'

'Well, it's for my school project.'

'Really?' said Nancy, looking at me. I shrugged. I hadn't got a clue what she was going on about. My school project was about pandas and elephants. The theme for us all being Endangered Species.

Night fell heavily. The smell of sugar and sausages and onions and stale perfume hung above the tables, warmed by tea-lights and chatting breath, and it merged into a giant scent that ebbed and flowed like a spring tide. Cardigans were pulled across shoulders, and neighbours – once insular, once shy –

leant upon those same clad shoulders and whispered boozy secrets into disbelieving ears. Nancy helped Joe and Charlie on the drinks table, ladling out the non-alcoholic punch called Silver Jubilee, and the much more popular alcoholic version called Jilver Subilee, and people danced and told jokes, all in celebration of a woman no one had ever met.

And cars were finally admitted and they came beeping horns, this time in solidarity, not annoyance, and they rolled by with hazard lights flashing, adding disco beams to our Motown tunes, and their open windows added laughing, singing voice to already tipsy banter.

Mrs Penny was as drunk as I'd ever seen anybody be. She lurched like a dying man from one dance move to another and disappeared occasionally down the alleyway to expel vomit or urine, only to emerge refreshed and almost sober, ready for another ladle of toxic punch. That night, though, the neighbours watched with care, not judgement, and hands were gentle as they rested on her back, guiding her to safe passage that was a chair or a wall, or sometimes even a lap. For that night they all learnt that the boyfriend had gone. Had taken a bag of his things and some of her things – things she wouldn't even know about until much later – things like an egg poacher and a jar of maraschino cherries. As I passed her dancing shadow, she reached out and grabbed my arm tightly and slurred a word that could have been *lonely*.

With the last record played and the last sausage roll eaten, Jenny Penny and I went with my mother in search of Mrs Penny. The street was virtually empty, now that the tables had been swiftly stacked on the pavement for the Council's removal.

We went up and down the street several times in case she'd taken refuge in a bush or in an unlocked car. But it was as we were heading down the alleyway for the second time, that we saw two shadows swaying towards us, and as they came close to the flare of a streetlight we could see that it was Mr Harris holding up Jenny's mother. She looked sheepish and wiped her mouth. Smudged lipstick, mouth of a clown. Sad not funny. Jenny Penny said nothing.

'I was simply helping the woman,' said Mr Harris tucking in his shirt. 'The woman', he'd said. She'd been *lovely Hayley* to him all night.

'Of course you were,' said my mother, sounding unconvinced. 'OK, girls, help Hayley back to the street and I'll join you in a minute,' and as we walked away, her weight evenly balanced on our small frames, I turned back and saw my mother poking Mr Harris angrily in the chest and I heard my mother say, 'If you ever *ever* take advantage of a woman in that state again, God help what I do to you, you arrogant shit.'

My mother and father didn't even get her anywhere near upstairs before she vomited in her hallway. Jenny Penny turned away embarrassed until my father's reassuring smile made her feel less alone. But she remained quiet throughout the clean-up proceedings, following my mother's orders like a besotted disciple. Bowl of hot water, towel, sheets, blanket, empty bucket. Pint of water. Thank you, Jenny, you're doing really well. My father helped Mrs Penny onto the sofa and covered her with lilac sheets, and as she slept my mother stroked her forehead, kissed it even, saw the child.

'I'm going to stay here tonight, Jenny,' my mother said. 'You go back to ours with Elly and Alfie. And don't worry about your mum, she'll be fine. I'll look after her. This is simply what happens when adults have so much fun. She didn't do anything wrong, Jenny. Just had fun, that's all. And she was a lot of fun, wasn't she?'

But Jenny Penny said nothing. She knew my mother's words were mere scaffolding holding up a crumbling wall.

Our slow footsteps echoed along the dark street. Jenny Penny reached for my hand.

'I wish my mother was like—'

'Don't,' I said harshly, interrupting her. I knew the word that was to follow, and that night it was a word that would have punctured my heart with guilt.

LOOKING BACK, IT'S QUITE CLEAR MY PARENTS HAD MADE
the decision to move by the time they returned from their trip to
Cornwall that Easter. They'd been on a second honeymoon,
Nancy said. They'd needed to reconnect, to find each other as
people once again and when they walked through the door,
ruddy and salty, there was an energy about them, an energy I'd
never seen before; a kindness not bound by familiarity or duty,
and when my father sat us down and declared that he had
decided to quit his job, I felt relieved that the fragility of
expectation that had hung over us during the last eighteen
months had finally turned into the decisiveness of action.

My father worked out his notice by the end of June and then,
shunning all goodbyes and celebrations, sat in his car in the
deserted car park and cried late into the night. The police found
him hunched over the steering wheel, eyes red and swollen like
boils. When they opened his door, all he could say was, 'Forgive

me. Forgive me, *please*,' and for a young policeman three weeks out of Hendon this appeared to be a shocking confession, as his imagination jumped from textbook to crime novel in one easy leap. He believed my father had murdered his family, and called for a squad of cars to rush over to our house. The door thundered under the blows of fists, and my mother, disoriented, torn from sleep, rushed down the stairs, fearful that the bearer of unbearable news had once again found his way to her door.

'Yes?' she said in a tone that was neither helpful nor passive.

'Are you Mrs Kate Portman?' said the policeman.

'I am,' said my mother.

'Do you know a Mr Portman?' said the policeman.

'Of course I do, he's my husband. What's happened to him?'

'Nothing serious, but he seems a little distressed. Could you come down to the station with me and collect him?'

And my mother did, and found my father pale and trembling in the fluorescent light under the care of a kind station sergeant. He was wrapped in a grey blanket and was holding a mug of tea. The mug was patterned with the insignia of the West Ham supporters' club and somehow made my father look more pathetic, my mother said. She took the mug from him and placed it on the floor.

'Where are your shoes?' she asked.

'They took them from me,' he said. 'It's procedure. In case I did anything to myself.'

'What? Like trip yourself up?' she said, and they both laughed and knew that it would be all right – for the moment, at least.

And as they walked out to the car park, she stopped and turned to him and said, 'Leave it here, Alfie. It's time. Leave her here.'

Her name was Jean Hargreaves.

My father had been working in Chambers at the time and was chosen to defend a Mr X against child molestation charges. It was one of his first cases and, emboldened by new fatherhood and the responsibility placed on his green shoulders, he undertook Mr X's defence as a sort of quest, a noble vocation against the dragon of slander.

Mr X was a known man, a respectable man of such gentle ways that my father found it unspeakable that he should be forced to defend himself against such heinous allegations. Mr X had been married for forty years. There was no whisper of affairs or marital grumblings, and their union was held up as the pinnacle to reach. They had two children; the boy went into the army, the girl into finance. He was on the board of directors of several companies; he was a patron of the arts and financed underprivileged children through university. But more importantly, he was the man my father wanted to be.

And then one day, a young woman called Jean Hargreaves walked into Paddington Green police station and unburdened herself for the first time in thirteen years, revealing the humiliating secret that liked to visit her at night. She had been ten at the time and subjected to a cycle of horrendous abuse, whilst her mother diligently cleaned the outer reaches of Mr X's house. The police would have thrown out the case if it wasn't for one mitigating circumstance: Jean Hargreaves could describe perfectly the heraldic ring her attacker wore on his little finger, and had noticed the smallest fissure across its shield.

The moment Jean Hargreaves took to the stand, her life was all but over, my father later told me. He broke her story down with swipes and body blows, and parried her uncertainty until she sat back slumped and unsure of everything including her name. It took the jury no time at all to say not guilty, and for

Mr X's firm cool hand to be thrust into my father's naïve palm.

And then came the worst of timings. My father was leading Mr X down the corridor, when all of a sudden they saw Jean Hargreaves sitting alone on a bench, awaiting the arrival of her best friend, who had disappeared ten minutes earlier to look for a taxi. My father tried to pull his client back, but it was as useless as dragging a baying hound away from a bloodied fox. Mr X pulled away and strutted down that silent corridor, his heels clicking as arrogantly as fingers, and at the moment of passing he didn't yell or vent his anger, instead he turned to Jean Hargreaves and whispered something and winked at her, and in that moment my father knew. Nancy said he stopped and reached for the wall; tried to pull himself free from his skin, something he tried in vain to do throughout the rest of his life.

Two weeks later Jean Hargreaves committed suicide, and in the time it took for her to fall twenty floors, my father lost faith in everything; but most of all in himself.

My father knelt down on the tarmac as cars came and went. The soft drone of traffic competed with his past. The June breeze billowed around his shirt and dried his damp skin – an illicit, welcome sensation to the memory of life. My mother stroked his hair.

'I love you,' she said, but my father couldn't look at her. It was the final chapter of his breakdown, the moment when his glass was drained of everything, and its emptiness awaited only the choices to come.

JUNE MOVED IDLY INTO JULY. THE SUN WAS HIGH AND
burning and would be for another four hours, and I'd wished
I'd worn my hat: the white hand-me-down cricket hat that
Charlie had given me last month. I knew I was late and ran up
the road panting for breath. I felt a trickle of sweat run down
my back and imagined it cool rather than hot and clammy. I
put my hand in my pocket and silenced the clinking coins, soon
to be exchanged for an icicle or two.

I'd just got back after escorting Jenny Penny home from the
recreation ground where she'd tripped and got her hair caught
in a fence. A large clump hung down like sheep wool and she'd
screamed in distress. She was convinced she was bald but I told
her a lot more would have to come out before she could use an
adjective like that, and this calmed her for ten minutes until she
fell howling into her mother's arms.

I turned the corner and ran towards the bus stop where my

brother was standing and pointing at his watch.

'You're late,' he said.

'I know. But Jenny Penny almost *died*,' I said.

'Here's the bus,' he said, uninterested in my life, and stretched out his arm to stop the chugging 179.

We sat upstairs. I wanted to sit in the front and he wanted to sit in the back and we sat separately until we got to Charlie Brown's roundabout, where I conceded defeat and went back amidst the stained seats and cigarette butts that had become the fantasy of every school child's life. 'Andy 4 Lisa', 'Georges a fat pig', 'Mike's got a nice cock'. My reading was succinct and brief, and I wondered who George and Mike and who Lisa were, and whether Andy still liked her.

I stood up and positioned my face next to the sliver of open window. The air was still and uncomfortable. I was uncomfortable. My brother was biting his nails again. He'd stopped for a bit during his happy phase, but now he'd started again. It was an action he should have outgrown, and whether it was out of nerves or comfort he still relied upon it and it made him look unnecessarily young. He hadn't seen Charlie for a week. Charlie had taken time off school, but he wasn't ill and he couldn't talk about it, but he would tell my brother everything later. And here we were *later*, and I felt sorry for my brother but I didn't know why yet.

By the time we got off the bus a breeze had picked up and made us more hopeful, and we laughed as we walked down the tree-lined streets with their low hum of mowers and sprinkler systems that flicked water over us, the passers-by. And then we saw it: the large removal van parked outside the house. We slowed down, delaying the truth, and I asked my brother for the time, trying to make him happy, but he ignored me and I understood why. The sun was hot; an irritant. So was I.

We stood and watched familiar items loaded into the van; the small silver television from Charlie's room, his skis, the large free-standing dresser he said was mahogany and came from France. My brother gripped my hand.

'Maybe he's moving nearer to us,' he said, forcing a smile. I could say nothing. Suddenly Charlie came out of his house and ran over to us as exhilarated as ever.

'We're leaving!' he said excitedly.

'What do you mean?' my brother said.

'My dad and I are going to Dubai. I'm already enrolled in school there,' he said, looking at me rather than at my brother.

I said nothing.

'He's got a new contract; new country; we've got no choice.'

'You could have come and stayed with us,' I said.

'When are you going?' my brother said, pulling his fingers out of his mouth.

'Tomorrow,' said Charlie.

'That's quick,' I said, my stomach starting to clench.

'Not really. I've known about it for weeks.'

'Why didn't you tell me?' said my brother quietly.

'Didn't seem important.'

'I'll miss you,' said my brother.

'Yeah,' said Charlie, turning away.

'It's really hot there, you know,' he added.

'It's really hot here,' said my brother.

'We're going to have servants,' said Charlie.

'What for?' I asked.

'I could come with you,' said my brother, and Charlie burst into laughter.

Two men carried a large leather armchair in front of us and noisily positioned it in the back of the van next to a large silver planter.

'Why did you laugh at me?' said my brother.

'He *could* go with you,' I said, reaching up for my brother's hand, 'if you wanted him to. All it would take was a phone call.'

'I'll ask my dad and maybe you can come and visit me one day. How about that?' said Charlie, folding his arms across his chest.

'Fuck off,' said my brother. 'I'd rather die.' And he swiftly turned to leave.

We strode up the road, the pace too fast in the murmuring heat, and I couldn't make out if it was sweat or something else coursing down my brother's face, but soon he was way ahead of me and my tired legs refused the fight, and instead I dropped my pace and sat on a wet wall, sprinkled intermittently by a flickering hose. I was expecting to hear a knock on the window, an angrily motioned hand waving me off this private wall, but I didn't; I heard his footsteps running towards me, and I didn't look up because I didn't care, because I hated him and I hated his desertion. He sat down next to me.

'What do you want?' I said.

'I don't know,' said Charlie.

'Then go away,' I said. 'You're an idiot an idiot an idiot an idiot.'

'Elly, come on.'

'*Idiot.*'

'Just wanted to say goodbye properly, that's all,' he said, and I turned round and punched him hard.

'Goodbye,' I said.

'Ow, fuck, Elly! What did you do that for?' he said, rubbing his shoulder.

'If you don't know then you're stupider than you look,' and I punched him hard again in the same place.

'Why are you doing this to me?'

'Because you shouldn't have done that to him.'

'I had to be careful,' he said. 'My dad, you see. He keeps watching me, he's really weird. Tell him that for me. Tell him . . . something nice.'

'Fuck off and tell him yourself,' I said, and started up the hill, suddenly revived, suddenly powerful; suddenly changed.

Had my parents ceased for one glorious moment, to stop and be still in the silence, they would have heard the sound of my brother's heart break in two. But they heard nothing except the sound of the Cornish waves and birdsong that were to fill their lives and ours to come. It was left to Nancy and me to pick up the pieces that my brother had become; to resurrect his shrunken spirit and pull his pale tear-stained face from beneath his pillow and give sense to a world that had given him none: he loved, yet wasn't loved back. Even Nancy had no words of comfort or explanation. This was part of life and she was sorry that the realisation had hit him so young.

We stayed with her at Charterhouse Square as the cavernous summer holidays opened up, and she kept us busy with continual visits to museums and art galleries and cafés, and gradually his lack of interest in everything except his wounded self started to wane, and he tentatively emerged, squinting into the late July sunshine, opting to give life one more chance.

'When did you know?' he asked her as we walked along the Thames, heading towards the South Bank complex and an old black-and-white film.

'A bit older than you, I suppose. Sixteen? I'm not sure really. I knew early on what I didn't want, and I got a lot of what I didn't want, so my choice became easy.'

'But it's not easy, is it?' he said. 'It stinks. All that hiding and shit.'

'Then don't,' she said. 'Don't hide.'

'Sometimes I wish I was like everyone else,' he said, and Nancy stopped in front of him and laughed.

'No you don't! You'd hate being like everyone else. Don't kid yourself, sunshine – being gay's your salvation and you know it.'

'Bollocks,' he said, trying to stifle a smile. He unwrapped a stick of chewing gum and checked out the dark-haired man who passed in front of him.

'Saw you,' I said, nudging him with my elbow.

He ignored me.

'I saw him look, Nancy. At that man there.'

'Shutup,' he said and walked on, hands stuffed in too-tight jeans, the ones my mum said would make him sterile.

'So, has your heart ever got broken?' he added nonchalantly.

'Oh God, YES!' said Nancy.

'Her name was Lilly Moss, actually,' I said, finally able to interrupt their conversation, 'the main one, that is. Everyone knows that story, Joe. She two-timed Nancy and tried to take her for all she was worth. Didn't get away with it, though, did she, Nancy?'

'No she didn't,' said Nancy, 'although she did get away with a rather expensive diamond necklace, if I remember rightly.'

'I'm never going to fall in love with anyone again,' my brother declared robustly, and Nancy smiled and put her arm around him.

'Never's a long time, Joe. Bet you won't make it.'

'Bet I will. How much?' he said.

'Tenner,' she said.

'Fine,' he said, and they shook hands, and Nancy walked on, safe in the knowledge that the ten-pound note would one day be hers.

'WE'RE MOVING,' MY FATHER SUDDENLY SAID OVER A FULL English breakfast. My brother and I looked at each other and carried on eating. The back door was open and August's heat was sending the bees wild, and their intoxicating buzz thankfully filled the silence that had settled in the wake of our cruel indifference.

My father looked disappointed; he thought his exciting declaration might have elicited more emotion, and he wondered if he really knew his own children; a thought that would trouble him many times throughout the coming years.

'To Cornwall,' he said enthusiastically, and he raised his arms as if he'd just scored a goal and said, 'Yay!'

My mother left her position at the grill and sat with us at the table.

'We know it's sudden,' she said. 'But when we were away at Easter a property came onto the market and suddenly we knew:

this was what we wanted. What we've dreamt of for our family. And so we bought it.'

She paused to allow the absurdity of what she was saying to slap us across our cheeks and to wake us up. It didn't. We carried on eating in a daze.

'We need you to trust us, that's all,' she said. (That book again.)

My brother pushed his plate away and said, 'All right. When?'

'Two weeks today,' my father said apologetically.

'OK,' my brother said, and he got up clumsily from the table, leaving two untouched rashers of bacon, and headed towards the stairs.

My brother was lying on his bed flicking an elastic band across his arm; rising red welts crisscrossed on his skin.

'What are you thinking?' I said from the doorway.

'I'm not,' he said.

'Do you want to go?' I said, sitting down next to him.

'Why not?' he said. 'There's fuck all for me here,' and he turned towards the open window and its view of all he would leave. The sky had turned a deep violet grey since the morning. The atmosphere was sticky. Starting to aggravate.

'What about Jenny Penny?' I said to him.

'What about her?'

'Do you think she can come with us?'

'What do you think?' he said, turning towards me and flicking my knee.

'Ouch,' I said. '*Un*necessary.'

'Of course she can't come, Ell. She lives here, with that dopey cow of a mum,' and he rolled back over to face the window.

'How am I going to tell her?' I said, suddenly feeling scared and sick.

'Dunno,' he said as he drew a line down the misted windowpane. 'We need a storm. Clear the air. That'll make things easier,' and as if prompted by his careless words, the first rumble of thunder rolled across the horizon, displacing startled birds and settled picnics as it went.

The rain fell immediately. Large drops – nearly sleet – saturated the parched gardens and soon gutters were spilling over and the wash of dusty overflow filed down pathways and pooled in craters of mud. The sky lit up, one fork, and then another, lightning stabbing at the horizon between the fence of poplars. We saw Mr Harris run out to his washing line, too late to save his drenched jeans. We ran down the stairs and out through the back door, another fork of lightning – the sound of a fire engine. My brother reached into the hutch and pulled out my shivering rabbit.

'About bloody time,' said god as I held him close to my chest. 'I could've died out here.'

'Sorry about that,' I said. 'Really I am.'

'Sorry about what?' shouted my brother.

Dogs barked three houses over and children danced screaming into the onslaught, laughing and awash with joyful terror. The thunder roared and shook the ground. Mr Fisk, at the back, ran out to secure a tarpaulin, its unruly edges billowing in the wind, wanting to take flight. And we stood in the middle of our garden, unsheltered, unprotected and looked around at the turbulence of the lives we backed onto, sat next to, the lives of the neighbourhood, and it shook clear our apathy until we saw again what our life here had been. There was the sledge our father had made, the one we took to school, the envy of all; and the ghosts of swings and climbing frames that had held us, and dropped us, the sounds of our tears. And we saw again the cricket and football matches that had scuffed bare the grass of the bottom lawn. And we remembered the tents we had made and the nights spent within; imaginary countries, us the explorers. There was suddenly so much to say good-bye to. And as the storm blew across and the first of the sunbursts lifted our corner of the world, there she was. Her face drenched, peering over the fence. Not smiling. As if she knew.

'Go to her,' said god.

'Why?' she asked, pulling the towel away from her face. The clock ticked loudly in the silence. She stared pitifully across the kitchen table, and I longed for my brother to reappear, to bring back the recognisable into this scene of disquiet. My chair felt hard. The orange squash, too sweet. Our ease, now awkward. Nothing was the same.

'Why?' she asked again, tears instantly appearing in her eyes. 'Why? Why? Why? Why? Why?'

I couldn't answer her.

'Is it me?'

I felt my throat clench.

'Of course not,' I said. 'My mum and dad said we have to.'

'Where are you going?' she said, gripping the rabbit so tightly, he started to struggle.

'Cornwall.'

'You may as well be dead,' she said, and let god fall to the floor.

'Fuck,' he said, and scuttled under a box.

She slumped forwards, rested her elbows on her knees.

'What about Atlantis?' she said. 'And all the things we were going to do?'

'It could be in Cornwall,' I said. 'Maybe we'll find it there.'

'It can't be in Cornwall,' she said.

'Why not?'

'Because it can't. It has to be a place that's *ours*. Can't you see that? Not something that's everyone else's,' and she began to stamp her feet as rage overtook her, a rage my brother had so often felt when playing with her. It was an excess energy born of the dangerous, an energy that could unexpectedly turn play into war.

'Don't leave me, Elly,' she pleaded. 'Please don't,' she said again. 'You don't know what'll happen.'

But what could I say? I reached out my hand. The gesture crass and dramatic.

'I really love you,' I said clumsily.

Pathetic.

'No you don't!' she shouted. 'You're just like everyone else,' and she got up and ran.

I followed her to the back fence, shouting her name, begging her to stop, pleading, but she never did. The shutter had come down. She would live behind it until I left.

We never did ask to see photographs, never did enquire about the village or the life we were to lead, not even about the schools we were to go to; instead we trusted our parents just like they'd asked us to, and allowed them to lead us blindly to an unknown place with an unknown future. I stood in the doorway of my room and looked around, feeling sad but strangely detached; I filled my favourite bag with Orinoco, my Womble, my hair brush and photographs, and my box of knick-knacks of very little worth but of surprising memory. I added my swimming costume and sunglasses, but not my flip-flops, intending to buy new ones in a shop by the sea. I realised I was happy to let the rest of it go. That at the age of nine years and eight months a child should welcome the chance to start again didn't seem particularly unusual at the time. I sat down on my bed with a beach towel wrapped around my shoulders. I was packed and ready to leave; only twelve days and three hours early. I closed my eyes and heard the call of seagulls.

The moving company did everything, packing our life away with the professionalism of minimal fuss. I looked inside the van just before they pulled the rolling doors down and thought we hadn't acquired much over the years; our belongings were scant and functional, almost forlorn. There was no piano to manoeuvre; no paintings to grace walls or heavy textured rugs to add warmth to slate floors, so cold and harsh on bare feet. There were no standing lamps that would soon cast shadows in corners like stowaways, or large wooden Victorian trunks that would house linen and sachets of lavender, and would work hard to keep out the damp over the winter months. No, these things were not ours yet; they would grace our life to come.

'Five minutes, Elly,' my father said, as he broke away from handshakes and well-wishers, and the teasing that accompanied their goodbyes. I placed god in his box on the back seat, and before I covered him with a blanket he looked up and said, 'Leave something here. You must leave something here, Elly.'

'But what?' I said.

'Something.'

I grabbed my brother and we ran back through the empty house, our steps loud and intrusive on the naked boards. I stopped and looked around. How easy not to exist any more. To just go and leave *this*; this that was my home.

'Come on,' shouted my brother, and I ran after him.

*

He closed the lid on the small red biscuit tin and buried it under the slatted back fence shaded by the wall. He covered it with extra bricks, a sprinkling of camouflage dirt and leaves.

'Do you think someone will find it one day?'

'Nah, never,' he said. 'Not unless they know where to look . . . What did you put in?' he asked.

'Photo,' I said. 'You?'

'A secret,' he said.

'That's not fair.'

'No,' he said, and looked at me strangely. I thought he might tickle me, or hit me even, but he didn't. He reached out and cuddled me and it felt weird. As if he was saying goodbye to me as well.

I never expected her to come and see me off – I'd tucked that hope away somewhere in the back between the towels and old linen – but when I heard the unmistakable sound of her unruly run, my heart leapt; and as she voiced my name – a shout verging on a scream – I ran towards her flaying arms.

'Sorry I'm late,' said Jenny Penny, breathing hard. 'It was my hair.'

We stood quietly looking at each other, frightened of speaking in case our words might wound.

'I've got new shoes,' she said finally in between quiet sobs.

'They're so nice,' I said, and I held her hand. They were red with small white daisies positioned on the toe, and I really liked them; they were the best shoes I'd ever seen her wear and I told her so.

'I wore them specially to show you,' she said.

'I know you did. Thanks,' I said, suddenly feeling wretched.

'I don't think we'll ever see each other again,' she said, looking up at me, her face red and blotchy from her tears.

'Of course we will,' I said, putting my arms around her and smelling the familiar scent of chips in her hair. 'We're linked,' I said. '*Inextricably* linked.' (Something my brother had said about us the night before.)

And I was right. We would see each other again, but only the once – as children, anyway – before our lives diverged like rivers separating and carving across new terrain. But I didn't know that as I waved to her from the car and shouted, 'See you soon, I'll miss you!' I didn't know that as I shouted, 'You're my best friend! Write to me!' I knew none of that as I looked back and watched her and our street recede like the point of light in a tunnel, until the moment we turned the corner and she and it were gone. I felt the air sucked out of my lungs like life itself.

TREES SURROUNDED US AS WE TURNED OFF THE MAIN ROAD and left the holiday traffic to chug along in Bank Holiday formation. We followed the single-lane track down towards the river, veering sharply left then right, following raggedy signs that said *Trehaven*.

The late afternoon sun hadn't lost its heat, and leaves from overhanging branches were dappled by its fractured intensity and flickered like broken mirrors onto my face. I breathed in this new air; it was damp; warm damp, and now and then I thought I could smell the sea, and could actually, because the tidal waters that fed the small river below were on the turn.

'We're nearly there,' I whispered to my brother as I leant back into the car, and for the first time during the six-hour journey, he sat up, interested. He started to bite his nails.

'It's all right,' I said to him, and he smiled at me and took his hand away from his mouth and concentrated on the green world outside. I lifted god out of his box and showed him his new home.

'You'll be safe here,' he whispered.

The road levelled out and as we took a sharp right, it lost its tarmac surface and soon the car was riding uncomfortably on rocks and gravel and compacted dirt. We stopped in front of a dilapidated wooden gate, *TREHAVEN* carved down the left-hand gatepost. Moss had bedded down within its curves and edges, and made the lettering vivid green against the damp darkness of the wood. My father turned off the ignition. I held my breath, not wishing to impede on the sounds of birds and forest life; I was still an observer, a participant not yet.

'We're here,' my father said. 'Our new home. Trehaven.'

We saw the removal van first and the clearing, and then finally emerging into sight came the house: large and square and off-white in the sunshine, and standing alone except for a small dilapidated outbuilding hiding in the shadow at its side. A small tree had taken sole occupancy of the neglected space within; its branches reaching for the sky.

I got out of the car and stretched, felt small in the shadow of our home. This was a house for rich people and as I stood looking at its grace and majesty, I suddenly remembered that we were.

I put god on a lead and ran down the lawn with him towards the river, carefully negotiating my footing on the flimsy mooring planks. They were rotten; eaten away by years of salt and wet and neglect, and there was a boat attached by rope, holed and half submerged, but clinging to its home like an elder with nowhere else to go.

'What do you think?' said my brother, suddenly behind me.

I startled and turned around quickly, for this was the land of spirits and sprites and other beings too light to elicit the sound of tread.

'Look!' I said, pointing to the river. 'A fish!'

And my brother lay down on the jetty and placed his hands gently into the cold water. The fish darted to the side. I watched him look at himself; follow the ripple of his reflection as the waters slowly rose around his fingertips. I heard him sigh deeply. A melancholy sound.

'How old am I?' he asked.

'Fifteen,' I said. 'Still young.'

A kingfisher flew overhead and landed on the opposite bank. I'd never seen one before.

IT WAS THE FIRST OF MAY, AND THE MORNING AIR WAS
trying hard to lift my sadness. It blew fresh through the trees, so
different from eight months before, when the forest was still and
musty, and encroached upon our house like heavy rain clouds
that refused to break.

For decades the house had been sheltered from light, and soon
its dampness started to camp out in our clothes, in our beds, and
in our bones and one lunchtime, five weeks after our arrival, my
exasperated mother issued the ultimatum that we either move
the house or we move the forest, and in a rare moment of purpose
my father went out and bought himself an axe.

It looked clumsy and sinister against his willowy frame, but
he was gripped by its fervent calling and strode into the forest
alone, shunning all offers of help, all offers of the more practical
chainsaws. This was his task, he said, and it would be carried

out alone. Penance, my brother reminded me, was a lonely place to be.

And as those oaks were thinned, so the clearing grew and receded from the house, taking the midges and mosquitoes too, and gradually sunshine came to our windows earlier, and light started to pierce that once thick canopy until a new shoot emerged, a flower maybe – a bluebell? – but something rare and unseen before. And soon those fallen trunks became planks, and the shelves our books leant upon, the table that held our fractious discussions, and the jetty that moored the surprise boat we were presented with that first Christmas.

From behind the stone wall I watched the school bus pull away, the second time that week. My parents didn't know I wasn't on it, and wouldn't, not until much later, anyway, when they lifted their heads out of the dust and chaos of renovation. They'd have something to say, of course – they always did – but I didn't care. That was a long way off and the day was mine.

I headed deeper into the forest where the oldest trees leant towards each other and formed a dome, and where the energy beneath hovered with the potency of a million words of prayer. For months I'd skirted the periphery of groups, laughing at jokes I never found funny, frowning at problems that never seemed insurmountable, only to have those self-same groups turn their backs on me beyond the stilted marker of school gates. 'Fuck 'em,' my brother said, but I didn't have the heart to. I wanted to be liked. But I was an outsider. And people didn't miss outsiders.

I sat down on the seat my father had built especially for my tenth birthday, and looked up at the dense interweaving of branches and leaves that obliterated the sky. I'd sat here through a storm once and returned home dry. I took the letter out of my schoolbag and looked at her familiar handwriting. She was left-handed and a trail of smudge followed her words across the envelope. I could see the ink now stretching down her little finger to her palm, where she would transfer it to her forehead in moments of hesitation and insecurity. But those moments must now be few, for she had a boyfriend and that's what she was writing to tell me.

His sudden presence omitted any mention of Atlantis, or the Christmas she'd just spent with us – that first, unforgettable Christmas at Trehaven – and my name and our once immutable friendship disappeared off the page to make way for Gordon Grumley, a new boy from Gants Hill. It was love, she said. I lowered the letter and quizzically repeated the word, as if such an emotion should have bypassed Jenny Penny as deftly as the gift of manageable hair. They'd met at a funeral, she said, and *he* now took her to the recreation ground to torment the man who played with himself in the bushes; *he* now walked her to school and *he* now plaited her braids with the patience of a god. The fact that she'd just been diagnosed with diabetes came as something of an afterthought right at the bottom of the page. She was OK, she said, but she always had to keep a bar of chocolate in her bag. She always did, I wanted to say.

'No school today then?'

Her voice bellowed through the trees.

'Nancy! You made me jump,' I said; a tone of admonishment in my voice.

'Sorry,' she said, sitting down next to me.

'I don't go to school on Tuesdays.'

'Is that right?' she said as she nudged my bulging schoolbag with her foot.

'Jenny Penny's got a boyfriend.'

'Really?' she said. 'That sucks.'

'It does,' I said, picking at a loose thread on my shirt, which quickly started to unravel. 'I don't think I like her any more.'

'Why's that?' Nancy asked.

I shrugged. 'Just don't.'

'Are you jealous?'

I shook my head. 'I just want my friend back,' I said, tears burning behind my eyes. 'I've become forgettable.'

I crouched down in the front seat until Nancy pulled away from our driveway and we sped out onto the open road.

'All clear,' she said, and I sat up and saw the yellow fields of rape to my left, beyond which, and out of sight, was the sea. The breeze whipped around my ears, around my hair, and I swallowed mouthfuls of it. We turned left down a narrow single-lane track and I pressed the horn around every corner, alerting oncoming cars to our presence, but it was unnecessary for we met no one except a lady and her dog, who pressed themselves against the hedgerow as we passed. I'd have an ice cream soon and all would be well; I'd have an ice cream with a double Flake and think I wasn't so bad.

'Morning, Nancy, morning, Elly,' said Mr Copsey. 'What can I do for you today?'

Mr Copsey owned the small kiosk at the back of the beach. He stayed open throughout the year, no matter how bad the weather was, and once Nancy asked him why he did it and he told her that without the sea he'd be nothing.

We sat in our usual place overlooking the rocky beach. The tide was out and rounds of slate and seaweed and pebbles stretched chaotically from the road to the water's edge. I looked up at the houses on the cliff and found it strange that three nights ago there had been a violent storm and waves had crashed over the gardens, depositing weed and, in one case, a dead seagull upon the lawns. Salt scum had to be scraped from windows to reinstate priceless sea views.

We'd met that particular onslaught as we'd met most unexpected things of that year, with doors bolted and shutters firmly drawn. And as the wind funnelled up the valley it brought with it the skimmed-off detritus of every life it touched: a briny stench of dead fish and damp nets, of shrimp heads and fishermen's piss, and trails of petrolstink and fear; an overwhelming scent that clogged our nostrils as efficiently as frost.

'That's an ill wind if ever there was one,' said my mother, and my father agreed; carefully adding to the smell with a voluptuous fart.

'Wait for me, Nancy!' I shouted as I raced after her, stumbling down the craggy beach. She was carrying an old canvas tool bag that clunked heavy against the rocks. I didn't know why she had it and could have asked, but actually I preferred to wait because Nancy was full of surprises and this was turning out to be a day of surprises. She stopped in the shadow of the furthermost cliff and dropped her bag. She took out a mallet and a chisel and scoured the surrounding area for thick plate-sized pieces of dark slate. I helped her and soon we had a pile next to us, stacked like pancakes. She sat down and took the top slate, positioning it sideways between her feet.

'Right,' she said as she carefully lined up the chisel against the edge of the slate. Two sharp taps and it separated cleanly in two, unfolding like two halves of a book.

'Nothing,' she said.

'But what are we looking for?' I asked excitedly.

'You'll know when you find it,' she said, and picked up another slate ready to place it into position.

*

Three hours later, the tide, together with Nancy's mood, started to turn; a sense of failure lapped at the edge of her frayed enthusiasm and even a freshly baked scone with jam couldn't lift her spirits. She was surrounded by mounds of splintered slate and unrewarded effort, but not unfortunately by the thing she was looking for. She stood up to call it a day.

'Just one more, Nancy,' I said, picking up the last and smallest of the pieces. 'Come on. Just one more.'

There was no clue that this might be the one. The mallet fell with the same heavy force and the chisel landed with the same perfect precision. Nothing was different, apart from Nancy's face as we prised the pieces apart and she saw that her search was over. For there, snuggled in the middle, was the coiled impression of a creature from another time, almost as old as the world. I gasped; ran my finger round and round its grooved spiral, and then held it close to my chest.

'Nothing stays forgotten for long, Elly. Sometimes we simply have to remind the world that we're special and that we're still here.'

2 May 1979

Dear Jenny,
I'm glad you're happy. Gordon sounds nice and I'm glad you have someone to play with. I miss you more than ever and I don't like school. I still haven't got any friends yet, but I never thought I'd make any as nice as you. I found this fossil on the beach and thought of you. Nancy says it's rare and precious. Nancy says good things. I hope you like it. Keep it safe for me.
Love,
Your best friend, Elly xx
PS. Sorry you've got diabeetis.

NOT ONCE HAD OUR PARENTS TOLD US OF THEIR PLANS FOR a bed and breakfast, and not once had they ever revealed this unnatural desire to house people who wouldn't normally be encouraged to share our lives. And yet here we were, looking down at the colourful magazine advertisement, placed just in time for the summer season.

'Well, what do you think?' they said.

Words like *idyllic, unique, peaceful* stood out next to the half-page photograph of our beloved home; a home that had exhausted our energies for almost a year whilst we transformed it into the idyllic, unique and peaceful space that it had stubbornly become.

'Do we need the money?' my brother asked quietly.

'No, of course not,' said my father. 'We're not doing this for money. We're doing this because we can and because it'll be fun. An adven-ture.'

Only nursery school teachers broke up words like that, I thought.

'Think of all the lovely people we'll meet,' said my mother, holding on tightly to the slab of pink quartz that hung around her neck, the one she'd uncovered at the clay pits in St Austell.

My brother and I looked at each other as we imagined Mr and Mrs Strange holding up the advertisement and saying, 'Look at this, dear, this looks nice. Let's visit and never leave.'

I reached for my brother's hand but it was already firmly in his mouth.

Our first two guests arrived just as the sealant had been placed around their bath. Mr and Mrs Catt pulled up in their sand-coloured Marina saloon and were greeted by my mother, who was wielding a bottle of champagne as violently as if it had been my father's axe.

They recoiled as she screamed, 'Welcome! You're our first!' and she led them into the living room where she introduced Joe and me. I only grunted and raised my hand because we had decided earlier that I should pretend to be deaf.

'Alfie!' my mother suddenly shouted into the hallway, and my father jogged in wearing a pair of flimsy red running shorts. He may as well have come in naked, since the discomfort of our guests would have been exactly the same. He leant towards them with his outstretched hand and said, 'Hi,' with an elongated *i*.

'Champagne, darling?' my mother asked my father, handing him an oversized flute.

'You betcha,' he said.

My brother and I looked at each other, quizzically mouthing the words 'betcha' and 'hi'.

'What about this *effing* travesty, eh?' said my father holding up the *Guardian*, showing a photograph of Margaret Thatcher.

'Two months on and still bloody with us.'

'We both think she's marvellous, actually,' said Mrs Catt in a crisp estuary accent, forcefully adjusting her bra strap. 'Doing a wonderful job.'

'And I'm sure she is,' said my mother sternly, looking towards my father.

'If you need anything, don't hesitate to ask,' said my father, about to swallow a large mouthful of discount-for-bulk Moët.

'Actually, all we really want is a bath,' said Mr Catt, placing his full glass of champagne onto the small table and rubbing his hands, as if the soap was in his palms already. My parents froze.

'A bath?' repeated my father, in a tone that suggested he was uncertain what a bath actually was.

'Yes, a *bath*,' said Mr Catt clearly.

'Right,' said my father, playing for time, but even he couldn't stretch *that* word for the necessary thirty-five minutes.

'Actually, do you know what's better than a bath?' my mother said with seamless reassurance.

'A shower?' said Mr Catt.

'No,' said my mother. 'A look at the garden,' and she marched the weary travellers down to the water's edge, where they gazed at nothing apart from their tired and vapid reflections. And at the precise moment when the sealant had set, my mother reached for their hands and shouted enthusiastically, 'Bath time!' and Mr and Mrs Catt looked at my mother in horror, suddenly imagining that she meant they'd all get in together.

They were harmless people who wanted no relationship with us, and only a very simple and private one with our house. They were up early whatever the weather, and had the same breakfast every morning. My mother could never tempt them beyond bran flakes and a small glass of orange juice, and my father could never tempt them beyond nine o'clock at night. He tried a film night and a cards night and a wine-tasting night, but nothing could lure them away from their own snug symbiosis. These were not the guests my parents had envisaged; they had envisaged guests who would be friends – a rather naïve and unrealistic aspiration – but one they would cling to over the years in their own impervious enthusiasm.

'Why does Mr Catt talk so loudly and slowly to you, Elly?' my mother asked one morning as I helped her to wash up.

'He thinks I'm deaf,' I said.

'What? Why?' asked my mother, and she pulled me to her and I nestled into her soft stomach. 'People are so different and wonderful, aren't they, Elly? Never forget that. Never give up on people.'

I didn't really know what she meant, but I said that I wouldn't, and clung to her scented clothes as fiercely as a hungry moth. I had missed this.

We were alone the day it happened. My parents had gone to Plymouth to order a new cooker and had left my brother and me to make wind chimes out of shells and metal scraps scavenged from the strand. The sky was an unblemished blue haze that morning and seemed to hypnotise all with its unstirring; quietening thrushes mid-song.

I heard the screech of brakes first, not the faint thud of impact; he was too small, you see. They had missed his head – the wheels, that is – and my brother had covered his body with his favourite shirt, the denim one Nancy had brought him from America. He looked like a discarded bundle lying at the side of the track; mislaid goods of the departed.

'I'm so sorry,' said Mr Catt, getting out of his car. 'I didn't see it.'

It, he said, not *him*. *It*, he said.

My brother wrapped god up and held him like a baby and carried him towards me as I waited by the gate. He was still warm, but where the firm rotundity of his body was supposed to be, instead there was something watery, something without essence, and as I held him I felt his warmth run from the shirt onto my leg until I looked down and my feet were covered in blood.

'What can I do?' said Mr Catt.

'You've done enough,' said my brother. 'Just pay and leave.'

'Leave?' said Mr Catt. 'Don't you think I should speak to your parents first?'

'No, I don't actually,' said my brother, picking up my father's axe. 'Just fucking leave. You're a murderer and we never wanted you here in the first place, so go on, piss off! I said Piss Off!' and he lunged for the car.

I watched the sand-coloured Marina spit and slide its way up the pebbled path, gear-straining somewhere between first and fourth, until it disappeared round the curve and left us to our unquenchable loss. My brother threw down the axe. His hands were shaking.

'I can't bear anyone to hurt you,' he said, and walked towards the shed to look for a box.

She picked up on the second ring as if she knew I'd call, as if she'd been standing by the phone waiting; and before I could say anything she said, 'God's dead, isn't he?' I never asked her how she knew – some things I preferred not to know – and so I said, 'Yes he is,' and promptly told her how it happened.

'It's the end of a chapter, Elly,' was all she could say after that, and she was right. His life meant more to me than anything, and now his death did, for it left an anguished hole impossible to fill. Jenny Penny was always right.

'He came back to you,' my brother said as I lay across my bed in the darkness. There was a pulse, *a faint miraculous pulse*, my brother said, that could not be felt before he laid the rabbit in my arms. And as he did, god opened his eyes and his paw brushed across my cheek.

'He came back to say goodbye.'

Then he should have stayed, was all I kept thinking.

'Maybe you'd like god buried in a special pet graveyard?' my mother gently said to me the following day.

'Why?' I said.

'So that he might be with other animals,' she said.

'He didn't like other animals, actually,' I said. 'I want him cremated. I want his ashes.'

And even though this was an unusual request in the late seventies, my mother scoured veterinary practices in the area until she found one agreeable to such a deed.

The memorial service was small and intimate, and huddled around his empty hutch each one of us had something nice to say. Nancy wrote a poem entitled 'Just When You Think It's All Over', which was really good, especially the last two lines, which she read out dramatically as if she was on stage: 'And if you think you can't see me, close your eyes and there I'll be.' Nancy was good with things like that; she always knew the right thing to say at memorials and other life-changing events. She made people feel better just by turning up. She went to lots of memorials in the eighties and most of her friends agreed that it wouldn't have been much of a memorial without her. She remembered things other people forgot. She remembered when

Andy Harman met Nina Simone in Selfridges and offered to sing a duet with her at Heaven, if only she could haul her iconic presence down to Villiers Street that week. She also remembered that Bob Fraser's favourite song was 'MacArthur Park' not 'Love to Love You Baby', as most people thought, and that his favourite flower was actually a tulip – a flower no self-respecting gay man would ever own up to. 'Memories,' she said to me, 'no matter how small or inconsequential, are the pages that define us.'

Joe said something about god being more than a rabbit and more like a god, which I liked, and Dad thanked god for making me so happy over the years, which made my mum cry in a way I'd never seen before. He said afterwards that she was still saying goodbye to her parents.

Mum put god's ashes into an old French peppermint tin and sealed it firmly with a red elastic band.

'Where are you going to scatter them, Elly?' she asked.

'I'm not sure yet,' I said. 'Somewhere special.' And until I decided, I put his ashes on my dressing table next to my favourite brush, and at night, when my room was secured in darkness, I saw lights dance in the air, which I knew were him.

'HERE,' MY BROTHER SAID, OFFERING ME THE TILLER FOR the first time. The river divide was just ahead and I steered towards the left-hand side where the river cut through dense woodland of scrub oaks and beech and sycamore too, and where I surprised a flock of Canada geese and sent them hurtling into distinctive formation.

Soon the river would narrow and carve through water rushes and overhanging trees still dripping with weed and flotsam from the previous high tide; it was the stretch I never trusted, the stretch of river that pulled my imagination as taut as rope around a cleat, and where I saw thick gnarled roots crawling across the mudflats like hungry arachnids.

'That's great,' my brother said. 'You're doing so well. Keep to the middle, let the boat search for deep water,' and I did, and only occasionally heard the sound of shingle against the wooden hull.

I cupped my hand across my brow; the sunlight was piercing and caught the surface of the water, highlighting the ragged spume. It was one of the last days of summer, and both nature and my brother responded. He lay down on the seat slats and placed his fishing cap over his face.

'Wake me up when we get there,' he said lazily, and in that one action I felt the responsibility for our safe return in my unsure hand.

I watched him doze. He seemed older these days, so much older than I was, and he'd grown into the landscape as if he'd always lived here and always would; but he would be gone by the following year, to finish his schooling in London, a sudden decision taken on a whim.

I looked at my watch; it was still early and they wouldn't miss us. We had the shopping for dinner and the guests wouldn't be back for hours. I cut the engine and let us float along with the tide, ducking under overhanging branches of trees that leant out at precarious degrees. I heard the faint sound of ducks gossiping in the weedy banks ahead.

'Everything OK?' my brother asked from under his hat.

'Yes,' I said, and picked up a small oar as a precaution against the shallow sandbanks that suddenly reared like seal backs.

A buzzard flew on the thermals overhead. I watched him hover against a backdrop of pink and violet heather until he swooped down into the hillside and emerged with a terrified vole clutched between his talons.

A grey mullet was flanking the hull, in search of company. It was large – four or five pounds, I think – similar to the one my brother caught the first autumn we arrived.

He'd taken so much pleasure in gutting it; he sliced under the gills and sharp along the belly, and soon the innards were floating downstream before being scooped up by a patient heron. My brother placed a small translucent orb into my palm.

'That's his eye,' he said. 'It still sees, even in death.'

'Shut up,' I said, and flicked it into the water.

He grinned and looked happier than I'd seen him in weeks. We cooked the fish on a makeshift fire next to the jetty and I said that if we were shipwrecked we'd do OK by ourselves now, and we wouldn't need anyone else. He smiled, but his eyes gave away that he'd always need someone else. No amount of self-sufficiency could dispel the craving he still felt for that person we no longer talked about; that person who'd taken him apart and left a piece missing that none of us could find.

I punted the boat under the branches and saw damson berries on the bushes ahead. I'd be making jam with my mother soon. I liked making jam. Swapping schoolbooks for activity.

'Joe,' I said, completely unthinking, 'Charlie would have liked this, wouldn't he?'

'Fuck off, Elly,' he said, suddenly sitting up, and I recoiled at his sharpness.

I lost my balance and fell onto the side of the boat, just missing a rowlock and a worse injury. The pain shot into my shoulder and I reached for my arm; rubbed it hard and stifled the tears wedged in my throat. I wanted him to look at me, to help me, but he wouldn't; instead his eyes narrowed as he looked into the sun, as if blindness was preferable to the sight of my betraying face. Unhelmed, the boat floated aimlessly and became wedged on a bank of shingle.

'See what you've done,' he said.

'Sorry,' I said, rubbing my arm.

'Fucking idiot.'

It was a fallacy that time had healed him; it had simply

allowed him to hide and file his experience away under the simple labelling of: Him and Me.

We waited silently for the tide to catch up, and as I rubbed the bruising on my elbow, I vowed never to mention his name again. To me he was dead. And he disappeared once again from our lives back into our convenient amnesia, until that strange night in December when he unexpectedly returned. And when his name was unexpectedly mentioned. But not by us.

The crisp smell of rime awoke me from my sleep and I got up swiftly to secure the window. I looked out onto the milky landscape; perfect, silent, eerily untouched except for the staggered imprints of a lone chaffinch in search of life. Winter had fallen heavily and precisely that morning across an unprepared valley. Everything felt slow. Movement, thought. Even breath. Until, that is, the frantic screaming of my name cut through the white like a saw through steel, propelling me downstairs on the swift tread of fear. The television was on:

'The sixteen-year-old boy was named as Charlie Hunter, our sources can reveal,' the newsreader said. 'He was kidnapped at approximately ten o'clock at night when masked men broke into what was considered a secure house on the outskirts of Beirut. He was with his father, an oil executive working for an American company in Dubai. They were visiting friends at the time. A ransom note was left behind at the scene, although this has not been confirmed. No group has claimed responsibility for the kidnapping and we are so far unsure as to whether the demands are political or financial. We shall keep you updated of any further developments.'

The scene suddenly changed and a reporter started to talk about fuel prices. My father turned the volume down until the room was left in silence and images flickered upon our faces.

'Good God,' said Nancy.

'I can't believe this,' said my mother. 'Charlie? Our Charlie?'

'Scrum half Charlie?' said my father.

'*Joe's* Charlie,' I said supportively, but it had the opposite effect, and Joe ran from the room.

'I'll go,' said Nancy, and she got up and followed him out. She sat down with him on the bed.

'I wanted him dead, Nance,' said my brother, choking for breath. 'I always wanted him fucking dead, like Golan.'

I stood and watched from the door. Waited for a command that might help to ease the situation or would have me running from room to room to kitchen on an errand that only I could fulfil. But none came.

'What are you talking about?' asked Nancy quietly.

'And now it might happen,' Joe said.

'It won't happen,' she said.

'How could I live with myself?'

'We just say these things,' said Nancy. 'It's not real. It's hurt and anger and tiredness, and a whole load of other shit, and it doesn't mean it'll happen. You're not that powerful,' she said, kissing his head.

'I don't care any more. He doesn't have to be mine, I just want him found, I want him safe, nothing more. He doesn't have to be mine.' And he pulled the pillow over his face. 'Please find him,' I heard him say. 'Oh God, please find him.'

I smelt her perfume first and that's what made me turn round and watch her tentatively climb the last of the stairs. She stood next to me in the doorway; in time to hear his truth.

'I loved him so much,' said my brother as he pulled the pillow away from his face.

His grainy image stood out from broadsheet to tabloid, and under any other circumstances it would have been exciting to see his dark, handsome face again, smiling out at us from beyond a beach; a beach we might one day have visited if only their hearts had taken a less potholed route. He looked happy (happier than us), and so unaware of the violence about to trespass on his life. I wondered how much his kidnappers thought he was worth; how much my parents thought I was worth, and wondered if worth was connected to things like goodness or usefulness or helping people less fortunate. I thought that probably I was worth more when I was younger.

At night, as I lay in bed listening to the owls, I saw him in a dark cellar, chained to a wall and surrounded by bones. There was stink on the floor and a cup of dirty water. Things crawled in the darkness, black backs shimmering green. I heard a chant, a call to prayer. A scream. I sat up. Just a fox.

They cut his ear off. They wrapped it in a handkerchief and sent it to his father's company; said they'd cut the other one off in time for Christmas Day, then his hands.

'How much do you think an ear is worth, Nancy?' I said quietly.

'Everything,' she said, as she layered cream onto a trifle that none of us felt like eating.

We sat in vigil in front of the television day and night, taking it in turns to relay news to those of us indisposed at the time. School took a back seat – I wouldn't return now until the following term – and the routine of our days was simply forgotten. We had two guests left, happy guests who stood out like our decorations, garishly cheap and inappropriate, and we neglected them like Christmastime itself.

'What goes on in other countries doesn't really concern us, does it?' they said.

'How can it not?' said my father incredulously.

My mother told them to help themselves to breakfast and anything else they needed. They did and then left without paying.

My brother no longer ate; nothing could tempt his stomach to unclench as he walked from room to room, pacing, bent double by the cold and his fear of what might come. He was shrinking, guilt was eating him, and only my father understood the power that such an emotion held.

I strode across the lawn, rudely disturbing the frost, and entered the forest like the early morning sun, so maddeningly awake. There was a metallic taste to the air, an expectant taste, and I ran through the undergrowth startling the squirrels and birds still lethargic with sleep, and slowed as I saw my seat up ahead. I sat down and shivered. I took the tin from my pocket and removed the elastic band. I prised off the lid and peeked inside. Just ashes, nothing more. No scent of peppermint, just ashes. I couldn't think of a prayer nor even a song as I scattered his dusty life across the woodland floor.

'Please find him,' I said. 'Please find Charlie.'

It was midday on 23 December. It was cold and overcast, and the whole village had awoken to news that a small fishing boat had been holed on the rocks out by the island. My parents and I watched the rescue from the shore. My mother had brought down flasks of tea and warm fruit scones for the rescuers and the inquisitives, and we watched the strange circling of the gulls, so predatory and foreboding, and their presence filled us with a nauseating doom.

We motored back solemnly, the high tide pulsing us towards

home on swollen crested waves, and as we docked and then made our way up the lawn, Nancy and my brother ran towards us screaming.

The television was on as we ran in and my mother immediately started to cry. He looked shaken but still the same, the same old Charlie. His hair was long and scruffy and his eyes receded deeper into their sockets as if they'd tried to hide away in there. No interviews were given. Instead he was shielded by a blanket and bundled into a car and media obscurity, where no details of his release would ever be given although we would one day learn that a million had changed hands, and that somehow seemed fair. And then he disappeared once more from our lives, but not this time from our memories. His name was uttered from time to time, and a smile returned to my brother's lips as he slowly let go of that joyless dance that had held *him* hostage over the years. He let it go and allowed possibility to once again enter his life.

Christmas morning. I looked out onto the lawn thinking that it was covered by a thick layer of snow, but it was actually mist and I could see it rolling up the river valley like white tumbleweed. I crept downstairs and peeked into the lounge and saw presents strewn under the tree. The smell of firewood was still so distinct; it was a smell that made me hungry, and I went to the hearth to see if the carrot and mince pie had been eaten, or if the sherry had gone. It was only half gone so I finished off the rest in one sweet mouthful.

I wandered into the kitchen to get a biscuit when out of the corner of my eye I saw movement on our lawn. I felt it had a larger presence than a bird or a squirrel and I quickly put on some Wellington boots and my dad's old jumper hanging by the back door and went out into the cold morning air. The mist hovered at knee height over the lawn and I found it hard to discern anything moving amidst its opaque haziness. And then I saw it. It bounced out of the mist and stopped about ten yards from me. His pointed skull and chestnut fur were so familiar, and those long legs and white-tipped tail.

'I knew you'd come back to me,' I said, and I crouched a nd went towards him but he immediately recoiled. I suddenly understood. This was the agreement, the same one my brother had made: I am here but I am not yours; and the rabbit hopped towards the forest and disappeared as quickly as an interrupted dream.

A NEW DECADE DAWNED, AND MY PARENTS WOULD eventually have guests who returned to them year after year, and who would all be a bit like us – a collage of the useful and impractical, the heady and the mundane.

It often occurred to me that normal people *never* stayed with us, or if they did it was certainly for no longer than the one eye-opening night. My mother loved this seasonal swell to our family, the ebb and flow of familiar faces that brought new stories and new delights to our door, just as the stagnancy of the everyday settled there like stubborn mould. Our lives had become tidal; friendships, money, business, love; nothing ever stayed the same.

It was a fine summer's day, the day I first saw Mr Arthur Henry striding through the village leaving a trail of open mouths and Cornish gossip in his colourful wake. He was wearing linen plus fours, a yellow and blue striped shirt and a pink and white polka-dot bow tie that was so large it almost obscured his neck. He carried a cane in one hand and a newspaper in the other, and now and then he would waft away wasps attracted to the sweet floral scent that exuded from his pale skin. I followed him only as far as the amusement arcade, where the sudden need to play pinball overtook me and where I reluctantly entrusted him to the day ahead. I watched him saunter along the quay next to the crabbers and the ferrymen. I watched him weave in and out of parents holding cigarettes and lager instead of their children's hands. He belonged to another time, a more genteel one; and yet he graced the modern with a simple inquisitiveness and charm that kept me spellbound for days.

The next time I saw him was in the forest. He was talking loudly to himself (Shakespeare, I later learnt) and danced like an aged elf in this unabashed green solitude. It was the type of dance not intended for an audience, for its form was wild and juvenile, and sprung from an uncritical source. He wore the same outfit but had walking shoes instead of polished brogues, and held a twig of leaves instead of his cane.

I felt shy watching his moment of privacy, and when my conscience could bear no more, I came out from behind a tree and said, 'Good morning, sir,' and held out my hand with an assurance beyond my years.

He stopped in the middle of a pirouette and smiled, and breathing hard said, 'Good morning, young lady,' and he shook my hand. He looked older up close but not that old; sixty probably, for his skin had the sheen of care and the trace of a long-forgotten vanity that once would have shone from mirrors with the radiance of sunrise.

'I like your outfit,' I said.

'That's very kind of you to say,' he said.

'This is my forest,' I said.

'Is it now? Then I am a trespasser and I am indeed at your mercy,' and he bowed in front of me.

I giggled. I'd never met anyone who spoke as eloquently as that and I thought he was probably a poet; my first.

'Where are you staying?' I asked as I sat down on the bench.

'I'm staying in a quaint bed and breakfast just behind the river on the east side,' he said as he sat next to me, still trying to catch his tired, exhilarated breath.

'Ah,' I said nodding, pretending to know which one he was talking about.

He took out his pipe and placed it comfortably between his teeth. He lit a match and held it above the bowl and puffed hard as gusts of nutty sweet smoke wafted from his mouth and made me feel hungry. I thought about the biscuits my mother and I had made earlier that morning – chocolate-covered shortbread fingers – and I could smell the scent of baking on my cardigan. My mouth started to water and I felt suddenly drawn to home.

'I live in the big white house just the other side of here,' I said, pointing in the general direction, hoping he'd be impressed, because I so wanted him to be impressed.

'I'm impressed,' he said, and I blushed.

'My house is a bed and breakfast too,' I said.

'Is it now?' he said.

'You can come and have a look at it if you want. We have some vacancies,' I said.

'Do you now?' he said.

'So if you stayed with us you could use this forest any time you wanted. *Legally*,' I said.

'Could I now?' he said, and he looked at me and smiled, and I knew immediately that his smile meant, Yes.

My mother loved Arthur from the start. She took great

pleasure in welcoming him under her orphaned wing, allowing him to mend the brittleness that had settled in over the years. She missed living her life with somebody older advancing ahead; somebody to shield her from the mortal wall that drew closer every season; someone simply to tell her that she would be all right. And he did that, all of that, from the moment he came to stay; and when he raised his cap and shouted his 'hellos', none of us had any clue that it would be the start of a rich and enduring relationship that would become as dependable as the quiet close of day; for Arthur simply paid a month in advance and installed himself in the outside cottage my father had completed just two days before. The smell of paint hung in the air, the vapours verging on nauseating, but it signalled newness to Mr Henry, not discomfort, and as he entered his new home, he opened his arms out wide and shouted 'Bliss!' (a word I soon adopted as my own; a word that endeared me to no one).

'What do you think of the shepherd's pie?' said Brenda, the dinner lady at school.

'Bliss,' I said, instead of my normal 'OK'.

'No need to be sarcastic,' she said, and put back the extra spoonful of peas that had hovered so enticingly above my plate.

By the time Arthur came to live with us, he had already retired from a life that had him yo-yoing between academia and the diplomatic service like an alternating current. He was disciplined, but hid it behind a camp frivolity that made people think he wandered unconcerned throughout the day. But he *was* concerned, about so much. He awoke unfailingly at six every morning and wandered down to the jetty to note the constantly changing aspect of nature. He noticed small things, particular things; the additional markings of a young deer that shyly appeared over the other side of the river, the last star to disappear at sunrise, (it was always the faint one to the right of the large oak), the minuscule erosion of the opposite bank as a new root became visible amidst the mud and sand. He opened my eyes to this subtle scene of change, and whenever I declared I was bored, he would march me down to the water's edge and make me describe all I could see in tones of enthusiasm and wonder, until my body again reverberated with the excitement of life.

He practised yoga on the grass just outside his cottage and could contort his limbs in the most extreme way, whilst his face remained a palette of calm and concentration. He said he'd taken up yoga at Mahatma Gandhi's ashram in Ahmedabad and had focused his mind by walking over hot coals for fun. Because there was always a twinkle in his eye, no one ever really knew if he stretched the truth as easily as he stretched his body, but I knew. I always knew the difference between truth and fiction. It was the subtle alteration of his tone, a resonance only I could detect as he traversed the borders between those two states. But ultimately who cared? Truth, as he always said, was overrated; nobody ever won prizes for telling the truth.

A yogi had once told him the exact time and circumstances of his death and with such information at his fingertips he had been able to calculate to the day, when both his money and breath would expire (although he told me he'd allowed a five-day leeway on the money).

'How are you going to die, Arthur? Tell me – how are you going to die?'

I asked him that every week for a year until he finally said, 'With a smile on my face.' An answer that seemed to silence my gory enthusiasm with an anticlimactic jeer.

During the years he had left, he planned to write his memoirs and relive them in what he referred to as 'impotent serenity'. They were stories of travels: racy, explicit accounts of a gentleman's tour of toilet cubicles and underground bars throughout the world, but in his hands they became a fantastic historical account of the changing template of society. And what soon became clear was that Arthur Henry had always been in the right place at the right time. He had just got off the bus when Rosa Parks decided not to, *and* he was in Dallas when JFK was shot. He was holed up in a moderately priced motel with an FBI agent he adored and knew only as Sly. When reports of the fatal shooting traversed those thin walls, Sly abandoned him like a discarded nightgown, and left him to his own spent company and the sweet rubbing of handcuffs toying at his wrists. He was found by a cleaner the next morning, a woman who seemed so inured to his naked predicament that she simply sat next to him on the bed and wept for the man who was once her American Dream. Arthur apparently did the same.

At weekends and holidays, I ran my boat taxi service to and from the village as a way to secure my pocket money. I loved ferrying Arthur about, and recently I'd been allowed to head out of the harbour into open water with him and hug the ragged coastline to Talland and back. I learnt to read the patterns the seagulls made and the encroaching smell of sea air, and could sense a heavy swell ahead of time. Arthur had never fished before, so this was the first time in my life that I could teach him something and I felt full of pride. I started to unravel the feathered, orange trailing lines that I promised my mother would catch our supper of mackerel that evening.

'Just let the rope run through your fingers, Arthur,' I said, 'and when you feel a tug, yell and start to pull in the line.'

'Elly,' he said, 'I shall scream!'

I scanned the waters ahead; pleasure boats were aplenty in this holiday season and I looked for a route that would lead us safely away from the dangerous holiday spirit that steered most of those erratic craft. I looked down into the waters and saw the shadows of rugged rocks beneath, waiting like crocodiles to emerge in the shallows. I'd caught a bass here the previous week. Five pounds of struggle and fear, but I'd landed it alone and sold it on the quay to a restaurant. But we were not fishing for bass today, we were fishing for mackerel, and what we needed was deeper water. I started the engine and soon we were heading out past the island towards a clear horizon, Arthur holding the orange line, never taking his eyes away from the task.

'Why don't you go to school?' Arthur asked as he attempted to light his pipe.

'I do,' I said.

'Oh, come on,' he said, 'not often.'

'No need,' I said. 'I can learn all I need to know here; by the sea, in the forest; building things. I can make jam *and* I can find edible fungi in the forest. I can do everything that would ensure my survival, should disaster unexpectedly strike.'

'And are you *expecting* disaster to *unexpectedly* strike?'

'I'm just saying I'm *ready*, Arthur.'

Arthur thought for a while and sucked deeply on his pipe. The sweet nutty plumes wafted towards me on the breeze and I opened my mouth, timed it well and swallowed mouthfuls of the thick edible smoke.

'Nature *is* a great educator; but not the sole educator. You do yourself a great disservice by not attending,' he said as he leant down and placed the fishing line securely under his foot. 'Don't leave it too late, Elly. Don't let the window of education pass you by. Even youth can have regret.'

'But I like learning,' I said. 'I just don't like *school*. I used to. But it's different here. I still want to play, Arthur. But everyone in my class wants to be grown up. I'm different. They tell me I'm different and I know I am, but only with them does it feel wrong.'

'I'm different,' said Arthur.

'I know, but you feel right,' and I leant over the side and let my hand trail in the coolness of the water. 'I'm unpopular and that hurts,' I said.

'Popularity, my dear, is as overrated as a large member,' he said, looking into the distance, lost in one of his other clandestine worlds.

'What member?' I asked, momentarily confused.

'How old are you?' he asked.

'Nearly twelve.'

'Don't ever stop playing, Elly,' he said, as he wiped his hands on a starched, white handkerchief that he'd ironed the night before. 'Never stop playing.'

I changed direction and took us further away from the pull of the island. Our drift had been deceptively strong, and the soft drone of the engine sounded strained against the tide.

'Arthur?' I said, shielding my brow with my free hand. 'No one needs to worry about me. I'll turn out all right in the end. You know I will.'

He slapped his knee and said, 'I said exactly the same thing at your age, Elly. And look at me now!'

'Well, there you go,' I said, beaming.

'There you go,' he said, falling back into the depths of thought. 'Actually, your mother wanted me to ask you something.'

'Oh?' I said, securing the tiller in a locked position and unravelling another fishing line.

'How would you like to be schooled at home?' he said.

'By who?' I asked suspiciously, as I tied the final knot.

'By me, of course!' he said, and a waft of smoke flew into my face and I coughed.

'I will take you to O level. English – Literature and Language, Mathematics, Geography, History – my favourite, of course; French and German. Your mother has a friend in the village who's prepared to cover the Art. So what do you think? Apparently it's non-negotiable and you'll have to work your bloody socks off. Take it or leave it?'

'Take it,' I said quickly, ignoring the darting line hanging over the edge; the line disappearing into the spumey wake with five mackerel thrashing to the depths with all their might.

The sun was low, and our quota of fish caught. I cut the engine and we drifted with the current – a moment of quiet – the slap of waves against the side, an overhead gull, the faint sound of a radio coming from a cove. I nervously placed the anchor over the edge. The rope uncoiled hastily and I was careful to keep my limbs away from its hunger, so present in my mind were the stories of children dragged to their deaths by a wayward foot or hand. The rope suddenly went slack and I relaxed.

We rose and fell gently on the wake of a passing motor boat, and as the sound of its engine settled beyond the cliffs, Arthur unwrapped the tin foil and handed me a piece of Victoria sponge, my favourite. Jam oozed from its sides and I licked my hand, a curious taste now of strawberry, butter-cream and fish. I looked over at the foil and wondered if we might share the last piece of cake, and as I was about to suggest the plan, the distant sound of a bell rang out across the waves.

'Don't tell me there's a church nearby?' said Arthur, pouring a cup of tea from his Thermos and looking about at the watery, empty surround.

'No, no. It's actually a bell on the water. Way out there,' I said, pointing to the faint line that was actually a light-house. 'Not many people know about it, but I do, Arthur. I've seen it.'

'Have you indeed? Well, I like the sound. It's rather eerie,' he said. 'Mournful. Grieving all those lost at sea, I suppose.'

'I suppose it is,' I said, never having thought of it that way.

It had been an adventure to me, that was all. An adventure most people said was make-believe, but I had seen it and so had my brother. A year before, it had loomed towards us out of the mist, a large brass bell floating on the waves as if it had been carelessly dropped from some heavenly steeple. It was a bell that called no one to prayer, and yet there we were, moored right next to it.

'This is creepy,' said my brother.

'More than creepy. We shouldn't be out here,' I said as I ran my hand across the rough cold metal, and as my brother started the engine, the bell suddenly struck its note and I fell to the floor in tears. I told my brother I had slipped, caught my foot on some rope. But what I never told him was that as the bell chimed, the metal suddenly felt warm; as if it had secretly craved the scanty touch of human contact and the sound it had so suddenly made was actually the sound of its pain.

'Do you believe in God, Arthur?' I said, eating the last piece of sponge.

'Do I believe in an old man in the clouds with a white beard judging us mortals with a moral code from one to ten? Good Lord no, my sweet Elly, I do not! I would have been cast out from this life years ago with my tatty history. Do I believe in a mystery; the unexplained phenomenon that is life itself? The greater something that illuminates inconsequence in our lives;

that gives us something to strive for as well as the humility to brush ourselves down and start all over again? Then yes, I do. It is the source of art, of beauty, of love, and proffers the ultimate goodness to mankind. That to me is God. That to me is life. That is what I believe in.'

I listened to the bell again, whispering across the waves, calling, calling. I licked my fingers and scrunched the tin foil up into a ball.

'Do you think a rabbit could be God?' I asked casually.

'There is absolutely no reason at all why a rabbit should not be God.'

IT IS DECEMBER AGAIN. MY BIRTHDAY. IT IS ALSO THE DAY when John Lennon was shot. A man went up to him and shot him outside his home in New York, wife next to him. Simply shot him. I can't understand it; wouldn't for days.

'The good die young,' says Jenny Penny during our phone conversation.

'Why?' I ask.

But she pretends not to hear me, pretends that the line is bad. She always does that when she doesn't have an answer.

I go to bed early that night, inconsolable. I don't even blow out the candles on my cake.

'One candle's already gone out in the world,' I say. I leave my presents for another day. There is simply nothing to celebrate.

I WAITED AT THE SMALL STATION, LOOKING DOWN FROM the bridge at the simple symmetry of tracking that went left or right: to London or to Penzance. I'd got there early. I liked to get there early, hopeful that the impossible might happen and the train would shatter its timetable, but it never did. The morning air was grey and freezing. I blew on my hands and misted breath streamed from my mouth. The cold had quickly got through to my shoes and was settling down into my toes; they would be white now and only a bath could give them back life.

I hadn't seen him for three whole months; locked away was he into term life and those London streets that stole him from me and left me instead with a pile of letters that were filed away in an A4 folder, with *PRIVATE* taped on the front. He was really good at Economics, he wrote, and he was really good at Art. He was in a choir and had started playing rugby again, now that he felt settled, now that he was happier. I thought 'playing rugby' was code for a new boyfriend, but it wasn't; he really had started playing rugby again. Love, it seemed, was as distant as memory.

There was nothing at this station; no café, no waiting room. There was only a shelter on the platform that became both useful and not useful, depending on the direction of the wind. I was too excited to wait in the van and listen to Alan's tape of Cliff Richard, which I seemed to know backwards and would have sounded much better to me had it been sung that way. Alan liked Cliff Richard, but he *loved* Barry Manilow. He'd listened to him in prison and the words had given him hope, he said. Even 'Copacabana'? I asked. *Especially* 'Copacabana', he said.

Alan had been our driver for a year now, and ferried our guests with the patience of a saint. He couldn't get any work before us, but he'd been honest with my father, who was the one man who believed in the redemptive power of a second chance. He put Alan on full pay, with the sole caveat that he should be ready for duty day or night. Alan agreed, and as the wage and respectability re-entered his life, so did his wife and child, and that faint stint of incarceration faded into make-believe, until nobody could really be sure whether it had happened or not.

The red and white signal marker suddenly raised its sluggish head. I saw the smoke first, as always, then the dark barrelled front barging its way across the countryside like some unstoppable bully. First class passed underneath me and then the buffet, carriage one, then two and then another until the train slowed into the station and I started to practise what I was going to say to him. Just as the train stopped, a door flung open and I saw his arm. He threw his kitbag out first (apparently they were all the rage at his school), and then he emerged wearing a Santa hat and sunglasses.

'Joe!' I shouted, and ran to the end of the bridge. He darted up the slope towards me.

'Stay there!' he yelled as he fought against the wind and attempted to get his heart pumping after three and a half sedentary hours in a forward-facing seat. And I felt myself lifted up into the grey morning sky, before falling into his wool-layered chest. He was wearing aftershave. I'd bought him aftershave for Christmas, damn.

'Hello,' he said. 'You look great.'

'I've missed you,' I said, as the first of my tears fell onto his sunglasses.

Alan always drove the long scenic route back to our house whenever my brother came home. It gave us time to gossip about my mother and father, and for my brother to reacquaint himself with the fields and hedgerows and vistas he once knew so intimately. Now and then, I would catch Alan looking in the rear-view mirror at us, eyes widening over information most normal families would have kept private and wouldn't have discussed until they were safely behind the confines of a closed door.

'Nancy kissed Mum,' I said to Joe.

Alan's eyes grew very big.

'When?' said Joe excitedly.

'About a month ago. When she broke up with Anna.'

Alan steered into the verge.

'She was really sad about that,' Joe said.

'Devastated,' I said.

'It was to do with newspapers and stuff.'

'Was it?' I said. 'I didn't know. Well, anyway, Nancy was crying outside on the patio and Mum was holding her and when Nancy looked up, she pulled Mum onto her lips and kissed her; *tongues* as well.'

Alan crunched the gears. He couldn't find third.

'No?' said Joe.

'And,' I said, now really trying to catch my breath, 'they didn't move. They stayed like that for ages. Mum didn't move.'

'No?' said Joe.

'And,' I said, 'when they finally pulled away, they laughed.'

'No?' said Joe.

'And,' I said, 'Mum said, "Oops," and they laughed again.'

Alan stalled.

'And guess what?' I said.

'What?' said Joe.

'I told Dad.'

'You didn't?' said Alan, suddenly taking his eyes off the road.

'I did,' I said to Alan.

'What did he say?' asked Joe.

'He laughed and said, "At last! At least we've got that out of the way."'

'Unbelievable,' said Joe.

Alan lost his wing mirror turning into our gateway.

My brother looked around his room, looking for differences, changes we might have made in his absence. But it was all there, exactly as he had left it: a room stalled by an interrupted moment; a grab-a-bag dash to catch a train; an exposed deodorant (now dry) awaiting his return; a newspaper, three months old, sprawled next to his bed.

I sat down and watched him unpack a bag full of dirty laundry.

'Did you know that Michael Trewellin died?' I said.

'Yeah,' said my brother as he folded one of his clean shirts.

'Drowned,' I said.

'I know,' he said.

'We went to his funeral,' I said.

'Oh, yeah?'

'They're weird, aren't they?' I said.

'S'pose they are,' he said.

'Everyone staring at the coffin,' I said.

'I didn't know they found the body,' he said.

'They didn't. Maybe that's why we were all staring at the coffin,' I said.

'Maybe,' he said.

'Wondering what was inside,' I said.

I reached for a magazine and opened it up at its centrefold: a tanned man in a very small towel. I was used to pictures like this when my brother came home. He'd probably give the magazine to Arthur and Arthur would say, 'Oh, you naughty, naughty boy.'

'I saw Beth in the village a couple of days ago,' I said, trying to sound lighter.

'Beth?' he said, stopping to look at me.

'Michael Trewellin's *sister*. I don't think you knew her very well,' I said. 'She was younger. About my age.'

I watched him fold a jumper.

'Is she all right?' he said.

'She looked very sad,' I said. 'Understandable really.'

He came and sat next to me on the bed, as if he knew where my thoughts were heading.

'Nothing will happen to *me*, Elly,' he said. 'I'm not going anywhere,' and he placed his arm around my shoulder. 'I'm not Michael.'

'I don't think I could bear it,' I said. 'She just looked so sad.'

*

My father asked for the lights to be turned off as he proudly held up the neon sign.

'There's *aways rum* at our *im*?' said my mother, trying to read the joined-up writing shining green in the darkened room.

'There's *always room* at our *inn*,' said my father, a touch of exasperation entering his voice. 'It's my Christmas message. I told you last summer I was planning something different,' and he had.

We'd been in the kitchen making lemon ice when he'd told us about his plans for a no-charge policy over Christmas.

'Our door is open to everyone, rich or poor,' he said, and my mother told him she loved him and led him out into the garden for a quiet kiss. For a man whose severe dislike of organised religion was notorious, his charity was becoming more and more Christian every day, and my brother looked at me and shook his head and said, 'This can only lead to a donkey, a stable and a real baby.'

'And don't forget the star in the east,' said Arthur.

'That'll be me then,' said Nancy, as she walked through the door, lighting a cigar.

My father quickly turned the lights back on and said he was going to affix his sign at the top of the pathway between the waving camel and the naked Santa, should anyone wish to join him. Strangely no one did.

Our one and only guest that Christmas was a Ms Vivienne Collard, or Ginger, as she liked to be called. She was Arthur's closest friend, and had first come to us four months ago with a broken foot as well as a broken heart (the two weren't connected). She was a Shirley Bassey impersonator, and with her red hair and pale skin, she stood out as one of the unique ones, if not exactly the best. When she sang 'Goldfinger' she curled her index finger in front of your nose and when you could finally focus, you could see that she had painted it gold. And when she sang 'Big Spender' she threw Monopoly money into the air. But when she sang 'Easy Thing to Do' no eye was left dry in our tinselled house. Arthur said he would have changed sides for a woman like that, until she sang a cover of 'Send in the Clowns', dressed as one.

Arthur and Ginger were inseparable when they got together. They had first met years ago on the London scene when their faces were smooth and devoid of experience, and had ended up sharing many things, including a flat in Bayswater and a ballet dancer called Robin. Their banter was rich and comfortable, their teasing intimate and profound; their 'I love you' without the use of those startling words.

Ginger arrived at our house at five o'clock on Christmas Eve, armed only with a suitcase full of champagne 'and a change of knickers', as she liked to whisper to Arthur, just to make him recoil into the darker recesses of our living room.

'Thank you, Alan,' she said as she tucked a five-pound note into his large palm. 'And a happy Christmas, pet.'

'That's not necessary, Ginger,' said Alan, attempting to tuck the note back into her coat pocket.

'You get something for that little girl of yours,' said Ginger, and Alan said he would, but never told her that the little girl was actually a chubby little boy called Alan junior.

'I love Alan,' said Ginger turning to my father, as the van disappeared up the drive. 'What was he *in* for again?' she asked nonchalantly.

'Can't catch me out that way, Ginger,' he said as he hugged her tightly.

Everyone wanted to know what Alan's crime was, but my father never told anyone, not even my mother.

'Hello, my treasure,' Ginger said to me as I carried freshly laundered towels to her room. 'Come and sit here and tell me your news,' and she patted her legs and I went and sat on her wide lap. I always worried that I'd crush her but when I felt her thick thighs beneath mine, I knew she was made of hardy stuff.

'Made any good friends yet?' she said.

'No,' I said. 'Not yet. Joe says I'm a loner.'

'Me too, kid. Nothing wrong with that.'

(She wasn't but I was grateful that she'd tried.)

'And how's that Jenny Penny? Is she coming for the holidays? Will I meet her at last?'

'No, her mum said she can't.'

'Strange one, that one.'

'Mmm. She's got her period now, you know.'

'Has she now? And what about you?' she asked.

'Not yet. Still waiting,' I said.

'Well, you wait on,' she said. 'You'll have that bloody thing clogging up your knickers for years. Lift up,' she added, clumsily adjusting the position of her skirt. 'So how's that big bad brother of yours?'

'He's OK,' I said.

'Still queer?' she said.

'Yep. It's definitely not a phase.'

'Well, good for him,' said Ginger. 'And you? Got a boyfriend yet?'

'No, I don't want one, actually,' I said.

'Why's that then?'

'Well,' I began, 'there was somebody who was a bit interested in me once. But I left it too late.'

'Oh?' she said. 'And what? He just buggered off, did he?'

'Sort of,' I said. 'He drowned.'

'Oh,' she said.

'He was called Michael,' I said.

'Well, good job you weren't with him, eh?' she said, 'otherwise you probably wouldn't be here now,' and she started to rummage around in her suitcase, obviously unable to think of anything better to say. But Ginger was like that: emotions embarrassed her except when she sang. My dad said that was exactly *why* she sang.

'Here,' she said, handing me a beautifully wrapped gift. 'I wrapped it myself.'

'Is it for me?' I asked.

'Who else?' she said. 'It's a ring.'

'Gosh,' I said.

'It was my mother's, but I can't get it on my finger any more because I'm too fat. Thought you might as well have it,' she said, not looking at me.

(Translation: *I love you and would like you to have something that's very dear to me.*)

I opened the box and saw a diamond- and sapphire-encrusted ring, which caught the overhead light and shone into my face like footlights.

'But this is so expensive, Ginger,' I gasped.

'Best you enjoy it now, rather than when I'm dead,' she said.

'Oh, I will, it's so beautiful, thank you.'

'That's all right then,' she said, and I felt her face flush with warmth as I kissed her and told her she was one of my most favourite people in the whole world. Because she was.

It was rare for Nancy not to be with us at Christmas, but we forgave her because she was skiing in Gstaad, allowing her heart to be mended by mountain air and a woman called Juliette. After lunch we called her and thanked her for our presents. She sounded ever so happy (drunk) on the phone, and Dad whispered to us across the table that Mum was probably a bit jealous.

'So what has *she* got that I haven't?' we heard our mother say to her down the phone.

'A girlfriend,' Nancy apparently replied.

I left them all in the dining room to their brandies and After Eights and stories of Christmases past, and I crept into the hallway, the flagstones cold and unforgiving beneath my bare feet. This was the moment I'd been waiting for, the quiet moment when Jenny Penny would tell me all about her day.

Every year I called her at the same time, always after lunch because she never woke up early on Christmas Day – probably the only child in the world who didn't – because she said she preferred to stay in bed and use the time to think.

'To think about what?' I said.

'About the world. About life,' she said.

'About presents?'

'No,' she said. 'I know what I get every year. A craft set, bigger and better than the year before,' (it never was) 'and an item of knitwear that my mum starts making in July.'

She'd spent that first Christmas with us, that legendary first Christmas we'd talk about for years, when she'd arrived by train with my brother with a small bag that held only a change of jeans, a change of underwear, and a long-held yearning for a change of scenery. And he told us how she'd stood transfixed in front of the carriage window as it left Exeter and hugged the coastline – the closest she'd ever been to the sea – and the waves lapped against her forehead, against her beaming smile as her reflection never moved, never faltered, until that shimmering coast disappeared behind crags and trees.

When she arrived, she ran down the lawn with me and fell into the river, and her squeals of glee shamed our privileged hearts, for what should have been a birthright was, in a single second, a brace of unattainable riches. Even as she was pulled from those icy waters, her lips turning blue, her teeth chattering, her joy was contagious and we all knew immediately that this would be a time to remember.

The night before Christmas we guided her carefully into the darkened living room so she could turn on the tree lights, and when she did her body shook with the excitement of the overwhelmed. The lights were of every shape, size and colour, and in the darkness turned a make-believe world into one of incandescent reality. 'Wishes come true in a room like this,' she'd said.

Later that night, as we lay in bed, she told me what she'd wished for – that she might one day come and live with us – and in the darkness we listened out for the sound of sleigh bells, and even though we were probably too old to still believe, we heard them outside and I saw her smile, wide and uncynical, and I was grateful that I had a brother who'd wanted to stand outside in the cold and dark and shake a small church bell simply to make her feel good. But we all did everything that first Christmas to make her feel good.

The following morning, I woke her up early and we crept downstairs and saw the pillowcases bulging with gifts and the part-eaten carrot and mince pies and the half-drunk sherry and the soot scattered on the carpet leading from the hearth. I looked at her as she stood transfixed, as tears ran down her cheeks, as she said, 'Father Christmas never visited me before. I don't think he ever really knew where I lived.'

I picked up the phone. I knew her number off by heart now, it had the rhythm of a poem with all those fives and threes, and it rang briefly and clearly before she answered.

'It's me,' I said, happy to hear my best friend's voice. 'Happy Christmas, Jenny Penny!'

'Elly, I can't talk for long,' she whispered.

It was hard to hear what she was saying, so soft was her voice.

'What's the matter?' I said.

'It's all gone wrong.'

'What?'

'We have to go,' she said.

'When?' I said.

'Now. Soon,' she said.

'Why?'

'Because we have to.'

'I don't understand,' I said.

'We just have to,' she said. 'I can't say anything else, I'm not allowed to. She won't let me.'

'But where are you going?'

'I don't know. Mum won't tell me. She said it's best that no one knows.'

'Even me?' I said.

'I've got to go, she's coming. I'll let you know when I get there,' she said. 'Bye, Elly.'

The line went dead and the last of my words disappeared into an unforgiving silence.

I summoned my mother away from the television marathon that had become as traditional to our family as turkey and mince pies, and told her what had happened. She didn't know anything for certain, she said. Just suspected.

'We have to wait and see,' she said. 'When they get there they'll let us know.'

'Get where?' I said.

'To safety,' she said.

Ginger stayed on with us after Christmas to perform at the Harbour Moon for New Year's Eve. She was topping the bill with a Tony Bennett impersonator who she called T. B. and who she hated because he made her feel ill.

'He doesn't even look like Tony Bennett,' she said when she got the news. 'I look more like Tony Bennett than he does,' and Arthur nodded in agreement. The money was good, though, and it was actually the party of the year for our village, which was a little bit like topping the bill at Vegas if you really used your imagination. The village became a playground for dressing up and people came from afar to show off their fancy-dress costumes, which had been planned months in advance. My father had started mine four months before and only he and I knew what it was going to be. All we said was that it was going to be bigger and better than the previous year's attempt, which wasn't going to be too difficult, seeing as I had been a thumb.

They were all in the living room, slouched around and unruly, and I could hear my brother goading Ginger and Arthur into another chorus of 'Why Are We Waiting?'. My mother crept out into the hallway to make sure I was all right.

'One more minute,' my father said to her, as he shook out my costume.

The trouble was, my heart wasn't in it any more. My worry for Jenny Penny had dulled all enthusiasm, and for a whole week I'd waited by the phone, waited for the news that never came. It was only because my father had made such an effort that I ultimately would too, and together we marched into the living room and waited for the lights to dim and the chatter to still.

I put on the shimmering grey dress with fin slits for hands

and attached the long fish-tail train. I could have been a mermaid, or even one of the Three Degrees, at this stage and it was fun to keep everyone guessing. Then my father carried in a very large box and the room hushed. He opened the box and took out something shaped like a helmet, which was covered by a beach towel. He placed it over my head and through the eyeholes I could see the striped towelling pattern and what I could only make out was a piece of dry seaweed.

'Da-nah!' shouted my father, and he suddenly whipped the towel away. Everyone gasped. Through my eyeholes I saw hands quickly reach for mouths.

'What is she exactly?' asked Ginger, downing an early Scotch.

My father turned to me and said, 'Tell them, Elly.'

'I'm a MULLET!' I shouted, and everyone went, 'Ah yes, of course.'

'TWO GIN AND TONICS AND A WATER FOR THE FISH,' SAID my brother for the fifth time that evening. He was dressed as Liza Minnelli, and looked really pretty until you saw that he hadn't shaved, either his face or his legs. When we left the house both my mother and father had shed a tear as their beloved son walked out into the cold night air dressed as a daughter, unsure as to what he might return as. That, my father would later say, was one of the unexpected gifts of parenthood.

By the time we got our drinks Arthur had secured the best seats in front of the fire by cleverly feigning illness. My brother moved my seat a little further back from the hearth, reminding me that I was still flammable and that it would be really embarrassing if I caught fire. It was about this time, I think, that I spotted the Womble in the corner watching us. He had been following us earlier because I saw him in the Jolly Sailor, where he'd had an altercation with a dog (a real one). He was standing alone next to the clock and it said half-past eleven.

Arthur nudged my brother and said, 'Womble, ten o'clock,' and before I could say no it's not, it's half-past eleven, the Womble made his way over to us.

'Hi,' said my brother, 'I'm Liza and this is Fish.'

I raised my fin and stifled a yawn behind my papier-mâché head, which was suddenly feeling very heavy.

'And I'm Freddie Mercury,' said Arthur, nervously securing his moustache.

'I'm Orinoco,' said Orinoco in a very deep voice; a voice that, had it really belonged to a Womble, would have frightened small children and would never have made them the popular creatures they became.

His name was Paul, I think, and he was from Manchester. When he took off his head, he had short brown hair – or maybe it was long; I can't really remember – but all I knew was that the energy of our wonderful evening suddenly changed and he was the cause. I tried to stay awake, tried to hear their whispered banter, the jokes they steered away from me, but it was useless; I wasn't part of them any more and my eyes started to close before the opening bars of 'Auld Lang Syne' gathered up the drunken, rolling voices. The worry about Jenny Penny, the glass of champagne, the subsequent sips of clandestine booze had ambushed my young mind and I couldn't remember anything after that; not the journey home, or Arthur leading me through the front door into my mother's arms. I didn't remember Ginger tap dancing on the flagstones, or Arthur telling the rude story about Princess Margaret. All I did remember was my father kissing me good night and saying, 'Have a wonderful year, Elly.'

I woke up four hours later, hungry and wide awake. The house still felt warm as I crept downstairs. I saw empty bottles and streamers strewn around the living room; Ginger's shoes and her feather boa snuggled in a chair. I went into the kitchen and poured myself a large glass of water and went to the cupboard for a piece of Madeira cake. And as I put the glass onto the draining board, I looked through the window and saw the hazy shape of my brother running into the forest, followed at the tree line by a haggard shadow. It must have been my brother because he still had on his patent heels and his wig, and both caught the light from the moon. I stuffed the remainder of the cake into my mouth, put on my mother's jumper and boots, and crept out into the cold, new January air.

I picked up a stick and ran as hard as I could to the edge of the forest. I stumbled twice until my eyes adjusted to the darkness, until I could again follow the sounds of breaking twigs up ahead. I wasn't scared, felt emboldened by my imagined role as protector, and I raced ahead, dodging the low branches of naked shrubs. The sounds of giggling were to my left, beyond a cluster of heavy oaks and when I came to their wide trunks, I crouched down and carefully parted a clump of ailing ferns. And then promptly threw up.

I sat on my bed and looked over at the Womble perched on the dressing table. It had come with me from my other life, a present from Jenny Penny for my seventh birthday. She had given it to me at the end of my party, when the guests and the cake had all gone, and she'd said, 'This is the best present you've ever been given. And I've given it to you.'

Now as I looked at it I no longer thought of her or the wrapping paper she made, or the poem attached to its scarf, entitled 'Best Friends'; no, I now thought of my brother on his hands and knees blurred in the forest dark with the unmistakable shape of a children's toy thrusting behind him; its deep Northern voice saying, 'Happy New Year, Joe. Happy New Year, ugh, ugh, ugh.'

I got up and put the toy in an old plastic bag, which still smelt of onions, and placed it at the bottom of a cupboard with all my old shoes. The following week I would take it to a charity shop, where it would sit in the window between a battered copy of *Jaws* and a tarnished silver toast rack. It would sit there for weeks. Retribution of sorts.

I never told my brother what I saw that night, not until years later, anyway, when we were sitting by the jetty as adults with adult lives. And he wouldn't remember that night, like so many others he wouldn't remember, and when I told him he buried his head in his hands and laughed and simply said, 'What's a fucking Womble?'

And I never did hear from Jenny Penny to say she was safe. Never received the call or the letter to say where she was or why they'd left, or what she was doing now. I called her old number not long after she disappeared and a man had answered and shouted at me and I hung up, scared. Wondered what he might have done.

Then another time, about a year later, I sat quietly on my bed and thought about her, attempting to mend that telepathic bridge that had fallen in her wake, and as the room stilled and the sun shifted beyond the trees, numbers appeared behind my eyes, the order deliberate and significant, the numbers constantly repeating. It was her, I was sure. My hands shook as I picked up the phone. I dialled the numbers and waited for her voice. It never came. Instead I heard a woman ask, 'Golden Lotus. What is your order, please?' It was a Chinese takeaway restaurant in Liverpool; a place that would actually have tentative relevance years later.

I simply had to accept that she'd been swallowed by that New Year and I had to let her go. But every anniversary I heard her harried breath whispering, 'I'll let you know when I get there. Bye, Elly. I'll let you know.'

I missed her. I would always miss her. I often wondered how it would have been if we could have experienced the coming years together. What would have been different? Could I have changed what happened to her? We were the guardians of a secret world; a lonely world without the other. For years I would flounder without her.

Part Two

1995

BRIXTON WAS ANGRY, BRIXTON BURNED. THAT WAS THE story I was meant to cover six days after my twenty-seventh birthday, but I didn't show, something I still can't fully explain. I'd had moments like that before – the sudden expiration of confidence or care – but never such a panic; one that gripped me with the hold of terror and made me feel both I and the world was all wrong. I told no one. Turned off the phones instead and hid at Nancy's. I lost my job. Not for the first time. Made up excuses. Not for the first time. And it was into this broken world that the card arrived. As if she knew. As if she'd been listening and waiting, like she always had. My lifeline.

I opened the balcony doors to the dull December morn and sat overlooking Charterhouse Square; sounds of children squealing, and playing catch. I watched a boy race behind a bench and tumble freely onto a pile of coats, which turned out to be a pile of friends. I stirred my coffee, sipped it from the spoon. It was a cold day, would get colder still. A yellow tinge to the overcast light. It would snow before the end of the year. I pulled the blanket tighter around myself. I watched a small girl hide behind a tree; it took ages for her to reappear.

It had been fifteen years since that strange Christmas Day, when the past tired of us and closed its fragile doors. *You won't remember me*, she wrote, but of course I did the moment I saw the scrawl of writing, black and unchanged and smudged across the envelope, and my joy was unchanged as I read the words *You won't remember me*. She'd made the card herself, something she always did because she was keen on crafts, and whenever she came to school with glue or glitter in her hair everyone knew she'd been making something – birthday cards or Christmas cards – and everyone secretly hoped to be the lucky recipient of those laughed-at creative efforts because they were good and they spoke loud, for they said, 'You are special. I have chosen you.'

But it was only ever I who received such a card.

It was a simple piece of blue paper folded down the middle with fragmented pictures of flowers and wine on the front, of mountains and smiles and cut-out letters like a ransom note, but saying *Happy Birthday* instead. And there between the letters I saw her again on the pavement in her favourite shoes, waving and receding, when she was nine, when I was nine, and when we vowed to keep in touch.

I looked again at the envelope. My parents had redirected it to Nancy's flat in Charterhouse Square where I was temporarily staying. Originally, though, it had been sent from Her Majesty's Prison.

THE SEAGULLS WERE LOUD THAT MORNING AND DREW ME harshly away from the stillness of the bed. I picked up my water and drank through the minuscule specks of dust that had landed on the surface during the night. The house was quiet, my room stifling and radiator hot. I got up and went to the window and opened it wide to spring. It was still cold, with not a hush of breeze, and the cloudless sky reached beyond the trees like the morning itself, suspended, unmoving, waiting. I watched Arthur down below slowly raise himself into a headstand, his small red satin shorts (once my father's) slipped to his groin revealing legs the colour and texture of bone. I had never seen his legs before. They looked as if they had lived a different life. They looked innocent.

Age had taken little from him and he still refused to reveal the time or circumstances of his earthly departure. Most mornings when I was home I'd sit with him at the water's edge and watch him look towards the opposite bank, as if death were waving to him like a teasing friend, and he would smile and his smile would say, Not today, rather than, I'm not ready.

His knowledge had freed him from fear, but had left us with the ultimate burden of waiting. Would he prepare us? Would he suddenly disappear from our lives to shield us from the ultimate loss? Would we play a ghoulish part in this final act? We knew nothing; and had he not moved his foot when I coughed, I would have believed he'd been taken there and then in that upturned state like a wingless angel who'd unexpectedly crashed headfirst to earth.

On my way downstairs I peeked into Ginger's room and could just make out her bald head nestled between the pillows like an abandoned egg. She was breathing hard, deep in sleep. This was her good phase, the phase between chemotherapy when she had energy and fun, just no hair.

The last round had been brutal, and the five-hundred-yard walk from the hospital to Nancy's front door was made in a cab, her face leaning on the open window's frame as her stomach churned over every bump. She liked to rest on the balcony, huddled in an eiderdown that barely kept her from cold, and there she flitted between wake and sleep with no concentration for anything except the occasional cup of tea, which she now took sweet.

I crept into her room and picked up the cardigan that had fallen on the floor. My mother laid out clothes for her every morning, because decision making had become hard and made her panic, and only my mother had noticed that. There was no left, no right any more in Ginger's world; life was lived straight ahead. I closed the door because sleep was what she needed most. Sleep and luck.

I stumbled into the kitchen and turned the radio off. More

about the massacre at Dunblane. The whys. The blame. The searing anguish of surmise. I watched my mother finish the last of her coffee. She was standing at the sink where a shaft of soft yellow light caught the side of her face, emphasising lines now permanently etched there. She had aged well, the process had been kind. And she had left nature alone, opting instead to banish vanity like the meddlesome, suffocating weed it was.

She was waiting for her only client of the day, a Mr A, as she referred to him (but who we all knew as Big Dave from the pub in Polperro). She'd been a qualified therapist for ten years, as well as the unqualified one for most of our young lives, and her practice was in the back room, which was really the front, depending from what side you entered the house.

We all knew 'Mr A' was secretly in love with her and hid his rather inappropriate behaviour behind thirty pounds an hour and the indefinable state of transference. He brought my mother flowers every session and she refused them every session. He brought her his dreams every session; she brought him reality. We heard the sound of bike wheels on the shingle outside. My mother peeked through the window.

'Roses again,' she said.

'What colour?' I said.

'Yellow,' she said.

'He's happy,' I said.

'God help me,' she said.

The bell rang.

'We're leaving as soon as I'm finished, Elly, so make sure Ginger's up and you're all ready,' she said in her therapist's voice.

I smiled.

'What is it?' she said.

'The poinsettia?'

'Oh. Put it back in the hallway,' she said, 'and I'll deal with it later,' and she marched quickly out of the room.

She'd been trying to get rid of the poinsettia since January, but it was stubborn and wouldn't die, and every week she'd place it on the kitchen table and wonder what she could do with it. 'Just leave it outside,' my father would say. 'Or throw it in the rubbish.' But my mother couldn't. It was a living thing; a step away from a human being. It could go back into the hallway. For another week.

'Hello, my darling,' said Arthur, skipping in from his yoga session and embracing me tightly. I felt the cold clinging to his sweatshirt.

'Hey,' I said, trying not to look down at his legs.

'I'll get Ginger up, shall I?' he said as he checked that the kettle was still warm and shoved a handful of leaves into the teapot.

'Oh, thanks,' I said. 'Need any help?'

'Not today, my angel, I'll manage,' he said as he poured the water into the pot and replaced the lid. I handed him the mug with the worn-out picture of Burt Reynolds barely visible on its side. Ginger had a thing for Burt Reynolds. Ginger had a thing for men with moustaches.

'This'll wake her up,' said Arthur, as he carefully carried the teapot and mug towards the door, halting only to let my father enter.

'Very smart,' said Arthur, disappearing into the hallway.

'Thanks,' said my father, adjusting his tie.

My father looked good in a suit and even though he rarely wore one he still carried its form with unquestionable style. I caught him admiring his reflection in the glass door, just as I noticed him the night before, quietly reading an old law book, and somewhere I wondered if two rivers were about to converge once again. I'd heard whispers, of course, mainly from my mother. She told me that he'd recently 'gone back to Rumpole', and had delivered this news with such secrecy that I could have been forgiven for thinking that 'Rumpole' was indeed code for an illegal drug rather than the entertaining book it was. 'It's not just a book, though, darling,' she'd said to me. 'It's a way of life.'

My father cleared his throat for the recital of the final line, and then delivered it looking at his shoes. I could do nothing except applaud and hide behind noise.

'Well, what do you think?' he asked. *'Truthfully.'*

I sipped my coffee and tried to think of something kind, something positive to say about a poem he hadn't chosen, but had agreed to read only because he was the godfather and that was his duty.

'It's really bad,' I said.

'I know.'

'Not you.'

'I know.'

'Just *it*.'

'I know.'

Chubby little Alan junior had grown up and become a father when his wife gave birth to a baby girl called Alana (they were expecting a boy). The child arrived three weeks late and weighed ten pounds and ten ounces, and apparently looked every bit of it. When she was presented to her parents' world at a small family gathering in St Austell, she revealed an astonishing head of curly hair that was quite particular to Alan's wife's side of the family. They all looked like they came from Naples, rather than Pelynt, and when Nancy commented that the baby looked like a fat Cher, it was only the careful addition of her laugh during the uncomfortable silence, that made people think she was only joking. (Over the years Nancy had lost interest in anyone less than three feet tall unless they were in pantomime and heading towards Snow White's cottage.)

My parents were often invited to these gatherings, a fierce indebtedness that Alan senior still felt as sharply as a switch across his back. Nancy was invited simply because Nancy was a star. And everyone loves to rub shoulders with a star. But it was at this increasingly boisterous gathering that events took an unexpected – and some might say, careless – turn, when Alan junior gave my father a cigar and asked him to be Alana's sole godparent, to the complete dismay of his wife's side of the family. An uncomfortable silence ensued, in which my father's mute embarrassment was somehow interpreted as a *Yes*. Whispers of 'Outsider!' and 'What was he thinking?' and 'What about us?' echoed around the small detached cottage, until Alan junior took his wife aside and put a halt to her family's empty protestations. It was the first time he'd ever put his foot down, and even though he did it with the lightest of treads – that of fear – he was unflinching in his choice. My father was a good man; the best in the valley. The decision was made.

We bundled into the car late as usual, but Ginger said we'd already waited three weeks for the fat kid, so it was only fair that the fat kid waited an extra half an hour for us. My mother looked at her in the rear-view mirror and I noted the slight worry on her face. Ginger had drunk only half a mug of marijuana tea that morning, but it was Arthur who had administered the heavy-handed dose and not my mother because she was still busy deciphering Mr A's erotic dream. And now Ginger was wearing a feather boa over the lovely dress and cardigan my mother had laid out for her, and had refused to take it off even when my mother reminded her that it was a christening they were attending and not sing-along night at the Fisherman's Arm's.

'I'm still going to perform,' said Ginger, grinning wildly.

'You are part of a church service, Ginger,' said my mother, 'not singing at Carnegie Hall.'

Ginger sucked her teeth and wrapped the feathers tightly around her neck, and with her accentuated nose she resembled a mighty bald-headed eagle looking out for prey; my mother's only fear was that she'd already found it and it was swaddled and curly haired and waiting for us at the font.

'Right,' said my father as he started the van. 'Are we all here?'

'Yes,' said Arthur.

'Yes,' said Ginger.

'Yes,' I said.

'Not quite,' said my mother wistfully, looking down at her hands, thinking of my brother. It's what happened whenever anyone said, 'Are we all here?'

My father reached across for her hand but she pushed it away and said, 'I'm all right, Alfie.'

My father shrugged and looked at us in the mirror. We sat there squashed and not daring to say a word, until Arthur finally did: 'I don't know why we have to be sad. There he is, having the time of his life clubbing and fucking in New York, and making obscene amounts of money on those trading floors, and here we are, attending a christening where the majority of people wished we were dead.'

'Shut up, Arthur,' said my mother, and he zipped his mouth shut like an infuriating child.

Ginger started to laugh. Not at anything in particular, but just because Ginger was stoned.

The postman waved us down as my father accelerated up the driveway, spitting shingle and dirt from his back wheels. He wasn't used to driving the van – Alan still did that – and on every hill he seemed to override third gear as if it never existed at all.

'Want these now then?' said the postman, waving a bundle of letters and bills in front of my father.

'OK, Brian,' my father said as he took them, and handed them to my mother, who quickly scoured them for the flimsy blue airmail envelope that brought news from her son. She handed me a letter that had been redirected by Nancy.

'Off to little Alana's christening?' said the postman.

Ginger rudely scoffed at the term 'little'.

'Yes,' said my father. 'I expect you've heard that I'm the godfather?'

'I did,' said the postman. 'And heard you weren't the most popular of choices round here.'

'Well,' said my father, as if he were about to say something more. But he didn't.

'Bye then,' said the postman abruptly, as he turned and struggled up the lane.

'Tosser,' said Ginger.

'Now, now,' said my mother.

'Run him over,' said Arthur.

'Oh for God's sake!' said my mother, stuffing a piece of chewing gum in her mouth.

The church wasn't full and our lateness was noted by each and every one of the Pelynt lot who sat in the front stalls, best seats in the house, as Ginger loudly said. Alan hugged us all and led us to a section he'd reserved for us, a section that was easy for my father and Ginger to get in and out from.

It was a simple service of promises and tears and child-appropriate readings. My father got up and did the best he could with the poem entitled 'The Child in my Arms Lays Quietly in your Heart', and Alan senior made an interesting speech that included words like, 'Lola', 'showgirl', 'diamond', and 'Havana', obviously hoping that the big bundle weighing down the vicar's arms could have been named after the heroine of one of the greatest songs ever. And as the opening bars to 'O God, our help in ages past' filled the air, I carefully pulled the letter from its prison envelope and started to read.

11 March 1996

I was so happy to get another letter from you, Elly. I know we're back in contact but its hard for me to trust – I have to pinch myself.

The Christmas we disappeared is still as clear to me as yesterday. We left as soon as Uncle Phil came back from the Red House and fell asleep and we took the car to an abandoned car park where Mum had booked a minicab. Everything was about covering our tracks you see. Mum had been advised by a womens refuge in Liverpool and they told her what to do. We stayed a couple of nights in a small hotel in Euston, I think, before taking the train up north. We lived in the refuge till Mum got back on her feet. We couldn't call from there or let anyone know the address, something about endangering the others. Thats why you never heard from me. Even when we got our own place, Mum said our previous life was dead. I had to forget about it all. About you. About all that had happened to her. She was so frightened. What she'd turned into no one should turn into and I couldn't tell anyone. I called you once. One Christmas about ten years ago. At the end of the day, like we used to. You said hello and I heard laughter. I put the phone down. I think it hurt too much. Hearing what I was once part of. What I could of been. Could of had.

I did get married. It wasn't a happy marriage although at first I thought it was. I thought it would give me everything I missed, or that my mum missed and thats all I can say really. I don't know if you believe in destiny but I know he was mine.

I looked up. Ginger was singing loudly and had managed most of the words, even though she seemed to make up a few of her own in the third verse.

I'd love to read Arthurs book when you've finished editing it, also any articles you've written for magazines. I've got plenty of time to read you see. I work in the kitchen here and its quite good. Before I came here I used to have a company called The Tranquil Path, just me and a girl called Linda. I did tarot reading and massage mainly – aromatherapy, intuitive, even Indian head massage. I got quite good. Quite successful. Funny how life turns out.

Oh, Elly, this feels so good writing to you again. I'm trying to forgive myself for what I've done and its proving the hardest thing for me to do. I'm down to serve nine years at the moment. They say I'll probably get out before with good behaviour. I should of got less, everyone said so, even the police. They didn't think it was murder

'Fuck!' I said, and the Pelynt lot turned towards me. So did Arthur and Ginger.

they knew it was self-defence and so I eventually got done for manslaughter. The judge was so nice, so understanding but as he explained to me, he had no choice. Its all about precedent you see and mitigating circumstances, but I expect your dad can explain more about that.

'What?' mouthed Ginger, who'd suddenly got bored singing. 'What?' she said again.

'I'll tell you in a minute,' I hissed, and continued to read.

'Tell me now,' she said, and started to laugh.

I hope this letter finds you well. Even though I said the M words please don't be frightened of me. I'm still me, Elly. Not the monster some people said I was.

Om shanti and cheerio.

Love, Jenny

PS. I do understand if you don't want to write to me again. Just thought it best to get it all out in the open. My diabetes is still under control. Thanks for remembering.

PPS. Stamps would be great. Legal tender in here.

I put the letter away as Ginger leant towards me and held my arm.

'Jenny Penny's murdered someone,' I said in time with the music.

'Ssh,' I heard from behind me.

'What? That strange girl with unmanageable hair?' said Ginger.

'Tell Arthur,' I said, and she moved towards him, grabbed his head and pulled it towards her mouth as if it was a first-of-the-season peach.

I nudged my mother and whispered in her ear.

'What?' she said.

I told her again.

'Murder?' she said. 'I don't believe it.' And as the music slowed to its desultory end, she grabbed my hand and sang loudly to the heavens, 'Be Thou our guard while troubles last, And our eternal home.'

Amen.

After a monotonous reading about the responsibilities of parenthood, the message of which, thank God, must have bypassed my own parents with the temerity of a stolen car, I was grateful when Ginger finally stood up to sing. Alan and Alan junior beamed. In their eyes Ginger was a star because she had sung with Frank Sinatra (which she actually had done), and therefore it was really only one step away from having the great man there himself. And so when Ginger unnecessarily bowed on reaching the front, Alan senior couldn't help but emit a tiny cheer. However, when she dedicated her song to, 'Jenny Penny, our friend who's been wrongly imprisoned for murder,' I winced, and couldn't have felt more exposed had I sat there naked. She'd been given *carte blanche* to sing whatever song she felt was right for the day, but as she sang the opening line to 'I Who Have Nothing', even I wondered what her thought process had been.

'A child comes into the world with nothing,' she said later, downing a large Scotch, as if she didn't know what all the fuss had been about.

No one ever turned in for an early night down there. It was unheard of, like a silent rule; it just wasn't done. We slept only when talk was exhausted, when we had wrung out its last vestiges and the space it left was empty, lifeless, *tired*. Many times I had sat with my mother watching the sky change from its French navy to a haloed hue, when the sun encroached upon the horizon, pushing upwards the blanketed dark to make room for its light that appeared golden and orbed and unnatural, and sometimes we would take the boat out down to the mouth of the harbour (sometimes beyond), and sit wrapped in blankets whilst a new day appeared.

But after the christening everyone seemed eager to retire, and by eleven the house was quiet and slightly forlorn. I made a fire because the spring dampness had intruded after the sun had gone down. I could feel it now, cool under my jumper, and I wanted to disperse it, and I wanted the comfort and the smell of flame. I held the match under the newspaper and fed slithers of dry wood, until they smoked and glowed orange and finally lit.

'Hey,' I said.

'Hold on,' he said. 'I'm gonna change phones.'

I heard a click. I heard him pick up the replacement.

'Hey,' he said, and I heard him swallow.

His voice was low, devoid of energy – his accent quite American when he was tired. He had a beer and I was glad about that. Something to lift him.

'What's new?' he said, and I told him about the christening, told him about Jenny Penny's letter.

'I don't fucking believe it. You're kidding me.'

'No. It's true.'

'Who did she kill?'

'I don't know anything yet.'

'Mum's old boyfriend?'

'Now there's a thought,' I said.

'Jesus, Elly. What are you going to do?'

'What can I do? Keep writing, that's all. Get the truth. God, it's so weird, Joe. She was my friend.'

'She *was* weird,' he said.

'Yeah, but *this*? This wasn't her. She had too much imagination for this.'

'Elly, you don't know her. You knew her as a kid. You can't freeze someone in time,' he said.

Silence.

I poured out more wine. I've frozen myself in time.

'What happened to the job, by the way?' he asked.

'Panicked.'

'That's it?'

'Can't settle. You know me, restless. Turned into Nancy. No big deal.'

'You sure?'

Silence.

'Sure, Ell?'

'Yeah. I'm good. Just hate being tied down,' I said and finished my glass. 'So what are you doing tonight?'

'Falling asleep with a beer in my hand.'

'Sexy,' I said.

'It just hasn't been a good day, or a good week.'

And I heard the darkness fall again across his back. Silence. I held my breath.

'Come back,' I said. 'I miss you. We all do.'

Nothing.

'You know I have to be here.'

'Still?'

'Yeah. Work. You know.'

'You hate your work.'

'I love the money.'

'You're an arse.' I laughed. I drank. 'That job's not you.'

'Maybe. But what's me, Ell?'

We both went quiet.

'You need to meet someone,' I said.

'Given up on that.' He yawned.

'Isn't there anyone in your choir?'

'We've done each other.'

'Ah.'

'It's what we do.'

'I know.'

'I have no friends,' he said, and I started to laugh again. Good, I thought, we're back onto this game, this game was familiar.

'Me neither,' I said. 'We're freaks.'

He prised the lid off another bottle.

'How's Ginger?' he asked.

'Hanging in there.'

'Fuck.' He drank loudly.

'You should call Mum and Dad.'

'I know,' he said. 'Send them my love.'

You could do that yourself, I thought.

'Just a bad day,' he said.

I put a log on the fire.

'We're singing at a mate's wedding next weekend,' he said, trying to sound happier.

'That sounds great.'

'Yeah, it will be. It's like our first proper performance.'

'Fantastic.'

'Yeah, it will be,' he said.

'Something to look forward to.'

'Yeah,' he said.

'I miss you.'

'Same,' he said.

The fire spat out minuscule embers onto the wide hearth where I watched them fade like dying stars. My brother had episodes like this, ones that eclipsed the brightness that he was; that he could be. My mother blamed it on rugby, on the frequent knocks to his head, the concussion. I blamed it on the secret I made him carry. My father simply thought it must be quite lonely at times, being gay. Maybe it was a bit of everything, I thought.

17 March 1996

Dear Jenny

I hope you are well. I can't imagine what life has been like for you and that has made it hard for me to write this letter. Thank you for your honesty; I feel no desire to turn away; on the contrary, I just want to know more – what could have happened to my friend that she ended up where she is? If you wish to tell me more, I am here. I spent the last week in Cornwall and have thought about you all the time. Everyone wishes to be remembered to you. Joe especially – he's in New York. Everyone sends you love. I'd like to see you, Jenny. My father said that you would need to send me a V.O., a visiting order, I think. Is that right? I really would like to visit you, but I don't want you to feel awkward. I know it's quick – maybe too quick. I've become like that. I find letter writing hard and have sadly lost the art. I have so much to say, so much to tell you, as if I've waited so long to tell only you what's gone on in my life. Have enclosed stamps and also a postal order. Dad says you probably need money to get your own duvet or stuff like that, anything to make your room more personal. It never occurred to me, the whole catalogue-shopping bit. Let me know if there's anything else I can do.

I hope people are kind to you. Stay strong.

Take care.

Love, Ell

THREE WEEKS LATER SHE TOLD ME EVERYTHING. IT TUMBLED from her pen like a confession, but not one she was forced to write because there were both sides to this story; intention and undertaking, freedom and consequence, she hid nothing.

The months leading up to the act were written unpunctuated as if every blow and insult ran from one to the other without a pause or break until she ended up bloodied on the bathroom floor with a shower nozzle forced into her mouth, drowning. She would have done it then, she said, as he leant over, playing with the taps. But there was nothing close to hand and anyway her wrist was broken and it dropped uselessly at a right angle and so she stayed leaning over the bath until the assault had passed, the footsteps receded, and the front door slammed shut.

I put too much salt in the spaghetti bolognaise! That's what she wrote; with an ironic exclamation mark. It had the power to break a heart.

She didn't report him. Instead, that night, she dragged herself into the rain to a secluded and notorious alleyway and emptied the contents of her bag over the ground and then stumbled to a phone box to call the police. She had been mugged, she said. They took her to hospital and looked after her and yet she knew they didn't believe her, because no one ever believed the catalogue of 'mishaps' that had befallen her third and fourth years of marriage – not even Linda, nor the neighbours, who hid their disbelief behind a stuttering veil of silence. And when he came to pick her up he wept and said he'd murder the bastard who'd done this to her, and that's when she realised what she was going to do and that's when it became nine years.

The night it happened he came home to a take-out meal rather than the beef stew she'd promised to make him, and it was a Chinese meal, something she liked more than he did, something she hadn't dared to order in months, but she needed his rage, you see. She got it from one of the oldest restaurants in Liverpool, the Golden Lotus. It was her favourite restaurant, which made her favourite dish – prawns with chilli, garlic and ginger – one of the few things that gave her confidence, together with a nice cold glass of Soave. Although her bruises had almost subsided (it had been six weeks), there were still dark rings under her eyes that made her look pitiful and harmless, which was quite useful, she wrote. He sat down and said nothing. She put rice on his plate and asked about his day and he told her to shut up. She ate a prawn cracker and handed him a beer. He smashed it over her head.

She fell to the floor, taking with her a bowl, a plate, a vase of budded flowers and her chopsticks. (She never used a knife and fork because it was important for her to be authentic whenever she ate Chinese food.) But that's why she'd used a chopstick: it was the only thing close to hand; a pointed, black metal one that had been part of an unrequested wedding gift. It was reflex, you see; he'd leant over her and spat and had forgotten to hold down her arms. She thought it was his shoulder at first. Only afterwards did she realise it was his heart she'd punctured fifteen times.

'Here,' I said to my father, giving him the letter. He put the saw to one side and sat down on an old armchair that was covered in wood shavings and dust. He felt around for his glasses in pockets crammed with everything but, until I pointed to his head and he felt for them and pulled them down over his eyes. Those were the sole moments that gave away his age; chinks in the armour of our eternal boy. I watched him read. His face was still, placid, as he read over the initial greetings. He hasn't turned the page yet, I thought.

I went outside and freed myself from the smell of sawdust and grease, the smell of his workroom. I hung out down there as a child, watched him make things: the shed, the jetty, climbing frames for our neighbours, cupboards, shelves, and our table, of course. I used to think it was just as well he didn't have a proper job, because he really was simply too busy making things. He used to give me solid cubes of wood that I would plane and sand smooth until they resembled pebbles, good enough to give. He taught me about the grains of wood, the textures, how oak was a pale brown wood whilst beech was sometimes reddish brown; how oak was coarse, and sycamore fine, and ash good for bending. My life was full of moments like that, moments I'd taken so wonderfully for granted. But Jenny Penny had never known her father. She'd never been around a man who'd taught her about wood or fishing, or joy.

'Elly.'

My father called to me. I went in and sat on the arm of his

chair. He handed me the folded letter and said nothing. I expected more: a sigh of disbelief, a wise comment, *something*; but instead he lifted his glasses and rubbed his eyes, as if he'd seen the brutality of her life, rather than had read about it. I put my arm around him in case his thoughts had gone back to Jean Hargreaves, the ghost we all thought he'd laid to rest, but maybe never had.

'She said she sent a V.O.?' he said.

'Yeah, for next Wednesday,' I said.

'Are you going?'

'Of course.'

'Good,' he said, and he got up and leant on his worktable. A nail fell to the floor and sounded like a tiny distant chime. He bent down to pick it up – never knew when he might need it.

'She might not—' he started.

'Can you help her?' I said, interrupting him. 'If we got the papers and stuff from her lawyer, if we knew more. Could you help her?'

'We'll see,' he said.

His voice promised nothing.

I WAITED IN LINE FOR THE GATES TO OPEN, SURROUNDED by excited chattering families about to see a mum, a sister, a daughter, a wife. It was cool in the shade, and instinctively I blew on my hands, as much as for my nerves as for the initial feelings of cold I'd felt, and yet no longer did.

'Cigarette?' said a voice from behind.

I turned and smiled into the face of a woman.

'No I'm fine – thanks, though,' I said.

'First time?' she asked.

'That obvious?' I said.

'I can always tell,' she said, lighting her cigarette and smiling at the same time; an action that turned her mouth into a lopsided grimace. 'You'll be all right,' she added, looking towards the gates.

'Yeah,' I said without any conviction, not really knowing if I would be or not.

'Have you been coming here long?' I said, regretting the line as soon as it had left my mouth, but she was kind and laughed, and knew what I meant.

'Five years. She should be out next month.'

'That's great,' I said.

'It's me sister.'

'OK.'

'I've got her kid.'

'That's tough.'

'Happens,' she said. 'Which of yours is in?'

'Friend.'

'How long?'

'Nine,' I said, suddenly getting used to the clipped edit of this conversation.

'Blimey,' she said. 'Serious.'

'I s'pose.'

A child suddenly shouted and ran forward as the gates opened up.

'Well, here we go,' she said, taking a last drag on her cigarette before flicking it to the floor. The child ran back and stamped on it as if it was an ant.

'Good luck, eh?' she said as we started to move forwards.

'You too,' I said, suddenly nervous again.

I'd been searched before, of course – airports, stations, theatres, places like that – but this time felt different. Two months before, the IRA had started bombing again – once in the Docklands and then on a bus in the Aldwych. Everyone was jittery.

The officer went through the little bag of measly items I'd brought for Jenny Penny, those memories from outside, and laid each one out on the table as if they were for sale: stamps, CDs, a nice face cream, a deodorant and a cake, magazines and a writing pad. I could have amassed more, I could have kept going, believing such acquisitions would make her room feel bigger, would make her days seem shorter, would make her reality seem more bearable. The officer told me there would be no kissing and I blushed, even though the normality of such a statement had been a constant throughout my life. I placed the items back into their bag as he called the next person over.

I went through into the visitors' hall where the air was still and remote, as if it too was living its own cloistered sentence, and I sat at my allotted table, which was number fifteen, and which gave me a good view of the rest of the room.

The woman I'd spoken to in the queue was near the front talking to a man at the adjacent table, adding to the low hum of expectant chatter. I bent down to my bag to pull out a newspaper and as I did, I missed the arrival of the first inmates. They came out in normal clothes, ambling and waving towards their friends and families, and their voices rose as normal, as normal greetings took place. I looked towards the door at the faces coming in. The thought that I probably wouldn't recognise her suddenly became real. Why should I? I had no photograph and people change; I'd changed. What was the discernible characteristic I remembered of her as a child? Her hair, of course, but what if she'd cut it – dyed it, even – what was left? What colour were her eyes? What was now her height? What was the sound of her laugh; I had no recollection of her smile. As an adult she was a stranger.

I was used to waiting for her. As a child I'd waited for her all the time, but it never annoyed me because I didn't have the one thing that unfailingly stole hours from her life.

'Sorry I'm late,' she used to say. 'It was my hair again.'

And she spoke of it as if it was an affliction like asthma or a limp or a problem heart, one that slowed her down. I'd once waited two hours for her at the recreation park, only to bump into her on my way home.

'You won't believe what just happened,' she said crying uncontrollably.

'What?' I said.

'I had to brush my hair twenty-seven times before it would tie up properly,' she said, shaking her head. And I instinctively put my arms around her as if she was hurt, or worse – had been dealt the cruellest possible hand that life could deal – and she clung on hard to me, stayed like that for minutes, until she felt the safety again of our uncompromised world and she pulled away and smiled and said, 'Don't ever leave me, Elly.'

A woman came through the door by herself. Most of the tables were deep in conversation; only mine and one other were still waiting. Her hair was quite short and wavy and she looked in my direction and I smiled. She couldn't have seen me. She was tall, slim, thin even, and her shoulders hunched forwards deflating her chest, causing her to stoop, ageing her by years. I didn't think it was her, but as I studied her movements I started to read into her face features that might once have been familiar, and could even be now. And then as she came towards me I stood up as if she was joining me for dinner, but she walked past to the table of two behind and said, 'How ya doin', Mum?'

'You look well, Jacqui. Doesn't she, Beth?'

'Yeah, she looks good.'

'Thanks. How's Dad?'

'Still the same.'

'Pain in the arse. Sends his love.'

'Send mine back.'

It happened quite suddenly, the moment I knew she wasn't coming. I heard her voice amidst the hundred others in that sealed room, and I heard her say, 'Sorry, Elly, I can't.' It happened before the prison officer came towards me, before he bent down and whispered in my ear, before everyone in the room stopped to look at me.

It was the same feeling I'd had when I'd been stood up for the last time, when his rejection sent a spiral of self-disgust coiling itself around my brittle self-image. I'd tried to become what he'd wanted me to become, which was impossible because what he wanted was someone else. But I still tried in my tired, misjudged way. And I waited for him. Waited until the bar emptied, until the staff headed wearily towards the exit; waited until his absence lodged itself in my heart and became confirmation of what I'd always known.

I got up with half an hour to go and made for the exit, conspicuous in my embarrassment. I dropped one of the bags and heard the face cream smash but I didn't care because it didn't matter any more, because I'd dump it in the bin at the station.

The train journey back felt tedious and slow. I was tired of eavesdropping. I was tired of the constant stops at the village-like stations 'just a stone's throw from London with the benefit of countryside'. I was tired of thinking about her.

The taxi across Waterloo Bridge revived me as it always did, and I relaxed as I looked east and took in the familiar sights of St Paul's and St Bride's and the disparate towers of Docklands glinting in the early evening sun. Commuters walked; buses were unnecessary. The old moored steamers were packed with drinkers, and the cool breeze that whispered through the city flicked the surface of the Thames, scattering sunlight as white and as piercing as ice.

We passed the Aldwych, the Royal Courts of Justice and

headed down Fleet Street, where I had lived during my studies. There was nothing there then, very little now, (the cafés would come later), and I used to have to walk to a shop on the Strand if I needed late-night snacks or that forgotten pint of milk. As we drove level to Bouverie Street I looked towards the river and saw the imposing building at the bottom on the right, near to the old *Daily Mail* works.

There were seven of us then, scattered in tiny rooms on the two uppermost floors: actors and writers, artists and musicians. We were a hidden ghetto away from the lives lived among the legal offices below. We were solitary and apart. Slept during the day, and uncurled at dusk like evening primroses; fragrant and lush. We never wanted to conquer the world, only our fears. We didn't keep in touch. Somewhere, though, our memories had.

I opened the balcony doors and looked out over the square. The sense of freedom and privilege the view offered was unimaginable in its calm and beauty, and never more so that evening. I undid my shirt. I'd felt dirty all day but now preferred a martini to taking a shower. Why hadn't she come? Why at the last moment had she faltered? Was it me? Had I asked too much of her? My disappointment was raw, as if she held the key to something unnamed, something vital.

I sat down and rolled the olive around the edge of the glass. Music from next door rose up and soared across the square, taking my thoughts with it; leading me once again to childhood rooms and rediscovered faces and games and jokes we once found funny.

I thought back to the Christmas she'd spent with us; her fierce belief in the strange declaration that left us sleepless the long night that followed. I saw her again on the beach, walking on the surface of the water in the moonlight, her hair wild and uncompromising in the briny squalls, her ears deaf to my pleas.

'Look at me!' she shouted, arms wide at her side. 'Look what I can do, Elly!' before she disappeared down into the dark sea, not struggling but calm against the billowing waves, and only emerging at the heaving pull of my brother's determined arms.

'What the fuck are you doing, Jenny?' he screamed, as he dragged her limp, smiling body through the surf, across the shingle. 'You fucking little idiot! We're all out looking for you, worried about you. How dare you? You could have drowned out there.'

'I was never in any danger,' she said calmly. 'Nothing can ever hurt me. Nothing can take me from me.'

And from that moment, I watched her. Watched her with different coloured eyes, until the raging energy that coursed through my body finally revealed itself and gave itself name: envy. For I knew already that something had taken me from me, and had replaced it with a desperate longing for a time before; a time before fear, a time before shame. And now that knowledge had a voice, and it was a voice that rose from the depths of my years and howled into the night sky like a wounded animal longing for home.

She never explained what happened, why she didn't show, and I never pushed; instead she disappeared for weeks, leaving my letters, my concern, unanswered. And then as June approached, her reappearance was heralded by a familiar scrawl across a familiar envelope, inside of which was a familiar hand-made card, this time with a solitary rabbit on the front.

I'm sorry Elly, she wrote in her minuscule cut-out lettering. *Be patient with me. I'm Sorry.*

'I'M SORRY,' HE SAID. 'I KNOW IT'S LATE.'

I'd just finished a magazine article, just got to bed and looked at the clock – three o'clock – and that was when the phone rang and that's when I'd considered letting the answer-machine pick up but I could never do that, because I knew it was him – he always called at that time – and so I reached for the phone and said, 'Joe?' and he said, 'Guess what?' and I said, 'What?' and he did something unusual. He laughed.

'What is it?' I said, hearing the sound of people in the background, the clink of glasses. 'What are you doing?'

'Out,' he said.

'That's great,' I said.

'Guess who's here?'

'Dunno,' I said.

'Guess,' he said again.

'I *dunno*,' I said, feeling suddenly irritated. 'Gwyneth Paltrow?' (He'd actually met her two weeks before at an opening, and had forced me to talk to her on the phone like a fan.)

'No,' he said. 'Not Gwynnie.'

'Who then?' I said, adjusting my pillow.

And he told me.

And on the line I heard a voice that might or might not have been him; a man's voice, not a boy's, surrounded by eighteen years of silence. But when he said, 'Hey, little Ell,' the thing he always said to me, I felt a sensation upon my skin as if I was falling through feathers.

Two weeks later, the sound of New York chatter and car horns rose from Greene Street as the sun poured through the large windows, filling the space with an abundance of light that seemed lavish and greedy. I rolled over and opened my eyes. My brother was standing holding a coffee, staring at me.

'How long have you been there?' I said.

'Twenty minutes,' he said. 'Sometimes on one leg, like this,' and he showed me. 'Or like this,' and he changed legs. 'Like an Aborigine.'

'You're so weird,' I said, and rolled over, tired, happy, hung over.

I'd landed quite late the previous night. Joe had met me at JFK as he always did, and held a big sign that said 'Sharon Stone'. He loved to listen to the whispers of the passers-by, the gorging anticipation of the star-struck, and he loved to watch their mute disappointment as I stood in front of him, dishevelled and casual and oh so not Sharon Stone. He relished this statement meant for the masses, and delivered it with precision that verged on cruelty.

As the taxi crossed Brooklyn Bridge (the bridge we always asked the driver to take), I opened my window to the smell of the city, to the noise, and my heart leapt as the lights illuminated my welcome, urging me onwards as it had done to millions of others, those wanting a different life. My brother had been one of the lured; brought by the promise of anonymity, not of gold, where he could be himself without the label of the past; without all those workings-out and crossings-out, the things we have to do before we come to an answer, the answer of who we are.

As I looked towards the financial district I felt a surge in my chest – for my brother, for Jenny, for the past, for Charlie, and I could feel the gnawing inclusiveness again; the *them* and *us* of my brother's world; the one where I was always an *us*. He pointed to the Twin Towers and said, 'You've never been up there, have you?' And I said, 'No.'

'You look down and you're so cut off from everything. It's another world. I went last week for breakfast. Stood against the window, leant against it and felt my mind pulled towards the life below. It's awesome, Elly. Fucking awesome. The life below feels so far away when you're there. The minusculeness of existence.'

The taxi pulled to a sudden halt. 'Yeah, yeah, you're fuckin' killin' me. Fuck you, asshole!'

We pulled away slowly and my brother leant towards the grille. 'Let's go to the Algonquin instead, sir.'

'Anything you want, buddy,' said the driver, and swerved dangerously into the inside lane. He reached down for the radio and turned it on. Liza Minnelli. A song about maybes and being lucky – even a winner – a song about love not running away.

His name had sat between us since my arrival like an odd chaperone, bringing a quaint propriety to our stories. It was as if he deserved a chapter all to himself, a moment when we turned the page and only his name was visible. And so with the drinks ordered, the bar quiet and our attention mutual and assisting, that chapter began when my brother finished chewing on a handful of peanuts and said, 'You'll see him tomorrow, you know.'

'Tomorrow?'

'He's coming with us,' he said. 'To watch me sing. Do you mind?'

'Why should I mind?'

'It's just so quick, for us, I mean. You've just got here.'

'I'm OK.'

'He just wanted to,' he said. 'He wants to see you.'

'It's OK, I understand.'

'You sure? He just wanted to.'

'I want to, too,' I said, and I was about to ask if they had become lovers again, but the martinis arrived and they looked perfect and tempting, and there would be time for that, and so instead I reached for my glass and took the first sip and said, 'Perfect!' instead of 'Cheers!' Because it was.

'Perfect,' said my brother, and he unexpectedly reached over and held me.

He had become like Ginger. You had to translate his actions, for they were seldom accompanied by words, because his world was a quiet world; a disconnected, fractured space; a puzzle that made him phone me at three o'clock in the morning, asking me for the last piece of the border, so he could fill in the sky.

'I'm so happy you're here,' he said, and I sat back and looked at him. His face was different: softer; the taut tiredness that had hung about his eyes, gone. His face looked happy.

'You are, aren't you?' I said, grinning.

The older couple by the palm looked at us and smiled.

'So,' my brother said.

'So?'

'Can I tell you all over again?'

'Of course,' I said, and he downed half his glass and started again from the beginning.

It was a Stonewall party, a charity party he always supported, and one that was going to be held that year in one of the large brownstones on the edge of the Village. They were intimate affairs that catered for the usual people, but which always made good money from the tickets and the silent auction, and the other silent auction that only the naughty ever knew about.

'But you didn't want to go?' I said, rushing the story ahead to territory I knew nothing about.

'No I didn't. But then I remembered I wanted to check out their renovations, because I've got my eye on a new place and I need an architect; which is also another story because I want you to come and see this house with me tomorrow.'

'OK, OK, I will,' I said, and drank a large mouthful of vodka, feeling its flush in my head. 'Now continue,' I said.

A string quartet was playing in the walled garden and he sat outside most of the evening, gladly cornered by an older gentleman called Ray, who talked to him about the riots of '69, and told him of suppers spent with Katharine Hepburn and Marlene, whom he used to know because he was involved in wardrobe at MGM and because he had association with von Sternberg too, because of his own German lineage (mother's side). And then the light faded and candles arrived, filling the atmosphere with scents like tea and jasmine; fig, too. People deserted as the music stopped, headed indoors to hear the results of the auction and to sample the Japanese buffet orchestrated by the events caterer *du jour*. And that's how they found themselves alone. There was no inappropriate suggestion, just the quiet familiarity of evenings he used to spend with Arthur, when they talked about Halston and Warhol and those seventies parties whose themes were as blurred as the preferences of the guests.

And then a man approached down the fire escape. A young man, it seemed, in the candlelit night; less young as he approached. But Ray looked over to him and smiled and said, 'And who might you be, handsome young brave?' and the man laughed and said, 'My name is Charlie Hunter. How're you doing, Joe?'

The waiter placed the second round of martinis down. I was hungry. I ordered extra olives.

They crammed years into those remaining hours before they tumbled out onto the sidewalks of the Village and wandered back to SoHo, happy and drunk and disbelieving. They spent the weekend at Joe's apartment, cocooned in movies and take-out boxes and beer, and voraciously ate away at the years, the lost years that had defined one another's name. And that's when Charlie told him he shouldn't have been at the party either. He should have been back home in Denver, but his flight had been delayed and a meeting had suddenly come up for Monday, and a business colleague he knew only as Phil had said, 'Stay – there's this party,' and so he'd stayed and hadn't seen Phil since; not since he'd left him by the silent auction, bidding for a dinner for two at the Tribeca Grill with an unknown celebrity.

Joe downed the remainder of his glass. 'And guess what, Ell? I think he's going to move to New York for good.'

And that's when I really thought I'd asked if they'd become

lovers; but maybe I hadn't because I couldn't remember, because that was when we ordered the third martini, the third martini that seemed such a good idea at the time; the third martini that stayed in my mouth as I awoke to that piercing sunlight and a brother standing on one leg, holding a double macchiato, pretending to be an Aborigine.

THE TOWNHOUSE WAS NESTLED IN THE HEART OF THE Village in a tree-lined street that was quiet and strangely remote, considering it was only a street away from Bleecker and two from Washington Square. We could see the realtor up ahead talking on the phone, standing next to a large ailanthus tree that offered little shade against the draining afternoon sun.

We ran the last fifty yards to meet him, a sudden race, a ready-set-go, which I won, because I reached and touched the black iron handrail first. The realtor seemed bemused; we looked hot and sweaty and, most of all, poor; as if we couldn't even raise the price of a hot dog between us, let alone prime New York real estate.

The odour from the ailanthus became strong as we climbed up the steps to the front door, and as we entered it mingled with the smell of damp, a smell the realtor immediately assured was only a slight problem, rather than the structural signifier we both imagined. It was dark as we entered, thankfully unfurnished, and the rooms were concealed behind wooden shutters, which stalled midway as they were pulled back, refusing to offer light beyond the realms of dusk. The house was rather poky inside, with a cumbersome layout that mimicked a chicken run. Walls were plastered with striped paper, an orange and brown and black theme throughout, with dark oak balustrades clumsily painted and now hidden behind the heavy gloss of mocha stain. I traversed the hallway and followed its narrow ascent to the upper two floors, the highest one nursing a hole and a bird's nest, and then precariously down to the kitchen and the small uninspiring garden beyond, which was landscaped with weeds and knee-high ailanthus trees, the seeds having been blown in from the front. There was so much wrong with this house, so much to do; but as I stood there, my brother secretly pointing to his watch, I immediately under-stood the layout, the how-it-should-have-been all those years ago, and the how-it-could-be now. And when my brother asked, 'Well?' with no enthusiasm in his voice, I said, 'I love it.' And I really did.

We got back just before six. I showered quickly and dressed; hid my nerves behind an article I needed to finish for the following day. It was a pitch, actually, a pitch for a regular column in a weekend newspaper which I'd hastily (and unimaginatively) entitled 'Lost and Found' – a name that would eventually and surprisingly stick. It was to be the story of Jenny Penny and her return to my life; stories cemented together by our correspondence and the memories of our past. And when I'd nervously written to her suggesting such an idea, asking for her opinion and maybe later her permission, I received a resounding *Yes!* by return of post, together with the new fictitious name I'd asked her to choose, to protect her fragile yet willing identity.

The buzzer rang; I wasn't finished. The buzzer rang and my brother shouted from his bedroom. I opened the front door and stood a few feet back. I suddenly remembered the towel around my head and pulled it off, throwing it over the back of a chair, letting my hair fall damp, unruly, free. I felt anxious. Wondered how he would enter. Would he run in shouting, happy to see me? Or simply knock? I heard his footsteps, heard him pause. And then he did neither; simply pushed the door gently and stuck his head round and smiled, and said, 'Hello, Ell, how're you doing?'

The dark features were the same, the smile the same, but his voice had lost the flat Essex tones I could still remember. And he'd brought champagne. We were going out but he'd brought champagne because it was a moment for champagne, and he stood there with his hands on his hips and said, 'You haven't changed,' and I said, 'You neither,' and we embraced, and he was still holding the champagne bottle as we embraced, and I felt it cold and hard against my back.

My brother came out to the sound of the cork popping. He came out still wet from the shower, wearing his choir T-shirt, a pink T-shirt that had 'The Six Judys' written on the front above a line drawing of that famous dame. And then underneath in smaller type: 'We'll Sing for your Supper'. It was something they did every time, had a new T-shirt printed for each new charity they supported. One year, they'd supported an elderly group and the T-shirt had said: 'You're Never Too Old to Sing'. This time, though, it was food for the homeless, and the provision of a new catering van.

I handed around the glasses of champagne. I'd filled them to the top, not something I usually did, but it had been distracting and I'd needed that because when my brother raised his glass and said, 'To us. Finally together,' I had to turn away as I felt the first of my tears, before I'd even had my first mouthful, before I could even join them to say, 'To us.'

I thought he was in the study with Joe helping with a finance problem, but as I began to close down the computer, I suddenly felt his hand on my arm and I startled and he said, 'Wait,' and began to read the opening paragraph.

'What do you think?' I said.

My brother ran in and said, 'The taxi's here. Are you ready?' before disappearing into his room for a pile of promotional CDs and photos.

'I want to be in this,' said Charlie quietly. 'Write about me.'

'In this?'

He nodded. 'You lost me and now you've found me. I should be in it too, don't you think?'

'You'll need to change your name,' I said.

'Ellis.'

'What?'

'That's the name I'd like. Ellis.'

'OK,' I said.

'What's Jenny Penny's?' he asked.

'Liberty,' I said. 'Liberty Belle.'

We sat at a small unoccupied table at the back of the suite, away from guests we didn't know, ignoring the ones we did, close to the ice-sculpted vodka bar and a never-ending supply of mini hamburgers and fat breaded scampi.

'I thought you might be married,' he said.

'No,' I said, finishing my drink.

Silence.

'That's it? No elaboration? No one special?'

'No.'

'Never?'

'In hindsight, no.'

'In *hindsight*. God, you're so like him,' he said, waving to my brother who had just peeped out from behind the makeshift red velvet curtain. 'Your own little club.'

'It's not like that. It's complicated.'

'We're all complicated, Ell. Do you remember the last time you saw me?'

'Yeah.'

'You were nine, ten, right? And really pissed off at me.'

'He never got over you.'

He laughed. 'Yeah, yeah.'

'Yeah, actually,' and I reached swiftly for a glass of wine as it passed by on a tray.

'We were what, fifteen? Fuck. Where did all the time go, Ell? Look at us.'

'It's as if it was yesterday,' I said, downing half my glass. 'So, are you fucking?'

'God, you are all grown up.'

'Yeah, happened overnight. Well?'

'No,' and he tried to swipe a glass of champagne from the tray, this time spilling it down his arm. 'He won't with me.'

'Why not?'

'He doesn't go back,' he said.

Bobby, the hairiest of The Judys, came out and introduced the rest of the group. He talked about the charities being represented that evening, talked about the artists exhibiting around the room. He talked about money and asked for lots of it.

'By the way,' I said turning back to Charlie, 'the last time I saw you wasn't then. It was when you were on television being bundled into a car.'

'Ah,' he said, 'that.'

'Well?' I said, but he pretended not to hear me as the opening bars to 'Dancing Queen' quickly filled the room.

I couldn't sleep. Buoyed by the latent effects of jet lag and coffee, I found myself wide awake at three in the morning. I got up, crept to the kitchen and poured out a large glass of water. I turned my computer on. The sound of breathing was loud and close. My brother never shut his bedroom door. It was a security thing: he needed to hear the sounds of his home, needed to hear if a different sound entered. I gently closed his door. Tonight he was safe; safe with me, and safe with Charlie asleep in the adjacent room.

It was then, in the three o'clock darkness, that I wrote about the moment Ellis re-entered our lives that evening in August, as shoppers gathered at corner bars, swapping tales of sales and divorces pending, of who loves who and holidays to come. I wrote about how he entered with a wallet crammed with fifties, and memberships to MOMA and the Met, and loyalty cards for Starbucks and Diedrich's too. I wrote about how he entered with a slight scar above his lip from an accident skiing, and how he entered with a wounded heart from a man called Jens; a man he didn't really love, but he was someone there, a late-night-talk-to; we've all had one of them. I wrote about how he entered with a letter in his pocket, which his mother had written a couple of days before, a letter more emotional than usual, wondering how he was, wishing they spoke more, stuff like that. I wrote about how he entered with a terrifying ordeal that he wouldn't talk about for years, with an empty space where once was an ear. And I wrote about how he entered with the knowledge that he was changing jobs, leaving the snow fields of Breckenridge and the Rocky trails behind, and swapping them for land in the Upstate quiet, where neighbours were unseen, and where the Shawangunk Mountains would watch over him like the eagles they unleashed; swapping it all to be with an unlikely someone from his distant past.

That's how he entered; how I remembered he entered.

5 July 1997

Jenny,

Every morning I pick up the Guardian *and the* News of the World *and walk through the double-arched gateway and enter the courtyard, with its fountain and car park and patients sitting on benches with drip lines for company. I never say hello to anyone, not even to the gatekeeper; just keep to myself and to the story that lives so quietly on that upper floor. Ginger has shrunk before my eyes; she stopped momentarily at a weight that would have thrilled her years before and given her what she would have referred to as a 'figure', before plunging her headfirst towards a skeletal state too weak now to support anything other than sleep.*

We'd got used to the cancer and so had she in many ways, or at least used to the habitual cycles of medication and chemotherapy and what it did to her body throughout those seven years. But we can't get used to this infection and the way it's decimated her frame and clawed so hungrily at her spirit. She's never once said her cancer was unfair, but this infection has eaten at her dignity, and the self-pity she banished from her life has appeared now and then, and made her hate herself more. She has been dealt a shitty hand, Jenny; the days she feels it pain us to the core. I feel inadequate.

As she sleeps, so I work at her bedside. I work on our column, which has become a surprising success. I say surprising, but you say you always knew. Liberty and Ellis are mentioned now on trains and on buses and in the chatter of work breaks. What do you think of that, Jenny Penny, my friend of old? Fame has found you at last . . .

I LOOKED OUT OF THE WINDOW; NIGHT WAS CLOSING IN ON the building works and the overgrown trees from Postman's Park. The shadows were large and grotesque. I didn't want to go home. This had become my home, the nurses my friends, and as the long nights stretched out before me, I eavesdropped on their problems as they talked about broken hearts and money, about rents and the price of shoes and how depressing London was before the change of Government.

I told them stories about Ginger; this woman who'd shared champagne with Garland and a secret with Warhol. I showed them old photographs because I wanted them to know this woman; this woman beyond the name and number and date of birth that was wrapped around her wrist. I wanted them to know this woman who still tingled when she heard stories about meeting Liza down Fifth Avenue, or seeing Garbo garbed in sunglasses and scarf on the Upper East Side, stories like that, for she still thrilled at such epic stardom; glowed in a fame that scoffed the talentless. She'd found hers; had had that moment, that golden moment, forever untarnished by advancing years.

'What's up, pet?' said Ginger, suddenly waking, reaching weakly for my hand.

'How're you doing?' I asked.

'Not too bad,' she said.

'Water?'

'Only with Scotch – you know me.'

I placed a cool cloth against her brow.

'What's going on in the world?' she asked.

'Gianni Versace was shot dead yesterday,' I said holding up the newspaper.

'Gianni who?'

'Versace. The designer.'

'Oh, *him*. Never liked his clothes,' and she fell back to sleep, content maybe, that there was at least some justice in the world.

The summer evenings unfolded and I longed to take her out into the courtyard to get the sun on her face and to see her freckles appear once more in tanned clusters. I wanted to take her back to my flat behind Cloth Fair, the flat she told me to make my home five minutes into a first viewing the November before. I wanted us to sit on the roof and look out over Smithfield in the early hours, watching the meat market open up like some giant nocturnal bloom. I wanted us to listen again to the bells of Bartholomew, as we ate croissants and read the Sunday newspapers and gossiped about people we knew and those we didn't. But most of all, I wanted wellness to seize her again and drop her running into the colourful wake of London life. But

Ginger never got to go outside again, and in the end I told her she wasn't missing much, because we'd done it all, lived it all, hadn't we? So there wasn't much point.

'I'd like my ashes to be scattered here, love,' she said to me one day, pointing to a picture of herself standing on the jetty, the river behind her full and bloated. 'So I can keep an eye on you all.'

'Anything you want,' I said. 'You just tell me what you want,' and she did, and I hid my tears behind a sheet of A4 paper and a hospital Biro.

I went home that night for a shower and a change of clothes. The ancient road behind the church was deserted, and the whisperings of bygone lives accompanied me into the alleyway, to the safety of my front door. I turned towards the sound of footsteps; a fleeting shadow retreating into shadow; a laugh, a conversation, the see-you-later echoing across the brickwork, and afterwards the silence. Silence. Turgid and soulful. Edible.

I looked at my body in the mirror, a body I'd once disowned with the currency of scorn. It had never been good enough – not for me, not for others – but that night, it looked beautiful, it looked strong, and that was enough.

I opened the drawer and took the ring out of its hiding place. The worn inscription on the inside band: *Las Vegas 1952. Our memories. X*

She never told me who he was, but Arthur reckoned he was a bad boy, a gangster, and so their memories would've been short. It fitted me now, fitted my ring finger. I put it on and held it up to the light. The diamonds and sapphires sparkled. I smiled like the child who'd received it, frozen in time. Frozen in time.

I picked up the phone and wondered what I was going to say to him. He'd last been here six weeks ago when she was first admitted. He'd flown back from New York and his boss didn't want him to, threatened to fire him, but he'd flown back because he loved Ginger, so of course he'd come back. And when I took him onto the ward and she saw his face, she lit up with such delight, you'd have thought his mere presence had caused the cancer to retreat. And that week she seemed to get well, *did* get well, but that was before the infection. He left vowing to see her in October. It was now the third week of July. It was ringing.

'Hey, Joe,' I said.

There was silence the other end.

'It won't be long,' I said.

'Right,' he said. 'Call me when you're with her.'

'Course I will.'

'How are you doing?'

'Wretched,' I said.

Neither my parents nor Nancy came back for that final week because Ginger asked them not to. They begged her, fought with her, but she said she 'didn't want them to remember me like that', but really it was because she couldn't bear to say goodbye. Age had softened her and authenticity now squired her feelings. Words, once saved for a song, became her own. My parents found it hard to accept her wishes but they reluctantly agreed and prepared quietly for a life without her. My mother had her hair cut into a very nice bob. Nancy signed up for a TV series in LA. And my father went back into the forest and chopped down a tree. The sound of the trunk fracturing and splintering and falling to earth was the sound his heart would have made, could it speak.

And as Ginger became weaker, so I made the final call, the one that brought him to Paddington Station the following morning, where I met his shaky descent with a resigned smile from beyond the barrier. He looked old and troubled, and the cane he once used as a prop, was now used as a walking stick. He was quiet in the taxi and we avoided all mention of her name until we came down Farringdon Road and he asked me again what ward she was on and did she need anything.

'OK?' I asked, reaching for his hand.

He nodded and as we turned into Smithfield, said, 'I used to have relations with a young butcher down here.'

'Fond memories?' I said.

He squeezed my hand and I knew exactly what that squeeze meant. 'I haven't written about him yet,' he said, 'but I will. Chapter thirteen, I expect; the one entitled "Other Distractions".' He was trying so hard.

He stumbled as we got out of the cab, and I heard him sigh deeply. 'How's she doing, Elly? Really?'

'Not good, Arthur,' I said, as I led him to the entrance.

He leant over her bed and touched the side of her face and said, 'Who's got cheekbones then?' and she smiled and tapped his hand and said, 'Silly old fool. Wondered when you'd get here.'

'Still our Ginger,' he whispered as he leant down and kissed her.

'You smell nice,' she said.

'Chanel,' he said.

'Wasted on you,' she said, and he reached into his bag and pulled out an almond tart.

'Look what I've got,' he said triumphantly, as he lowered it under her nose.

'Almonds,' she said. 'Just like Paris.'

'For us to share,' he said. 'Just like Paris.'

I never knew if she had any real appetite or not, for she hadn't eaten solids for days. But he broke a piece off and held it to her mouth and she ate hungrily; for it was the memory she was tasting again, and the memory tasted good.

I moved a chair close to the bed for him and he sat down and held her hand. His own death he'd made peace with years ago, but everyone else's still frightened him and so he held her hand to not let her go. He held her hand because he wasn't ready to let her go.

I watched them from the door and listened to the stories billowing from youth to middle age and back again; stories from the little hotel on Saint André des Arts, where they drank into the early hours and watched the couple opposite make love, a sight so beautiful, it was still talked about forty years later. They were best friends, telling best-friend tales.

I left them and headed towards the stairs, and as I walked down I was overwhelmed with the gratitude of wellness. I walked out and breathed fresh air. I felt the sun on my skin. The world is a different place when you are well, when you are young. The world is beautiful and safe. I said hello to the gatekeeper. He said hello back to me.

Jenny

Something happened that I thought you'd like to know about. Last afternoon, riding painlessly on a wave of morphine, Ginger told us about a visit she'd had earlier in the day. That was strange because neither Arthur nor I had seen a visitor and we'd been there all morning. He'd brought her flowers, she said, this man; he'd brought her favourites, white roses; flowers that adorned her dressing room in her heyday and whose scent made her feel that anything was possible. I looked at Arthur and we shrugged, because there were no white roses, just a small vase of freesias that one of the nurses had brought in a couple of days before. But she made us smell the white roses, and we did and she was right, the scent was strong. Ginger said her visitor was an older man, sixty, maybe, but still handsome, but age didn't matter because he'd found her and he was exactly as she'd imagined. His name was Don and he was her son. She'd given him up years ago, she said, but she knew it was him when he walked in. He'd brought her flowers, you see. Roses. White roses. And his name was Don. He'd come looking for her and he'd found her. And now she felt good. She was calm and now she could go.

We'll never know the truth of that story, and I don't think either of us wants to really. It was a story that began and ended in that room. Arthur says everyone takes something to the grave . . .

There were no long speeches or great goodbyes in the end; Ginger simply slipped away at four in the morning whilst we were sleeping. I awoke soon after – an intuition, maybe? – I looked over at her and knew she'd gone, as if the very air that once inhabited her body had been sucked out and replaced by a contoured landscape of concavity. I kissed her and said goodbye. Arthur stirred; I knelt down and gently woke him up.

'She's gone, Arthur,' I said, and he nodded and said, 'Oh,' and then I left him to say his farewell, as I went to find a nurse.

I walked down the one hundred and thirty-one steps that I had walked four times a day for six weeks and went into the square. It was dark, of course; sporadic lights and the sound of the fountain. I looked up at the sky. 'There's a new star tonight,' my brother would have said, had I been younger, had he been there; and for forty minutes I looked for it. But I had become too old. I couldn't see her anywhere. Where she had been, was now just space.

She died a month before Princess Diana.

'So as not to steal her thunder,' we all said.

Dear Elly,

The whole prison watched the funeral yesterday. Those poor boys walking behind. It was very quiet in here. Everyone had their own sadness. For many it was the wasted time – the time they'd spent inside away from families or the time spent drinking or on drugs or the death of Loved Ones they never got to see again. Or the children taken away from them and put into care. Westminster Abbey looked beautiful. I've never been. Never been to St Paul's either or the Tower of London. So many places to see.

There are lots of conspiracy theories in here. Always are. I said people should have stopped calling her 'Di', that would of been a start.

You mentioned Mr Golan in your last letter.

I had a Mr Golan in my life too.

One of my mums old boyfriends.

Sometimes when I'd arranged to meet you and I was late, it wasn't because of my hair. I wish I'd told you of all people. Im sorry. Their helping me in here about it. Its good. Talking. Lots of talking.

I shaved my head two days ago. I thought I might look like a man but everyone says I look pretty. I feel strangely free. Funny what hair can do to you.

Sorry about your last visit. Never stop being patient with me Elly.

Take care always

Your Liberty, your Jenny x

THE LAST AUGUST OF THE MILLENNIUM DREW UPON US AND
my father suddenly cancelled all reservations and refused
all bookings, and instead left our house empty and yawning
and waiting, in preparation for us, his family. It was the first
time we would all be together since the scattering of Ginger's
ashes, and it was an action so out of character for this man
who flourished in the presence of guests that my mother
found herself constantly monitoring his every move in case
he should once again plummet to those unknown depths,
where he would become a mere trophy to the power of
the unresolved.

And yet it was simply excitement that had gripped him,
nothing more sinister; the same excitement that had him wake
us up as children in the middle of the night to watch his favourite
film, a Western usually, or to watch Muhammad Ali box into

legend in our sleepy minds. His excitement was the taper that ignited our sluggish souls, and drew us all towards him that summer; that summer when the light went out.

Joe flew over with Charlie on the red-eye and I met them at Paddington station, where we performed a ten-minute turnaround to catch the nine o'clock train to Penzance.

We dozed intermittently, fuelled by a passing buffet trolley. The boys started on beer as the coastline met the tracks, and I watched them – intrusively, I felt – for signs of burgeoning love, for signs of a commitment to a shared future. But the paralysis that had taken hold the moment of their reunion still remained, and they shared nothing – no home, no dreams, no bed – nothing, except the can of lukewarm beer now traversing the table. My longing was left unresolved; my meddling heart again dissatisfied.

Alan was waiting for us at Liskeard, as usual. But when he came down the slope with hands outstretched for handshakes and bags, I could tell he was different; the robust joviality was gone, his eyes heavy and dull. And as he was pulled towards my brother's chest and embraced in a tight unforgiving clasp, he didn't blush or pull away as he normally did, but offered himself up to the safe warmth of another's hold.

'All right, boys?' he said as he took their bags and placed them in the boot.

'Yeah,' they said. 'You?'

No answer.

We weaved through the familiar lanes with their tightly banked hedges and scattering colour of yellows and blues, and faintly tinged pinks, and we stopped and reversed more than usual as holiday-makers panicked in the face of an oncoming car. We passed the monkey sanctuary where years ago I saw an unprovoked attack on a man's wig. And then as we turned onto the main road, Alan quietly reached for one of his fabled CDs, blew on its underbelly before slipping it seductively into his new state-of-the-art CD player, the one my father had bought as a surprise last Christmas.

It was a song about a depressed man and his longing for a girl and her selfless love. We joined in as the second line began, and captured the mood – the anguished tone – in a frenzy of descant; and even the hairs on Alan's forearms rose, in, what I believed to be at the time, indescribable pleasure.

It was at the point, however, just after Mandy came, of course, and gave without taking, that Alan suddenly turned the music off. He said we were *ruining* it for him and he didn't speak to us for the rest of the journey.

(My father later told us that there was trouble in Alan's marriage, or rather he'd brought trouble into his marriage in the form of a foxy little hairstylist from Millendreath. Her name was Mandi.)

They waited for us at the top of the driveway, all four of them, like a motley picket line, holding tall glasses and a jug of Pimm's instead of placards and banners, and sharing a roll-up cigarette, which at first we thought was a spliff, but soon realised it couldn't be because my mother still had her top on.

'What kind of shoddy welcome is this?' said my brother as he jumped out of the car, and everybody laughed as if he'd just told the funniest joke in the world, as if that roll-up cigarette had actually *been* a spliff.

We tried to persuade Alan to follow us down to the house for drinks but he wouldn't, he just wanted to unload the bags and sulk. He drove back up the slope with the music blaring, and crunched into third gear a little too quickly and immediately stalled. In the heavy silence that surrounded him, the music echoed through the trees, pitiful and forlorn, wailing like an ill-disguised omen. Oh Mandy.

Oh Alan, I thought.

I strode down to the jetty alone, disturbing a heron quietly lazing on the bank in the afternoon sun. I watched him take flight, groggy and lethargic, low over the water. I looked back up to the house and saw my mother framed in an upstairs window, preparing the rooms as she always did. And I remembered again the house as I first saw it as a nine year old, with its off-white peeling façade like a tatty crown on an uncared-for tooth, shadowed by ragged trees, and grieving the frail ruin at its side. I remembered again the sense of adventure that flooded my thoughts, the breathlessness of the what-ifs, the connection, the infinite connection to a horizon that reached beyond and whispered, *Follow, follow, follow.*

I sat down on the grass, lay down until my back was wet, uncomfortable and wet, and the aching gratitude that burnt my eyes had rolled away. I'd been feeling like this for a while, the continual looking back, the stuckness of it all. I blamed it on the coming New Year, only four and a half months away, when the clocks would read zero and we would start again, could start again, but I knew we wouldn't. Nothing would. The world would be the same, just a little bit worse.

My mother leant out of the window and waved; she blew kisses to me. I blew kisses back. She was about to embark on an MA, the secret dream that had so recently found voice, and she no longer saw Mr A and the contents of his wayward mind. Three months before, he'd fallen in love with a holiday-maker from Beaconsfield and had stopped his sessions immediately, giving credence to the myth that love cures everything (except perhaps the settlement of an outstanding bill).

I stood up and ran back up the lawn towards the house and that upstairs room where I would shake the pillows and smooth the sheets and fill the jugs and arrange the flowers, and all just to be with her; to be with her with the something I could never tell her.

'ARTHUR!'

I shouted his name again and just as I unleashed the rope from its mooring loop and was about to give up, he appeared from his cottage and ran towards me with an empty, old rucksack bouncing on his back like a deflated blue lung.

'Sure you want to come?' I said. 'You could stay with Joe and Charlie.'

'They're napping again,' a touch of disappointment in his voice.

'OK then,' I said, and helped him carefully into the boat.

He loved it when we all returned; he was nearly eighty but became a chameleon around us, and our youth became his. I pushed away from the bank. I didn't start the engine immediately, but let us drift towards the central tidal flow where we said out loud as we always did, 'All right, Ginger?' And where we both felt the slight jolt of the boat; the swift acknowledgement of our words, caused not by wake, nor wind, nor shallows, but by the something other that outwitted proof.

I slowed along the bank to pick blackberries and early damsons, and we hid under overhanging branches to look out for the large male otter my father reckoned he'd seen a few days before; a figment of his imagination really, a ploy I believed, to get us to really look once again, to soften the impenetrable gaze of the harried.

'I've been getting dizzy,' Arthur said, as he trailed his hand in the cool clear water.

'What kind of dizzy?'

'Just dizzy.'

'Have you fallen?'

'Of course not,' he said. 'Dizzy, not *doddery*.'

'Have you changed your diet yet?' I said, knowing full well he hadn't; and he scoffed at such a suggestion, for it was as unworthy to him as a life without bacon and cream and eggs, utterly unthinkable.

His cholesterol and blood pressure were as high as they could be; something he delighted in as if it had taken the utmost skill to get them to such dizzying heights. And he refused to take the tablets prescribed, because a few months before he'd secretly told me that he wasn't going to die that way and so he didn't need to take them, and instead reached for another scone dripping with jam and clotted cream.

'Are you worried?'

'No,' he said.

'So why are you telling me?'

'Just filling you in,' he said quietly.

'Do you want me to do anything?'

'No,' he said, drying his hand on his sleeve.

He'd started to do that, started to inform me of everything; the inconsequential, the meaningful; conversations that ended in a cul-de-sac of unanswerable rhetoric. I think it was because I knew everything about him, had read it all – the beautiful, the sordid, the all of his book. I had been his editor for five years, and now it seemed, had become his editor away from the printed page.

'I'll be back here in ten minutes,' I said as I took the rucksack and climbed the vertical, rusty steps of the harbour wall. At the top, I stopped and watched him nervously manoeuvre the boat around two red buoys before he zigzagged out to sea, and I wondered if I'd see him again, or if he'd suffer once again the indignity of being led back into harbour by an irate coastguard deaf to his consoling pleas. In his imagination Arthur Henry was a seaman, competent and brave; but in reality nothing except terra firma could provide those qualities, and I knew he'd stop just beyond the harbour mouth and go round in circles until the ten minutes were up. And sure enough, by the time I'd descended the ladder weighed down by my order of packed ice and crabs and langoustines, sweat had appeared across his forehead and in the cleft of his bony chest, and he moved back swiftly to his position at the bow of the boat in a manner that said, Never again.

We glided effortlessly across the glassy surface, the *phut phut phut* of the engine quiet and considered against the bustling backdrop of the tourist-crammed village.

'Here, Arthur.'

He sat up as I handed him an Orange Maid.

'I thought you might have forgotten.'

'Never,' I winked, and he pulled out a handkerchief to catch the first of the drips.

'Fancy a bite?'

'It's all yours,' I said, as we veered left up the open sprawl of river towards home.

They were dozing on the lawn when we returned and, seeing Charlie engrossed in a proof copy of his book, *Benders and Bandits, Busboys and Booze*, Arthur walked briskly up the slope and flopped eagerly into the unclaimed chair next to him.

He leant towards him and said, 'Where are you up to, Charlie?'

'Berlin.'

'Oh dear me,' said Arthur, rather strangely adjusting the right leg of his oversized desert shorts. 'Close your ears, Nancy!'

'Oh, yeah right, Arthur,' said Nancy, not looking up from her *American Vogue*. 'Never lived, have I, sweetie?'

'Not in a dark little room on Nollendorfstrasse,' said Arthur, leaning back blissfully into his chair.

My brother was in my father's workroom. He didn't turn round at first, so I watched him carving and chiselling, practising a simple tongue-and-groove joint. He'd made two already and they were balanced on the ledge above his head. He looked like my father in that dim light, the father I knew when I was small; the same silhouette, the hunched, curved back that never seemed to breathe, for breath disturbed precision, and precision in woodwork was everything.

He was going to night school, learning furniture restoration, might learn more, he said. He'd given it all up, the life he'd run away to. Left his job on Wall Street, left the space in SoHo that sucked thousands every month, and he'd bought the townhouse in the Village, with its bird's nest and ailanthus and its brown hall wall that we knocked down after Christmas. And he was restoring it by himself; had been restoring it room by room, month by month, in an unhurried tribute to its former state. This slow pace suited him, because there was now weight around his middle and the weight suited him, but that I would never say. And it was really only Charlie now who was his connection to the old life and the trading floors, to the constantly changing numbers and those early breakfasts at Windows on the World. Because it was Charlie who now worked in the South Tower, overlooking Manhattan from the eighty-seventh floor, an untouchable presence as I flew over New York, him King of the World.

My brother rubbed his eyes. I turned on the light; he turned to me.

'How long have you been there?'

'Not long.'

'Come here, sit down.'

I went to the fraying armchair and brushed away the wooden curls that he'd planed from a piece of oak.

'Drink?' he said.

'What's the time?'

'Time for Scotch. Come on, I found Dad's stash.'

'Where?'

'Wellington boot.'

'So obvious,' we both said.

He poured out the Scotch into stained mugs, and we downed them in one.

'Another?'

'I'm all right,' I said, feeling my stomach recoil and churn at the smoky heat. I had eaten too little that day. I stood up, suddenly needing water.

'Wait,' he said, and held out his arm; told me to look behind. I turned, and there framed in the doorway was a large buck rabbit. It watched us with dark eyes as it nuzzled its way through sawdust and cuts of wood, debris and dust clinging to its chestnut-coloured fur. And as we watched it, the years peeled away and we became small again, and it brought something in with it, something we never talked about, the something that happened when I was almost six, when he was eleven. It was there as we watched it, and we knew because we both became quiet.

I knelt down and held out my hand. Waited. The rabbit moved closer. I waited. I felt the cold twitching nose upon my hand, something warm, breath.

'Look at this,' said Joe.

The sharpness of my turn caused the rabbit to run. I stood up and went over to my brother.

'Where did you find it?'

'Back there. Behind the shelving. Dad must have kept it.'

'Why would he keep it?'

'Souvenir of a memorable day?'

I took the large arrow head from him and turned it over. My father had encouraged Jenny Penny to make it that first Christmas. Helped her to saw the scrappy pieces of oak and to nail them together into the large pointed formation before me. She'd decorated one side with empty limpet shells and grey-only pebbles from the shore, and sprinkled it all with glitter. The surface of my palm shimmered in the light.

'She'd wanted to be found,' he said.

'Everyone wants to be found.'

'Yeah, but that's the bit I always forget. We didn't guess where she might be, we didn't find her. She led us there.'

'Where was it found that night? D'you remember?'

'On the jetty. Pointing downriver . . .'

'To the sea.'

'I always thought she disappeared to hurt herself, or to kill herself. You know, a grand gesture, her refusal to go home. But now I see she simply led us to a place, to a moment, where she could show us how special she was. How different from everyone else she was.'

'How *chosen*.'

I felt uneasy. I clambered over the rocks to the furthermost point, where the craggy strand joined the sea. The tide was out – far out – and it wouldn't have been an impossibility to have walked over to the island that afternoon; I'd done it before. I looked east over to the Black Rock, to its familiar shape rising from a bed of heaving dark. Prawning had been good this season; always sparked my childhood enthusiasm. Buckets full of the translucent greys, boiled on the beach. We could in those days – not now, of course.

The sun felt hot. The familiar fetid arsestink of low tide. A strong briny smell on the wind. I threw a stone for a scampering mutt. Turned back; carefully retracing my footing. I realised the memory of that Christmas was as imprecise to my brother as it was to me. It was Jenny Penny who had instigated the search, and instigated her discovery, just as she had provoked the conversation the night she arrived.

'Do you believe in God?' she'd asked loudly, silencing the hum of our familiar chatter.

'Do we what?' said my father.

'Believe in God?'

'That's a big old question for a night like this,' said Nancy. 'Although to be fair, quite relevant for this time of year.'

'Do *you* believe in God, Jenny?' asked my mother.

233

'Of course,' she said.

'You seem very sure of that,' said my father.

'I am.'

'Why's that, honey?' asked Nancy.

'Because he chose me.'

Silence.

'What do you mean?' asked my brother.

'I was born dead.'

And the table fell silent as she intimately described her birth, and the prayers, and the resuscitation that followed. And no one in our house slept that night. No one wanted to be absent in her presence – not through fear, but that she might show us something we weren't ready to see.

I sat on the wall and looked across the flattened tops of weed-draped rocks and knew how she'd walked on water that night. I'd known it for years now, but I saw how carefully she must have noted the staggered formation, the isolated pathway that had collaborated with her that night, and had given her momentary surety of footing.

I'd come over the hill, I remember, breathless from my panicked run. She's here! I shouted to my brother; and I saw her looking back at us; not running from us, but waiting for our audience, before she started her slow trajectory across the barely submerged rocks, into the oncoming waves.

'I'm never going home, Elly.' That's what she'd said the day before, but I didn't take her seriously – thought it was the anticlimax, the malaise of Boxing Day that was affecting her.

She'd left notes around the house, around the garden, tied onto the bare branches of fruit trees. We thought it was a game – it *was* a game – but we thought it was a game whose ending would bring a joyous relief; a shared Well done! My turn now!

But then it changed. It grew dark, and we grew fearful. My parents and Nancy headed into the forest and up the valley into neighbouring terrain, where boggy earth could ambush even the careful-footed-sighted. Alan took the roads leading to Talland, Polperro, Pelynt. He later took the road that carved through the village, intending to follow its winding path into Sandplace. We were on the bridge when we flagged him down. The three of us. Joe, me and her. Silent, shivering, unimpressed.

She would give no answers to my parents' anguished questions. Sat in front of the fire instead and lifted a blanket over her head, refusing to talk. Her mother was called that night – my parents had no choice – and her fate was seamlessly sealed.

'There'll be no train ride home for her now, no way. No, Des's back. You remember Des? My ex of a few years ago. He's been with me a while now. Oh, didn't she say? Well, he said he'll drive down tomorrow and pick her up.'

Des, Des. Uncle Des.

The one who chose her.

THE KITCHEN TABLE WAS CARRIED OUTSIDE AND COVERED with newspaper secured by three tarnished silver candelabras, dripping trails of melted wax over the printed stories of yesterday and beyond. By the time we'd carried out the glasses and the wine and the trays of crabs and langoustines, the sky had turned dark, a fearsome dark, and we huddled around the candles like a pack of strays. We were about to start, but then we realised that someone wasn't with us and so we shouted her name until out of the darkness she appeared, like a beautiful wandering ghost dressed in a white silk shirtdress, the buttons of which were undone so low it was hard to decipher if it was going on or coming off. And as she strode across the dew-soaked lawn like the character in her new TV series, Detective Molly Crenshaw (Moll to her friends), her swagger was now a cop swagger, as if her gun was hidden somewhere awkward, and only the lucky few knew where.

As she reached the table she triumphantly held up two bottles of champagne as if she herself had picked and fermented those grapes and had bottled them all in the space of a day, and we couldn't help but cheer and applaud this feat. The sound brought an unmistakable glow to her cheeks, dismissing instantly the lie that she had taken her last bow in Theatreland.

'Let us begin,' she said, and as if on cue the quiet of the Cornish air was fractured by the sounds of shattering shell and the first '*Ah*'s as the sweet white claw meat found its way to our mouths.

'You're quiet,' whispered my father as he leant across to refill my glass. 'Everything all right?'

'Of course,' I said, as Nancy reached across Arthur for a large langoustine. It was decapitated in seconds, its jacketed skin parted and cast aside and its flesh dipped into a pungent bowl of aioli, before the ascent towards open mouth. She licked her fingers and said something but it was lost in the chewing, in the licking; she said something like, 'I'm thinking of getting married,' and a sudden silence fell upon the table.

'What?' said my mother, trying hard to disguise the horror in her voice.

'I'm thinking of getting married.'

'You're *dating* someone?' I said.

'Yup,' she said, filling her mouth this time with bread and dark crab meat.

'Since when?' I said.

'A while.'

'Who?' my mother asked.

Pause.

'A man.'

'A *man*?' my mother said, no longer bothering to disguise the horror in her voice. 'But why?'

'Hold on there,' said my father. 'We're not all bad.'

'Tell me – it's not Detective Butler, is it?' said Joe.

'It is,' said Nancy, giggling.

'No way!' said Joe.

'Who's Detective Butler?' asked my mother; her voice getting higher, the more agitated she became.

'The really hot, young one in the show,' said Charlie.

'But he's so queer,' said Joe.

'He's not queer,' said Nancy. 'I should know, I'm sleeping with him.'

'You're queer,' said Arthur.

'That's different, Arthur,' said Nancy, pulling apart a large claw. 'My sexuality is fluid.'

'Is that what you call it?' said Arthur, randomly hammering at a crab's head.

'But why?' asked my mother, filling her glass with wine and draining it almost before the answer had been given. 'Why after all these years?'

'I've changed, and it feels nice. *We* feel nice.'

'Nice?' my mother said, refilling her glass, her face pale and tortured in the flickering candlelight. 'Nice? *Nice* has never been grounds for marriage,' and she sat back, folded her arms and excluded herself from further discussion.

Nobody said much after that. There were a couple of banal comments about the size of the crabs and a discussion about whether whelks could ever rival oysters in gastronomic cuisine, and it would have stayed like that all night had my mother not softened and leant forwards and gently said, 'Is this a phase, Nancy?'

'Mid-life crisis, more like,' said Arthur. 'Why don't you buy a Ferrari instead?'

'I have.'

'Oh.'

'I don't know,' said Nancy, reaching for my mother's hand. 'All the best women are taken.'

(My mother suddenly looked a little happier and blushed, although I can't be sure of that because of the light.)

'And,' Nancy continued, 'he doesn't speak about his feelings, he doesn't cause any dramas over exes, he doesn't want to go shopping with me, he doesn't wear my clothes and he doesn't copy my hairstyle. It's refreshing, to say the least.'

'Nance, if you're happy, we're happy. Aren't we everyone?' said my father, and the table answered him with a pathetic scattering of 'no's and 'suppose so's.

'So, congratulations,' he said, 'and I can't wait to meet him.'

'And neither can we!' said Joe and Charlie a little too enthusiastically.

We raised our glasses and were about to toast the queer union, when all of a sudden we were interrupted by the sound of a heavy splash coming from the riverbank; a sound that propelled our drunken selves to the water's edge.

We shuffled carefully along the jetty, huddled behind my father as he held the candelabra over the water, illuminating the black river with yellow. The overhanging trees danced grotesquely. Shadows of reaching arms and groping fingers came towards us. We heard another splash. My father turned to his left and it was then that we saw the frightened darting eyes; not the eyes of an otter this time, the size, the stroke of its paddle all wrong; no, what we saw was the gently lined face of a baby deer struggling to hold its head high above the water. It went under. Re-emerged. Its eyes terrified, staring into mine.

'Get back, Elly!' my father shouted, as I jumped into the shimmering cold.

'Elly – it's dangerous! For God's sake get back!'

I waded towards the drowning beast; I heard another splash behind me and turned to see my brother thrashing towards me, water spraying as he kicked out towards me. The deer panicked as I drew near and it quickly turned and flailed towards the opposite bank. Its hoofs soon connected with an unexpected sandbank that had formed in the channel of the shallower waters, and I watched as it stumbled up the muddy edge, exhausted. It disappeared into the shadows of the forest opposite, just as the candles flickered and drowned in their own liquidity. We were left alone in the black.

'Idiot,' said my brother as he flung his arms around me. 'What were you trying to do?'

'Save it. What were you trying to do?'

'Save you.'

'If you didn't want me to get married, Ell,' bellowed Nancy across the Cornish valley, 'all you needed to do was tell me, honey, not try to fucking kill yourself!'

'Come on,' said my brother as he guided me back to shore.

I sat in front of the roaring hearth and watched the men play poker badly and loudly. My mother bent down and filled my wine glass. Maybe it was the angle or the light, maybe it was simply her; but she looked so young that night. And Nancy must have noticed it too, because I caught her looking at her as she carried in a tray of teas, and it was a gaze, I could see, that extinguished all thoughts of her erratic marriage (a marriage that, incidentally, would never happen due to Detective Butler's shameful 'outing' by *National Enquirer* magazine).

Later, as my mother entered my room to say good night, I sat up and said, 'Nancy's in love with you.'

'And I'm in love with her.'

'But what about Dad?'

She smiled. 'I'm in love with him too.'

'Oh. Is that allowed?'

She laughed and said, 'For a child of the sixties, Elly . . .'

'I know. Bit of a letdown.'

'Never,' she said. '*Never*. I love them differently, that's all. I don't sleep with Nancy.'

'Oh God, I don't need to know that.'

'Yes you do. We play by our own rules, Elly, always have. That's all we can do. For us it works.'

And she leant over and kissed me good night.

THE FOLLOWING DAY, THE PARTIAL ECLIPSE BEGAN JUST before ten. The sky was overcast, which was a shame, because the lessening of light became a subtle phenomenon rather than the dramatic occurrence of ancient times. We were out in the bay with other boats, surrounded by cliff tops dotted with hundreds of observers, their faces looking towards the cloud-masked sun, protective mirrored viewers held up like 3D glasses. Gulls were singing, and land birds too from the island haven, but there was chaos in their voices, melody gone. They were sensing the unusual, I was sensing the cold. The diminishing light felt like the approach of a storm, like something harmful, inexplicable. And then just before eleven fifteen, the last of the sun disappeared, and the darkness and silence were total, and the cold descended upon the water, and us, and the whole bay locked down into this ravenous silence; the birds quiet, confused into sleep.

I thought this is how it would be if the sun died; the gentle shutting down of an organ, sleepy, no longer working. No explosion at the end of life, just this slow disintegration into darkness, where life as we know it never wakes up, because nothing reminds us that we have to.

The sun started to reappear a couple of minutes later, slowly, of course, until colour once again saturated the sea and our faces, and birdsong filled the air, songs this time of joy, of relief. Cheers rang out from the cliff tops and the *ra ta ta ta* of applause. Yet we were all quiet for so long after, touched by the magnitude, the beautiful unfathomable magnitude of it all. This is what we are connected to. What we are all connected to. When the lights go out, so do we.

A MONTH LATER, ARTHUR WOKE UP AT SIX LIKE HE DID every morning; and yet on that particular morning his eyes didn't. I looked out from my window and I saw him stumble onto the lawn like a drunk. I ran down the stairs and into the fresh morning air and caught him as he knelt groping for direction.

'What is it, Arthur? What's happened?'

'I can't see anything,' he said. 'I'm blind.'

Non-arteritic anterior ischaemic optic neuropathy – that was the term the specialist used; an optic nerve stroke that lessened the blood supply to the eyes and instead deposited large shadows across both fields of vision. It was something that happened to older men with heart disease; one of those tragic, unfortunate things.

'Heart disease,' scoffed Arthur. 'It must be something else.'

My mother reached for his hand, held it tight.

'But I'm fit. I always have been; have never had any problem with illness whatsoever, and certainly not with my heart.'

'But your results say something different,' said the specialist.

'Then you can shove that difference up your tight little arse,' and he got up to leave.

'Come on, Arthur,' said my mother, leading him back to his seat.

The specialist went back to his desk. He looked at his notes, then out of the window; allowed his mind to wander back to similar occurrences and strange side effects filed under Coincidence, rather than the red of *WARNING*. He looked at Arthur again and said, 'Do you take a drug for erectile dysfunction?' At which point, seeming to know what the answer was already, my mother got up and said, 'All yours, Alfie,' and she left the room, leaving my father to deal with the sexual fallout of octogenarian practices.

The answer, apparently, was *Yes*; for a whole year now. He'd been one of the first to take it, of course, and had waited for its arrival like a child waits for Christmas. The specialist believed there was a link; the 'something else' that he'd heard about before, but he had no proof, so it was goodbye to the pills, Arthur, and a slow hopeful wait for sight.

They came back the following day, tired but relieved, and I waited for them in the kitchen, mugs filled with Scotch, not with tea, because it was late in the afternoon and only Scotch would do.

'I'm sorry, Arthur,' I said.

'Don't you worry.'

'It's not necessarily permanent,' said my mother. 'The specialist said your sight could come back at any time. They know so little about this.'

'But I must prepare for it not to,' he said, reaching for his Scotch and finding the salt cellar instead. 'I simply like having erections. I haven't been doing much with them, but I find them a comfort. Rather like a good book. It's the anticipation, really. I don't even have to get to the end.'

'I know exactly what you mean, Arthur,' said my father, before being cut short by a withering look from my mother. 'You're not a man,' he added bravely. 'You can't possibly understand,' and he leant across the table and held Arthur's arm in solidarity.

I led Arthur back to his cottage, which was warm and smelt of the previous day's coffee, and I helped him to his favourite chair, which we'd positioned by the small hearth, now that autumn was upon us.

'A new chapter, Elly,' he said, and sighed deeply. And a new chapter it truly became; a chapter when I became his eyes.

I'd had years of practice as a child, when he'd led me down to the river or into the forest to describe the seasonal changes and the smells each brought with them. I told him about the increased migration of egrets and described how they behaved, white and sullen, in the scrub oaks beyond. And we picked fungi in the woods and he truly smelt for the first time their earthy scent and felt the spongy sensation between his fingers and we fished, quietly at first, in the river waters until he could almost sense a fish upon his hook, as his fingers played on the line, like gently strumming fingers on a guitar string.

And it was my eyes, too, that led him nervously to his book launch that cold December night, as a sharp wind blew through Smithfield, chasing stragglers to the warmth of a bar. And it was my eyes that led him through the long, white entranceway of the once-upon-a-time smokehouse, through to the high minimal surrounds of the restaurant where everyone was waiting for him, and where his hand tightened around my arm as the sounds of voices and echoes and movement descended upon his ears in a crescendo of disorientation. I felt the fear pulse throughout his body until my mother came up to him and whispered, 'Everyone's saying such wonderful things, Arthur. You're a bit of a star,' and his grasp relaxed, and his voice relaxed, and he said rather loudly, '*Champagne pour tout!*'

It was late. Most people had gone. My father was cornered by a young artist who'd come down from dinner and I heard them discussing the importance of depression and jealousy on the British psyche. My mother was tipsy, flirting with an older gentleman who worked for Orion; she was showing him how to make a chicken by folding a serviette. He was engrossed. As I came up from the bathrooms, I looked around for Arthur, and, rather than seeing him crowded by people, I saw him sitting alone by the exit doors, a forlorn figure part hidden in shadow; a deep frown set across his brow. I thought it had been the anxiety of the evening that had ambushed his ebullience; the anticlimax of a project completed, and completed well. And yet as I approached, I could see it was something else, something much deeper; its resonance present, frenetic and cloying.

'It's me,' I said. 'Are you OK?'

He smiled and nodded.

'It's been a good evening.' I sat down next to him.

'It has.' He looked down at his hands; ran a finger along a vein, plump, swollen, a green worm buried under his skin.

'I've run out of money,' he said.

'What?'

'I've run out of money.'

Silence.

'Is that what's worrying you? Arthur, we've got plenty, you know that. You can have as much as you need. Tell Mum and Dad.'

'No, Elly. I've. Run. Out. Of. Money,' he said, clearly intonating each word, wringing out meaning until he could sense the understanding and implication spreading across my face.

'Oh my God.'

'Exactly.'

'Who else knows?'

'Only you.'

'When did you run out?'

'A month ago. Six weeks.'

'Fuck.'

'Exactly.'

Pause.

'So you're not going to die?'

'Well, I am some day,' he said rather grandly.

'I know,' I said, laughing. I stopped. He looked sad.

'I've become mortal again. Human. I have the not-knowing again and I feel scared.' A solitary tear ran from his eye.

We sat like that, quietly, until the stragglers left; until the cavernous room echoed with the sound of table-clearing and chair-scraping, rather than the sound of good times, good cheer.

'Arthur?'

'Mmm?'

'You can tell me now. How was it going to happen? How were you going to die?'

And he looked towards the sound of my voice and said, 'A coconut was going to fall on my head.'

248

I ROSE WITH THE SUN AND HAD MY COFFEE ON THE ROOF, wrapped in an old cashmere cardigan that Nancy had bought me years ago – my first adult possession, a cardigan that cost more than a coat. As I watched the meat market close down for the day and the workers discard their whites and head instead for a breakfast pint before sleep, I read again Jenny Penny's letter and finished the 'Lost and Found' article for that week.

7 September 2001

Elly . . . I've been making some extra money doing my tarot readings again. It gives people hope. I try to explain that its not just the reading itself, but the psychology behind it. But some people have never looked back you see. For some its simply too far to see. I'm quite popular with the lifers you know! I've recently been seeing 'freedom' in whatever cards they choose be it

Strife or the Princess of Wands or even Death. I never see freedom in Justice though. Justice is a difficult card for the imprisoned.

I pulled a card this morning – a random card – one for me and a moment later, one for you. I usually get Adjustment or the Five of Cups. But this morning I pulled The Tower. The Tower! And then I pulled it again for you. Two towers Elly! One after the other. What's the chance of that?

Its the most powerful of cards. The Tower falls and nothing can be the same again. Nows the time for true healing. The old is destroyed to make way for the New. We mustn't hold on to anything any more because all will be destroyed by this transformative power. The world is changing Elly and we must trust. Fate is beckoning. And if we can accept the laws of the Universe, the ebb and flow of joy of tragedy, then we have everything we need to embrace our true freedom . . .

I stopped reading. Could hear her words exact and persuasive, like her explanation of Atlantis all those years ago. The surety. The hypnotic lure of belief. I closed the computer and finished my coffee.

I felt restless, started to feel something that I'd known for a while: that we were finally coming to an end. It had been five years now, five years of Liberty and Ellis, and I felt their stories were now told, but I'd been putting it off, that final goodbye, especially when I found out that Jenny would be eligible for parole soon, something my father had told me the week before. And although some things were still to be decided, she would soon learn that it would be he who'd be representing her at that final hearing, leading her outside, to where life had progressed six years without her. And so I would wait a little while longer; for that final column; the one she would write herself, sitting on this roof with me by her side.

I skipped breakfast and made my way instead towards Soho for a lunch of cappuccino and croissant. I liked the walk; simply west along Holborn from Chancery Lane to the divide at New Oxford Street. The sun climbed higher and shadows shortened and the city awoke, spewing people onto the streets from all directions. I came to Cambridge Circus and suddenly veered off down Charing Cross Road towards the National Gallery and the Vermeer exhibition, an exhibition I'd been sloppy and procrastinating in my desire to see. Time was running out; only six days left. I didn't even stop in Zwemmer's, as I usually did, or the second-hand bookshops whose bargain basements filled most of my shelves; no, I continued on fast and dodged tourists slow to browse.

I could see the lines at the ticket desk already. The exhibition had been sold out for most of its run and I soon resigned myself to yet another wasted opportunity, but as I joined the end of a slow-moving queue, I heard the whisper that there were tickets available for that afternoon, and sure enough as I reached the desk, the assistant said, 'Three o'clock OK?' and I said, OK. And in the cool air-conditioned entrance hall I stood holding my ticket, feeling lucky that my day was now planned.

Soho was quiet and I sat outside; something I always did, even in winter. Deliveries were late and trolleys piled high with cans of oil and wine and tomatoes trundled carelessly towards doorways and disappeared into kitchens, only later to return. This would always be a working street to me. Elsewhere all the old shops had gone or were going, greedy landlords waiting for the brand names, the names that could afford the hefty rents, so byebye the rest. I looked to my left; Jean's hairdressing was still there and Jimmy's, of course, and Angelucci's too, thank goodness. They still sent coffee down to my parents, an espresso blend that the postman loved to deliver, for the smell made his day, he said. This corner was safe, for now at least. I took out my newspaper and ordered a double macchiato with a *baci* on the side. This corner was safe.

It was hard to imagine we were heading towards dark mornings and the long cold haul of winter that would turn my skin the colour of greying whites. I knew this mild autumn would send the leaves into a riot of frenzied colour, more golds and reds dominating many a wood, the colours of Vermont, the place we'd gone to the previous year.

We'd driven up from New Paltz, a spur-of-the-moment thing, just the three of us. We went to ride horses but hiked instead, and on the way there we picked someone up, a young woman who looked more like a girl. We picked her up because it wasn't safe to hitch-hike – and we all said that, not just me – and she said, 'Yeah, Yeah,' as she scrambled into the back. Her odour smelled strong; it was an odour that said, Don't fuck with me, as she sat next to me with her black garbage bag on her lap. And the youthfulness we'd imagined from the roadside disappeared inside the car, because there under the rim of her Dodgers cap, was the face of a tough life: eyes tired and harder than her years. She said she was going on holiday. We knew she was running away. She took nothing from us except a big break- fast. We watched her disappear into a bus station, engorged by a carelessness she took for adventure. She said her name was Lacey; after the cop show. We became quiet after she left.

I must have heard the shout, but I just wasn't aware of it at the time. But looking back I remembered I'd heard *something*, but I had no context, you see. But then someone tapped me on the shoulder and pointed to the screen inside and I turned round and saw four people already watching. I couldn't see clearly what was going on because it was quite dark, and so I got up and followed inside; slowly, horrifically, drawn to the solitary image that filled the giant screen:

Blue sky. A beautiful September morning. Black smoke and flames billowing from the gaping wound in its side. North Tower, the caption said.

Gotta call Joe. North. Charlie's South. South's safe. I dialled his number, straight to voice mail.

'Joe, it's me. I'm sure you're all right but I'm watching TV and I can't believe this. Have you spoken to Charlie? Call me.'

It came in low and banked and it was the noise, a haunting whine that greeted its target as it exploded into a fireball, sending thousands of gallons of burning fuel rampaging through the lift shafts, melting its spine. Your tower. Charlie. Yours. The woman next to me started to cry. Straight to voice mail. Fuck.

'Charlie, it's me. I'm watching it. Phone me; please tell me you're all right. Please phone me, Charlie.'

My phone rang immediately and I picked up.

'Charlie?'

It was my mother.

'I don't know. I'm watching it now. I can't get through either. I've left messages. Yeah, of course keep trying. Let me know. Of course I will. I love you too.'

The café was packed, silent. Strangers comforted strangers. The impact zone was lower than the North Tower and that was a bad thing. Maybe he was downstairs buying a newspaper or in the bathroom, not at his desk. Not at your desk, Charlie.

People were now waving at the windows, looking for rescue.

They were leaning so far out, straining away from the black smoke creeping towards them. I dialled Joe again. Fucking voice mail.

'It's me. Call me. We're all worried. I can't get hold of Charlie. Tell me he's OK. I love you.'

They tumbled out, just a couple at first and then more, like wounded archers from distant ramparts. And then I saw them, the two people of my future dreams. I saw them hold hands and jump; witnessed the last seconds of their friendship and they never let go. Who reassured who? Who could do that? Was it done with words or a smile? That brief moment of fresh air when they were free, when they could remember how it was before; a brief moment of sunshine, a brief moment of friends holding hands. And they never let go. Friends never let go.

I picked up.

'No I haven't,' I said. 'Not yet.'

I sounded tired, I knew I did. I heard the fear in her voice and I tried to reassure her, but she was a mother and she was scared. She'd heard from Nancy, she was trying to get from LAX to New York but the airports had shut down. A plane had crashed into the Pentagon.

'Joe,' I said again. 'Call me – just a quick, I'm OK.'

'Charlie, it's me again. Call me. Please.'

People all around were on their phones, the lucky ones had located friends; others waited, pale; I was one of them.

Two fifty-nine p.m. South Tower sucked to the ground amidst a flurry of millions of bits of paper, of memos and drafts with names of those now lost, until it was gone, and all those inside were gone and their nightmare was over, now handed to those who were left, those left waiting, now mourning by their phones.

I rang again. No voice mail now, nothing. Another plane had

crashed outside of Pittsburgh; a rumour that it was shot down – conspiracy was starting already. *Conspiracy breeds conspiracy.* That's what Jenny Penny would have said.

The Tower is falling. Nothing can be the same.

Three twenty-eight. North Tower gone. Scenes of dusty moonscape where once was an avenue of people holding coffees, and smiling and rushing to work with thoughts of lunch maybe, or what they'd be doing later, because at that time of the morning they still had later. And as the dust cleared, survivors from the street crawled out dazed and covered in ash, and a man whose shirt had ripped across his front revealed a bleeding chest, but he was oblivious as he concentrated on smoothing his hair to the side, because he'd always smoothed his hair to the side – it was something his mother had started when he was young – so why should that day be any different? It was his search for normality. Call me, Joe. Call me, Charlie. I want normal again.

And that's when I could've done it. Could have wandered down to the Vermeer and reminded myself of beauty. I could have gone down there and been normal. I could have lost myself in a joy I could still remember from that morning, because it was still so close, and I could remember everything before the world changed.

I could have done all that and would have, had I not picked up my phone instead and heard his voice and I started to shake when I heard his voice, and he was talking fast, and he sounded panicked but he was OK. He'd never gone to work that day, had got up late and couldn't be fucked, and I was telling him about the reports here, stuff I'd heard, but he kept telling me to stop, and I didn't hear him at first because I was so happy. But then he shouted at me and I heard.

'I can't find Joe,' he said, and his voice broke.

I SAT ON THE ROOF AS THE LIGHT FADED. NO MORE
remnants of summer. The murmur of the television rose from
below. I felt so cold. I wrapped an old picnic blanket around
me; it was my parents' and I'd never returned it because I never
knew when I might need it. It smelt of grass and damp wool. It
smelt of Cornwall. I remembered again the silence of the call
with them, when the numbing possibility descended upon their
thoughts, when I told them, Your son can't be found.

I tried to get on a flight, but most were grounded or diverted
to Canada. A couple of days and then back to normal, the
operator said. That word again. I put my name down on the
reservations list. I'd be first out, I'd be there to see for myself,
because I couldn't go back to my parents without something to
shatter their silence at least. Either a scream or a smile.

I finished another glass of wine. Waited for the phone call
he'd promised to make. I watched the trucks arrive and park,

heard the soft drone of the engine feeding the refrigeration. I poured out more wine; emptied the bottle.

It had been hours, must have been. I looked at my watch. He'd said he was heading to Joe's house, the police had cordoned off below 14th street, but he'd get there, he'd said, just to check. The smell, Elly; that was the last thing he'd said to me. The smell.

My phone rang. The battery was low. It was him at last.

'Hey,' he said, his voice thin and empty.

'How are you?'

'OK.'

'What is it, Charlie?'

'I found his diary,' he said, his words barely audible. 'It puts him there.'

Duke/Office/8.30.

The diary entry was brief. Written in turquoise ink, the turquoise ink from the pen he took from me last February. We called around, of course, but there were not many to call. Those who were there, the ones who got out, could barely remember him, still in shock. 'Yeah, think he was there,' they said, or, 'No, didn't see him.' We were left none the wiser, left guessing.

Duke didn't make it. Some said he was at the point of impact, others said he'd gone back up the staircase to look for a colleague. That would've been like Duke; gone back to help someone else. That's why they called him The Duke.

By the time I got to New York, Nancy and Charlie still hadn't touched anything in the house. They didn't want to move anything in case I saw a clue, an overlooked clue to his missing.

But all I saw was a full fridge and a half-drunk bottle of his favourite wine, both clues that said, I am coming home, going nowhere.

They'd checked hospitals, Nancy in Brooklyn, Charlie in Manhattan, took turns in New Jersey, took turns in the temporary morgues. She left his name, said it twice clearly, but was asked for it again as voices battled with phone lines. She leant against a wall outside and tried to cry, but tears, like comprehension, were stuck and of the past. She was comforted by no one. Everyone had a story of grief. Everyone else's was worse than yours.

The smell was acrid: burning rubber and fuel, and the other unmentionable that sat in the nose and sent images of horror to the mind. Charlie had warned me about it, but I could still smell it every time I went out, even in the garden, because there was nothing in bloom to mask the stench, because ultimately it was the smell of shock that dosed this city, a sour smell as potent as week-old urine. I pulled out one of his old foldaway bistro chairs and wiped it down. It buckled as I sat on it. The left hinge was broken; he still hadn't mended it.

We'd planned this small garden together, planned the perfumes, the colours, the pots of densely sown lavender, the larkspur, the lemon myrtle in the shade beneath the kitchen, the overflowing squares of voracious red peonies, and the rows of white stocks whose scent said, Forever England; and of course the blue-violet rose, a repeating pattern that coiled and draped around the iron staircase and crept along the wall like a seductive tom; the rose that had bloomed so abundantly all summer, the envy of every guest whose green fingers suddenly paled against my brother's haphazard and uninformed passion. He could create oases in deserts with the sole fertiliser of belief. He'd created a home out of his wanderings.

A helicopter swooped overhead. The rhythmic chopping of the air. The sound of a police siren, or an ambulance racing through the city. The something found, the identifiable at last; and then the devastating phone call to follow, but still, something to bury.

He'd been too lazy to deadhead the plants – never understood the point. 'Let nature be,' he'd said. I picked up a small bucket and started to prise the dried brown trumpets away from their hold. I could let nothing be. Music played next door. Bruce Springsteen. It had been Frank Sinatra before. Only the New Jersey boys allowed to crest the patriotic airwaves.

'Your mum said something strange the other night,' said Nancy, as she opened takeaway cartons of food no one had any appetite for.

'What did she say?' I said, reaching for a fork instead of chopsticks.

Charlie looked at Nancy.

'What is it?' I said.

Silence.

'Don't take this the wrong way, Ell,' she said.

'What did she say?'

'She said that maybe Joe went missing, just took off and disappeared, you know, like people do, when accidents happen. Because they're presented with the chance to start again.'

I stared at her.

'Why would he want to start again?'

'I'm just telling you what she said.'

'It's bollocks. He wouldn't do that to us.'

'Of course he wouldn't,' said Charlie, breaking open a fortune cookie. 'He wasn't depressed, he was happy.'

He said *happy* the way a child would.

'It's fucking bollocks,' I said angrily. 'He would never put us through that. He just wouldn't. She's going mad.'

We watched Charlie read his fortune. He screwed it up and we never asked him what it was.

'Why the fuck would she say it?' I pleaded.

'Because she's a mother. She needs to keep him in the world, Ell.'

We had little to say after that. Ate in silence. Ate in anger. My stomach hurt, I couldn't digest. I tried to concentrate on a flavour, any flavour, to pick it out from all the others and exercise my sense, but all I could smell and taste was burning. Nancy got up and went to the kitchen. She said, 'More wine?' We said, 'OK.' Charlie finished the remainder in his glass. She didn't come back.

I went to find her. She was bent over the sink with the taps running, her face contorted, the bottle on its side, the cork still embedded. She was crying silently. Small muffled sobs, hidden in the sound of falling water. She was ashamed to cry, crying was grieving, grieving was for the lost and she felt she was letting him down. I lay with her that night. She on her side; her hair damp around her neckline, her cheeks moist. Too dark to see her eyes. My father's little sister. Holding his pain.

'You are not alone,' I said.

I got up in the middle of the night and went to my bed. I hadn't taken his room, Charlie had his room; I took the bird's-nest room, the last room we renovated, the room with the working hearth and the front-facing windows flicked by tree branches, their *tap tap tapping* pleading for entry. This was the room always left for me, the bed always made, my clothes in the cupboards, the one of every two that I always bought and kept here. I thought about lighting a fire, but I couldn't trust myself to get it right; the rogue rolling cinder that might hide under a drape and count to twenty before making itself known. And I wouldn't notice it, wouldn't find it, not that night. Restlessness wasn't vigilance. It was distraction. I was everywhere with him, just not here.

I heard the front door open and close quietly. It was Charlie. His footsteps echoed in the silent space, the space that held its breath for news. Footsteps in the hallway. The muted sounds of the television. Then off. Down to the kitchen. The running of water. Filling a glass. And then the footsteps climbing the stairs, the creak of the door to his bathroom, the flush of a toilet, the heavy thump of an exhausted body on the bed. That was the routine. But it changed that night; a minuscule variation. He didn't come back up the stairs; opened the back door instead and went out into the garden.

He was sitting at the table, smoking. A candle flickered in front of him. He didn't often smoke.

'I can leave you alone if you want,' I said.

He pulled out a chair and threw me his sweater.

'I loved him,' he said.

'I know.'

'And I keep listening to messages he left me. I just want to hear his voice. I feel like I'm going mad.'

I reached for a cigarette and lit it.

'I told him a few days before all this happened,' he said. 'Simply told him what I wanted. What I wanted for *us*. Asked him why he couldn't make that jump, why he couldn't be with me. I knew he loved me. What was he so frightened of, Ell? Why couldn't he do it? Why couldn't he fucking say, Yes? Maybe all this would have been different then.'

I let his questions evaporate into the darkness, where they joined the million other unanswered questions that hung above Manhattan that night; burdensome, and irredeemable; ultimately cruel. No one had answers.

The breeze seemed cooler as it filtered through the shutters. I emptied the box of photographs onto the floor and we edited for two hours until we found the one we all agreed on, the one that looked most like him, as we all saw him: smiling, with the pool at the Raleigh shimmering behind. It was the trip when he stole my pen with turquoise ink. Just last February. When we met in Miami for some winter sun. The most expensive kind of sun.

We chose the words and I went down to the print shop and made some photocopies and the man looked on respectfully. He'd seen hundreds of these and I was just one more. When I finished he wouldn't take my money. The gesture made me cry.

I needed to see it for myself, and by myself, give the other two a rest because they'd seen too much, and so I went alone. Just walked south, kept going to where they used to be, marking the skyline. There was no preparation. I hid behind dark glasses and separated myself from hell.

> *Have you seen my husband?*
> > *My daddy was a waiter*
> > *My sister's called Erin*
> > > *My wife and I just got married.*
> > > *She's missing . . .*

The downtown walls were plastered with verse and words and pictures and prayers, and they stretched into the distance like a grotesque fable, one of unprepared despair. People moved along slowly reading, and when a fireman or rescue worker passed by there'd be a moment of applause, but they wouldn't look up because they knew. They knew there'd be no survivors. Had known before everyone else. And they wouldn't look up because they were so tired and hadn't slept, and of course they couldn't sleep, they were surrounded by photographs saying, *Find me, find me*. How could – how would – they ever sleep?

I found a space next to a woman who had worked in the restaurant. She looked nice, she was a grandmother, and I put him next to her. I never expected people to find him, not really. I simply wanted people to look at him and say, He looks like a nice man, I wish I'd known him. Someone stood at my shoulder.

'My brother,' I said, smoothing the crease that crooked his smile.

IT WAS LATE. LATER THAN I USUALLY WENT OUT, AND I SAT at the bar and faced bottles and optics, and a distorted reflection of myself in between. Behind me were quiet stragglers; ones left thinking and drinking, no pause in between. In front of me, whiskey.

I didn't know this part of town, could be anonymous in this part of town and moments before, I'd come back from the bathroom with an extra button undone. It felt crass, I felt awkward, but I hoped for a pick-up, a date or something, but I was out of practice, out of touch with a world like that. Cut off from a world that required behaviour like that. A man looked over. He smiled, I smiled, my standards were dropping. I paid the tab and headed out into the sobering air. My heart tore. I'd had no one for so long.

I walked the block, passing couples, a dog walker, a runner

too. All had direction; me, aimless. I turned up a tree-lined street, its symmetry halted by the red and white lights of a neighbourhood bistro.

It was warm inside, and smelt of garlic and coffee. The owner was cheery. I was his only customer, he might have been waiting to go home, but he didn't show it. He brought over my coffee, enquired about my evening, gave me a piece of *Torta di Nonna*. 'You won't be disappointed,' he said. I wasn't. He handed me the arts section of the weekend *Times*. Kind.

The soft bell above the door rang. I heard a brief conversation and the subsequent groan of the espresso machine. I looked up. A man. He looked at me. I think he smiled. I looked down, pretended to read. He pulled out a chair and sat down behind me. I wanted another coffee but I felt wired, didn't want to get up, could feel him behind me. The man went to the counter and paid his bill. Don't go. Look up. I listened for the sound of the bell. Nothing. Footsteps towards me.

'You look how I feel,' he said, his face tired, sad. He handed me another coffee, a *baci* perched on the saucer.

We barrelled through his front door, a heaving mass of peeling clothes and reaching hands, and we crawled from floor to sofa to bed, but slowed at bed. The startling intimacy of perfume and photos, this once-shared life, stemmed our need, and that's when he said, 'We can stop if you like.' No stop. His mouth tasted of cinnamon and sugar. Coffee too.

I unbuttoned his shirt. His skin felt cool and pimpled as I ran my fingers across his chest and down the hairline of his stomach. I stopped at the elastic of his pants. He sat up awkward, shy even. His cock between us, hard and ready. I held it against the fabric. Outlined the shape with my fingers, grasped it. He didn't move, no thrust, waiting to see what I would do. I lifted his hips and peeled off the white shorts. I bent down. He tasted of soap.

I buried my head in the pillows as my cunt clasped around his fingers, as they slid deep in me, wet and fast, thrusting fast until his cock took over, until he rolled me over and faced me. This sad face, this gentle, beautiful face that had no name. He bent down and kissed me, kissed her. I reached for his hair, lank and wet. I grabbed his mouth, sucked his tongue. He pushed me into the sheets, my knees tight around his ribs clinging to this shared moment, faster shunting as he moved deeper in me, expelling all that had been buried, all that had been hidden, faster fucking, until I felt the surge of energy and reached for him, this stranger, and bit hard on his shoulder as my sound – as his sound – filled the room, and brought back life to a bed, coated in ache.

Five o'clock. Life was beginning outside. I rolled over, exhausted; felt sore between my legs. I dressed quietly in the twilight and watched him sleep. I would leave no note. I made my way to the door.

'This wasn't nothing,' he said.

'I know.' I went back and held him. This was breath.

THE DAYS SPREAD OUT BEFORE ME, INTERMINABLE, SENSELESS hours, and I went to a French café where I wasn't known and where I didn't have to deflect the 'Any news?' with polite 'Not yet's. I sat in the window and watched life pass, watched it head Uptown. I saw three young women walking arm in arm and they were laughing, and I realised that I hadn't seen that in days; it looked so strange.

I wrote there. Wrote the column and wrote about the Lost. I wrote about the flowers at every fire station, piled three, five high, and the candles that never went out; prayers burning through despair, because it was still early days and you never knew, but of course most people did. People knew as they lay alone at night, that this was the beginning, the raw beginning that was to be their Present, their Now, their Future, their Memory. I wrote about the sudden embraces in the middle of shops, and the funerals that appeared everyday for fire-fighters and cops, funerals that stopped the streetflow with a volley of salutes and tears. I wrote about the lost cityscape as I sat on our favourite bench along the promenade by Brooklyn Bridge; the place we went to to think and where we imagined what our lives would be three, five, ten years hence.

But most of all I wrote about *him* – now called Max – my brother, our friend, missing now for ten days. And I wrote about what I'd lost that morning. The witness of my soul, my shadow in childhood, when dreams were small and attainable for all. When sweets were a penny and god was a rabbit.

Nancy went back to LA to work. She wasn't ready, but they called her back and I said she'd never be ready so she had to go.

'I'm thinking of coming back,' she said.

'To here, New York?'

'No. To England. I miss it.'

'It's not perfect.'

'Seems so after this.'

'This could happen anywhere,' I said. 'Nowhere's safe. This will happen again.'

'But I miss you lot,' she said. 'The everyday.'

'You'll feel different when you get that holster back on.'

'Idiot,' she said.

'So come home,' I said as I held her. 'We need you.'

And as she opened the front door and headed down the stoop she turned and put on her sunglasses. 'I'll be all right, won't I?'

'What do you mean?'

'Flying. I'll be all right?'

'You'll always be all right,' I said.

She smiled. Fear was catching. Even the immune were suffering.

We went out to eat that night, just Charlie and I, the first and only night since I'd got there. We went to their place, to Balthazar, and we sat where they always sat, and people were discreet but still asked how we were and Charlie said, 'We're OK, thanks.'

We ate from platters of *fruits de mer* and drank Burgundy and ate steak frites and drank more Burgundy and did as they used to do, and we laughed and got drunk, until the restaurant thinned out and we were allowed to stay in the corner like the Forgotten, as they cleared around us and told jokes about the evening. And that's when he told me. So unexpectedly. Told me about that room in Lebanon.

'You can hold on to anything, Elly, to make you carry on.'

'So what did you hold on to?'

Pause.

'The sight of a lemon tree.'

He proceeded to tell me about the small window high up in his room, no glass, just open to the elements, his only source of light. He would climb up to it and hold himself in the draught of fresh air, the scented fresh air that made him feel less forgotten. He couldn't hold on to the wall for long, and would drop back down into the darkness, where the smells were then his; humiliating and dirty, clinging.

A few days after they had taken his ear, he awoke very late in the afternoon and climbed up to the window and saw that a small lemon tree had been brought into the yard. And in the fading light, the lemons seemed to glow and they were beautiful, and his mouth watered, and there was a breeze and he could smell coffee, perfume, even mint. And for a moment he was all right because the world was still there, and the world out there was good, and when the world was good, there was hope.

I reached for his hand. It was cold.

'I have to go back to England,' I said. 'Come with me.'

'Not without him,' he said.

I knew they'd want something with his DNA in case they found him, found something of him. I went into the bathroom before I left and bagged his toothbrush and a hairbrush, but not his favourite brush, in case he came back, you see; I left that on the side next to his aftershave, next to an old copy of *Rugby World*. I sat on the edge of the bath and felt so guilty that I was to go home and leave him there, but I had to go; had to go and bridge the distance that now separated my stricken parents. And so I left Charlie there, in the house we spent months working on, the house with the bird's nest and the ailanthus tree and the old gold coin we'd found whilst digging out the garden. I left Charlie there to man the phone line, to make calls to the Embassy, and to be there when they called. Charlie, the old hand at trauma; Charlie, the unexpected proof that life can sometimes turn out all right.

IT IS ALL SO MUCH SMALLER. THE SHOPS HAVE GONE, WIPED clean except from memory. The deli, the newsagent, the butcher with its sawdust floor, and the smart shoe shop we never went in, they've all gone. I don't feel sad, feel nothing, simply nothing. I drive along, signal left and turn into the street where we all began.

I don't stop outside, but a few houses before, and I see the swish of saris now, the changing constellation of immigration. I imagined that I would walk up the path, the path that cut through the grass and the flowerbeds, and I would stand in front of the door and ring the bell. 'I used to live here,' I would say and there would be smiles and an invitation inside, and maybe even a cup of tea, and I would tell them stories of our life and tell them how happy we were, and they might look at each other and think, I hope their joy and luck rub off on us too.

There is a loud knock on my window. I look into the face of

a man I don't know. He seems angry. I lower the window.

'Are you going yet? 'Cause I live here and I want to park.'

I say nothing to this man. I don't like him and so I say nothing. I turn the ignition and pull away. I roll slowly down the street, until I see it. I stop outside. The wall has gone, garden gone, and a car is parked where the flowerbeds used to blossom. There is a porch, and I can see coats suspended in the condensation. I am a stranger. I drive on. Nothing is as it should be.

I look at my watch. Late. I am cold. Waiting for house lights to retire. The alleyway smells the same; I am alone. I see the movement of a fox. It comes closer – they're urbanised now – I kick stones its way and it saunters off, unafraid but irritated. I look over the fence. As I do, the last light disappears. Now I feel nervous; definition of shadows all around. Is that a man? I move against the old gate. Blood pounding. *Move on, move on, move on.* I hear his footsteps recede on the gravel. I count the silence that remains.

I lift the latch easily and secure the gate with a brick. The small torch beam is surprisingly strong, and the jumble of junk at the bottom of the garden appears untouched, apart from the addition of fox faeces and an old trainer. Half a chicken carcass.

I dig through moist leaves until I hit the dirt. I follow the line down from the slatted fence and measure a hand's-width away. I scoop out handfuls of earth until I feel the chilly sensation of tin. I pull it free and wipe the lid clean: Biscuit assortment (we ate them all).

I put nothing back, don't cover my tracks. It will be blamed on a fox. I want to get away from here. I kick away the brick and secure the gate. I stride quickly away. Darkness enfolds the wake of my presence. I was never there.

The Polaroid is surprisingly clear in the early morning light. The girl who became a boy. I am smiling, (I am hiding). The Christmas of my rabbit. Leave something behind, he had said.

I reach for my coffee. I put on another layer and look out over the familiar of my adult world. I unfold his letter. The scrawl of his fifteen-year-old handwriting grips my throat – to my eyes, a jumble of ciphers. To free, to explain.

> *Golan   choice.   were only young.   else die.   tell someone,   not you Elly,   fault.   Coward.   perfect always look after   YOU   always.*

I ARRIVED AS A GREY AFTERNOON CHILL DESCENDED UPON the station and heralded my arrival with the promise of nothing. The station was quiet; only one other passenger disembarked with me, a passenger who carried his home on his back and who strode up the hill with the practised gait of a professional walker. I let him go ahead.

I'd told no one I was coming, not even Alan, and had simply picked up a local cab outside the station. In truth I'd wanted to stay in London, away from everything that said, This is Joe; for the views and the smells and the trees were all him as they were also me, intertwined as we were in this landscape, forged and rooted and held.

I asked to be dropped at the top of the roadway by the old bar gate, by the mossy indented word *TREHAVEN* that we'd first seen twenty-three years ago, when we were poised on the edge of adventure, me with a timid yearning to start my life again, him with a broken heart that had never healed.

It was cold and I wore too little, but the cold felt good and it cleared my head, allowed me to stop and listen to the faint drilling of a woodpecker. And as the hill took me down towards the house, the space he'd left seized me and something somewhere in that space whispered, *He's still here*. I heard it as the hill propelled me towards the silence of meal times and the masked pain, and the open photo albums no longer stored away in musty drawers. *He's still here*, it whispered as my pace quickened and my tears fell, *still here*, until I started to run.

They were in the kitchen, all three of them, drinking tea and eating sponge cake. It was Nelson, Arthur's guide dog, who noticed me first, the little chocolate-brown Labrador who'd become his eyes a year ago when mine could no longer commit full time. He bounded towards the door and barked, and I saw Arthur smile because he knew the bark, knew what it meant, and my mother and father got up and ran towards me, and everything seemed strangely normal that first moment when I arrived. The cracks appeared only after I went up to my room.

I hadn't heard her behind me; the weight she'd lost made her tread lighter, or maybe I was distracted by the sudden emergence of a photograph on my dresser, a photo of me and Joe at Plymouth Navy Days, when we were young, a photo I hadn't seen in almost fifteen years. He was wearing a sailor's hat and I had wanted to laugh, but it hadn't been placed in irony, and so I didn't. My mother picked it up and looked at it – ran her fingers across his face, ran them across her brow.

'We were so lucky that he was ours,' I said.

My mother carefully replaced the photograph.

Silence.

'I've never been a crazy person, Elly, not hysterical. I've been rational all my life and so when I say, he's not dead, it's not wishing or hoping, it's rational; it's clear thought.'

'OK,' I said, and started to unzip my bag.

'Your father thinks I'm mad. Walks away when I say such things, says it's grief making me mad, making me say such things, but I know it, Elly. I know it I know it I know it.'

I stopped unpacking. Halted by the desperate grip of her words.

'Where is he then, Mum?'

She was about to answer when she saw my father standing in the doorway. He looked at her and came towards me and handed me a pile of old *Cornish Times*.

'Thought you might like these,' he said, and backed out of the room, hardly looking at my mother.

'Stay,' I said, but he chose not to hear me and I heard his footsteps heavy and sad on the oaken staircase.

I found him in his workroom. A stooped figure, suddenly old. A makeshift lamp was clamped to an overhead shelf just behind him, and his face appeared soft and masked in the illuminated dust, his eyes dark and sad. He didn't look up as I came in and I went over and sat on the old armchair, the one we'd brought from our old terraced house in Essex, the one that was re-covered in burnt-orange cotton twill.

'I'd do anything,' he said, 'anything to have him back. I pray and I want to believe her, I so do. And I feel I am betraying her. But I saw the images, Elly. And every day I read about the fatalities.'

He picked up a sheet of sandpaper and started smoothing the edge of the bookcase he'd almost finished.

'I've always known something like this would happen. Something has always hung over this family. Something, just waiting. I can't hope any more. Because I don't deserve hope.'

He stopped working and leant over his bench. I knew what he was talking about again and I quietly said, 'That was all a long time ago, Dad.'

'Not for her family, Elly. It's still like yesterday for them,' he said. 'Their grief is my grief now. The circle's complete.'

I LAY ON THE BENCH, SHIVERING, UNTIL NIGHT LAY WITH me and the moon struggled to penetrate the canopy above. The leaves were unyielding, hanging on firm in the sudden chill that succeeded sunset; they would not fall yet – not tonight, at least.

The sounds of unseen creatures and movements – once the sound of creeping dread – were now familiar to me, and kind, and I breathed in the dank mustiness, the earth-laden chill, and filled my nostrils and put out those fires that raged still within. Sleep was mine. Unencumbered by dreams, I slept long, long into the early hours when I awoke to rain. It was almost morning as the sun haloed the outer reaches of the forest. I sat up on the bench; my underside dry. I felt in my pocket and pulled out a half-eaten bar of chocolate. It was dark chocolate, bitter, Arthur's favourite. I always took it with me when we went out for a walk. I broke off a square and let it melt in my mouth. A little too bitter for breakfast, but I was grateful.

I heard the sound of rustling first and knew what it was before I saw it. I hadn't seen it in months, almost a year maybe. The dark intense eyes came out of a pile of leaves, followed by the chestnut fur, the pointed nose twitching in recognition. It stopped in front of me, as if wanting something. I tried to shoo it away with my foot but it didn't flinch this time; stayed staring at me. It didn't even startle at the sound of my phone, the loud ringing harsh in the feeble dawn. Its eyes never left mine as I picked up and nervously said, 'Hello?' And it stayed staring at me as I listened to her voice – now so much older – as she whispered the words, 'Elly, I can't talk for long,' just like she said twenty-one years ago. 'Listen to me, don't give up. He's alive, I know he's alive. Trust me, Elly. You must trust me.'

Its eyes never left mine.

I didn't shower, just changed into an old fishing sweater bought almost fifteen years before. The elasticity had gone, and it hung straight across my hips, hung from the neckline too. Joe used to say it was my comfort. Maybe he was right. It felt coarse and rustic after the cottons of summer; it felt defiant; as if winter was within reach.

Arthur was at the breakfast table when I came down and he was listening to his pocket radio, a single wire dangling from his left ear. The other two had left a note: 'Gone to Trago Mills to buy paint.' Buy paint? I didn't know whether to be glad or not. It was a start, was all I kept thinking. Something they were doing together.

'Coffee, Arthur?' I said, as I pulled apart a croissant.

'No, I'm fine, dear. Had three already and I've got palpitations.'

'Better not then.'

'That's what I thought.'

I bent down and Nelson came towards me. I nuzzled him, rubbed behind his ears and gave him a piece of the pastry, which he tried to refuse but couldn't. He tried so hard to be conscientious, but we as a family had ruined him. From the day he arrived, earnest and full of intention, all we ever saw was the prettiest of souls and treated him as such, until his single-mindedness turned into flighty, everyday distraction. And as I rubbed his belly, the sleekness was now replaced by rotundity, for he had become the receptacle of my parents' grief and ate whatever was offered; preventing them from feeding their own gnawing heartache.

I brought my coffee to the table and sat down.

'It's so quiet here without you all,' he said, turning off the radio. 'Your absence has made me old.'

I reached over and held his hand.

'I can't believe all this. I thought I'd left such violence behind,' and he took out his neatly pressed handkerchief and quietly blew his nose. 'I'm ready now, Elly. Ready to depart. The fear has gone, together with my desire for life. I'm so tired now. Tired of saying goodbye to those I love. I'm so sorry, my darling.'

I kissed his hand. 'There's a new family of herons on the river, I believe. Dad heard them the other day. The young should be ready to leave soon. How about we go and find them?'

He squeezed my hand. 'I'd like that,' he said, and I finished the last of my coffee and dropped the remainder of my croissant into Nelson's grateful mouth.

A brisk wind blew up the valley, carrying occasional rain and the smell of salt, and the water chopped and slapped at the sides of the boat as Arthur yelled in delight. Nelson stood at the bow like a figurehead until a flock of Canada geese startled him as they unexpectedly took flight, and he jumped down and hid behind Arthur's warm spindly legs. I turned off the engine and paddled along the riverbank in search of the large nests the herons always built at water level along this stretch. We hid under overhanging branches, paused to listen to distinct river sounds, and as we beached momentarily on a shingled shelf, the leathery greens and the grey-greens and the black-greens of watergrowth surrounded us, and merged with the dark front that suddenly rolled up the river like thick dark smoke. I barely managed to pull the heavy tarpaulin over us before the first of the lightning flashed and the sleeting rain fell.

'Oh, I see it all!' shouted Arthur, as he staggered out into the rain and lifted his face to the onslaught, squealing as the mad urgency of nature whipped his eager senses. The air rumbled with the cannon sound of thunder, and the lightning bounced from field to tree to field.

'Arthur! Get back!' I shouted, as he fell close to the side.

Again thunder and lightning triumphed, the splintering sound of fractured wood tore through the valley; the loud thump of rain as it hit the river surface before being enveloped by the rising mass. Nelson shook behind Arthur's legs, and again Arthur shouted out into the storm and railed at the loss of his boy, his hallowed gentle boy he'd feel and know no more.

I didn't hear my phone ring, not the first time – the thunderous noise maybe, or the inconsistent signal that faltered during storms. But as the storm moved over and left us with the feeble spray of sunlit rain, that's when I heard it, the ring suddenly echoing amidst the quiet exhaustion of the scarred river valley.

'Elly,' the voice said.

'Charlie?'

'Elly, they've found him.'

The moment I'd waited for. I held my stomach. My legs suddenly shaking. I reached for Arthur's hand. What had they found? What thing had they found that had declared him, him? And as if he could read my silence he quickly said, 'No, Elly. They've *found* him. He's alive.'

... *to a passer-by he might have looked like a man sitting on a bench overlooking Lower Manhattan, enjoying a quiet moment of aloneness away from the wife, from the kids maybe, from the pressures of work. He might have looked like an insomniac, just like the joggers who ran the promenade in those early hours. He might have looked like either of those things, because he was shaded by the trees and nobody would have been close enough to see that his eyes were shut; not close enough to see the trickle of blood from his ear or the dark wet patch that matted his curls on his swollen head; because they weren't close enough to see, he could have been a drunk, sitting on a bench in the early hours of the morning. And nobody was interested in a drunk.*

He was found unconscious at three o'clock in the

morning on 11 September 2001, on a stretch of the promenade at Brooklyn Heights, a place he always went to, to think about life.

It was quite a walk from his house, Jenny, but he did it at night, often instead of a run. He loved the bridge, loved to walk the bridge and never felt afraid of the city's vacant aggression that hugged darkness, because it thrilled him and emboldened him. Could quite simply arouse him. And he was found by a young man who approached him for a light, a man who saw up close the bruising around his mouth, the swollen features of a bursting head. This young man phoned the police and saved his life.

They found nothing on him. No wallet, no phone, no keys, no money, no watch. Nothing to say who he was or where he was from. He wore only a faded red T-shirt and old chinos and brown Havaianas on his feet. He never felt the cold. Not like me. Remember how I'd shiver.

They rushed him to the ER, where they drained the fluid and worked on his head until the swelling retreated. They took him up to the ICU where they put him with four other patients and there he stayed, waiting for his mind to return to gently inform the rest of his body to awaken and live. And there he stayed, quite peaceful, apparently, and immune, until the morning he awoke and tried to pull the tube from his mouth. He didn't know his name or where he lived or what had happened. Or what would happen next. He still doesn't.

All this is fact. What we've just learnt. Will let you know more, Jenny, as it comes.

Ell xx

HER NAME WAS GRACE. GRACE MARY GOODFIELD, TO BE exact, and she was a registered nurse, and had been for twenty-six years with no thoughts yet of retiring. Her folks were from Louisiana and she still holidayed there.

'Have you ever been?'

'No, not yet,' said Charlie, the first day they met.

She lived alone in Williamsburg, had the ground floor apartment in an old brownstone, a happy place, good tenants above and below. 'Space enough for me,' she'd said. 'Kids long since flown; man long since gone.'

Like so many others she wasn't supposed to be at work on 11 September. She was doing mainly night shifts that week, and her morning was to be spent changing over the curtains to heavier ones in preparation for the coming fall. But even before the Towers fell she rushed to the hospital to take up her position like all those others, waiting for the mêlée of survivors and their tales of luck from those upper floors. But, as we know, that didn't happen.

She wasn't needed in ER, and so she went to her office on the ICU floor, and went around the rooms to boost morale, to hand out cookies, and always with a smile, because she was the best shift leader and she knew her staff and she knew her patients. Just not the new one, though, not the unconscious one. No one knew him.

She called him 'Bill', after an old boyfriend who liked to sleep. She would sit with him when the others had visitors, and she would hold his hand and tell him about her life or tell him about what she'd cooked the previous night. She'd tried to look for him on the Missing Persons websites, but it was useless because thousands were missing. The police wanted to help but there was nothing they could do whilst he was under, their minds and resources directed elsewhere; directed to the horror unfolding beyond those safe walls.

She looked at his clothes, those meagre belongings bagged in his locker, and she could piece nothing together of his life. This useless anonymity scared her. She worried he might die lost, with no one knowing; parents and friends not knowing. I'll be there for you, she said one night, as she left after a particularly hard shift.

She brought in different smells and oils and placed them under his nose, anything to flick the switch of memory. She introduced lavender and rose and frankincense to his mind, coffee too, and her latest perfume – Chanel No 5 – which Lisa from emergency had brought back from Paris. She encouraged the other four patients to talk to him if they felt well enough, and soon stories of wars and sex and baseball rebounded across the floor, and only quietened if a nurse was present, something more reminiscent of an old bar than the care unit it was. Sometimes she would bring in music and hold a headphone gently to his ear. She thought he was in his thirties and calculated what songs may have travelled with him throughout his life. She played Bowie and Blondie and Stevie Wonder – all borrowed from her neighbour's collection, the neighbour who lived upstairs.

Almost three weeks later she got the call. Janice ran in and said Bill had woken up. Grace called for a doctor. When she entered he was grabbing for his breathing tube, panicking, his left arm sluggish. 'It's OK,' she said. 'It's OK,' and she stroked his head. He tried to sit up on his own and he asked for water. They told him to sip it slowly, they told him not to speak. His eyes darted around the room. Gerry in the bed by the door said, 'Welcome back, son.'

When he was strong enough, the police returned.

'What's your name?' they asked.

'I don't know.'

'Where are you from?'

'I don't know.'

'Where do you live?'

'I don't know.'

'Is there someone we can contact?'

He rolled over.

'Don't know.'

He did well over the next few days. Ate well, slowly started to walk, but still remembered nothing. He recognised the Twin Towers as structures of architecture, not as places he'd visited for meetings, places that housed people he'd lost. They moved him out of ICU to a single room. They heard nothing from the police. Grace kept an eye on him, tried to see him most days, took him flowers and kept calling him Bill; he didn't mind. And they would talk about magazine articles and watch films. He watched a film with the actress Nancy Portman and he decided he liked her and thought she was funny, and he would have been thrilled at that moment, had he known she was his aunt, but he didn't, of course. He remained locked into a world solely of the present.

When he improved, Grace knew he'd eventually be transferred to a public psych hospital, and that would conceal him deeper, mire him further in a system from which, without memory, he could never return.

He was standing at the window, a forlorn sight, singing a tune he'd picked up from TV. He turned to her and smiled.

'Know how you lost that tooth?' she said, pointing to his mouth.

He shook his head. 'A fight probably.'

'You don't seem like a fighter,' she said. 'Too gentle.'

Then one night, as he lay sleeping, Grace went to his locker and took out his clothes for the last time. They were the only clue she had. She picked up the faded red T-shirt and saw again the faint drawing of a woman – a starlet maybe? – with the words *Six* and *Judy's* above it, barely visible. She turned it over. Could hardly read it: *Sing with all your Hear* across the back.

It was all she had.

She typed in *Six Judy's* and pressed SEARCH. Waited. Nothing on the first page. She reached for her coffee. It tasted stale. She stood up and stretched.

Clicked on the second page.

The word was *Heart*. It was the nineteenth entry:

Choir Sings for Sweet Charity
The Six Judy's are an all-male choir specialising in show tunes and the era of Old Hollywood. We are a non-profit-making group and have supported various charities, including Unicef, HelpAge USA, Coalition for the Homeless, Cancer Research Institute, as well as more personal projects like fundraising for kidney transplants and heart by-passes. If you're interested in us, please contact Bobby on the number below.

It was late, too late to call, but she called anyway. A man answered. He wasn't angry, just tired. She asked him if any of his singers were missing. One, he said. I think I've found him, she said.

'He has a gap in the front of his teeth.'

HIS BACK WAS TO ME, FRAMED BY THE WINDOW. THE TREES beyond were starting to change colour. A plane flew from right to left, skimmed the top of his head, trailed a plume of white lit by intermittent sunshine. It was a normal day outside. Inside, there was a vase of flowers, simple pink roses that Charlie had brought in a few days before; they were all he could get. I'd brought nothing. I suddenly felt shy, frightened maybe, of all he wasn't. He was wearing the shirt I brought him from Paris, but he didn't know that; he didn't know me.

I'd had days to think about this moment. From the time of the phone call when we steered our storm-wracked boat back to shore and hauled our excited selves up the slope towards the house and my parents within. And from the moment I stood in front of them and told them all that Charlie had said and my mother said, 'It doesn't matter, we have him and that's enough.'

And from the moment my father looked at her and said, 'I'm sorry,' and she held him and said, 'He's come back to us, my darling. No sorry.'

Charlie let go of my hand and motioned me forward.

'Hi,' I said.

He turned round and smiled, looked exactly the same; more rested, perhaps, but no bruising, just the same.

'You're Elly?' he said, and put his hand to his mouth, started to bite his nails; a gesture that made him, him. 'My sister.'

'Yeah.'

I went towards him, went to hold him, but he held out his hand instead and I took it and it felt cold. I pointed to his mouth.

'You did that playing rugby, by the way.'

'Ah, I wondered,' he said.

I hadn't seen the gap in years, since he broke the crown on a rogue piece of crab shell. I wondered if I should tell him. I didn't.

He looked at Grace and shrugged. 'Rugby,' he said.

'See, I says you were no fighter, Joe.'

She said 'Joe' as if it were a new word.

We had to go slow. The doctors said that. He was a blank photo album. I wanted to replace all the pictures, but the doctors told me it was important for him to create new ones. Go slow, they said. My parents entrusted Charlie and me to bring him home. But not just yet, the doctors said. Go slow. Work backwards. Allow him to unravel by himself. Go slow.

I saw her in the corridor as I was speaking to my parents. She was relacing her sensible black shoes, styled for comfort, not for fashion. What would I do with fashion? I could hear her say. My parents made me put her on the line, thanked her, invited her to Cornwall, to stay as long as she wanted; 'For ever,' my babbling father shouted, and he meant it, of course. Grace Mary Goodfield, who smelled so wondrously of Chanel and hope. I will know you for the rest of my life.

Charlie and I had already said our goodbyes, and we sat on the bed and waited.

'Well, Mr Joe,' said Grace. 'This is it.'

'I know.'

She reached for him as he moved towards her.

'Thank you,' he said. 'Thank you.'

And he whispered something neither of us could hear.

'You keep in touch now. Get that aunt of yours to send some signed photos for us all. Item of clothing for the raffle would be nice,' she added, laughing.

'We'll send her over in person. Get her on a few ward rounds,' I said.

'Do her good,' said Charlie.

'Even better,' said Grace.

Awkward silence.

'And don't forget – Louisiana – always nice in spring.'

'Spring it is then,' we said.

'I'll never forget you,' said Joe.

'Told you, you were no fighter,' she said, pointing to his mouth.

I am here but I am not yours.

*

He leant against the cab window, distant, quiet, non-reciprocal. We crossed the bridge and the lights lifted the dusk, and Joe eased his face towards the view beyond.

'My God,' he said as the illuminated world fired his imagination until I realised, naïvely, that this was probably the first time he had ever seen it.

'And where were the Towers?' he asked.

Charlie pointed. He nodded and we didn't say any more after that; not about that day or where he was found or how that bridge used to be his favourite bridge – there would be time for that. Instead, we followed his gaze and quietly re-experienced the awe of the city neither of us had felt in years.

Charlie paid the driver and as we got out I felt a sudden chill I hadn't prepared for.

'This is home,' I said to Joe, and ran up the steps expecting him to follow. He didn't. He wandered into the middle of the road and looked up and down the street; trying to get some bearing, I imagine. He was nervous about entering an environment that would give clues to who he was.

Charlie patted his back, encouraged him towards the door. 'Come on,' he said naturally.

The hallway was lit and I could still smell the candle scent of two nights before; the night Charlie had filled me in on what to expect, the night we'd got stinking drunk into the early hours.

The house felt warm and the lighting cast shadows around the hearth and stairwells, and made the rooms look strangely bigger. Joe followed me in; he stopped and quietly looked around. He looked at the photos on the hall walls – a set of three Nan Goldins he'd paid thousands for – but he didn't say anything, and instead ran upstairs and we heard him pacing on both sets of landings, until he ran back down to us and then beyond to the kitchen below. We heard the back door open. The sound of footsteps on the fire escape.

I met him again in the living room. I was kneeling in front of the hearth with a small pile of sticks in my hand.

'I can do that,' he said, and started to place them on the bed of newspaper, awaiting only a taper. It was one of the many moments where his memory divided at a crossroads and allowed him the knowledge of how to light a fire, but not to remember when he last did it, or who he was with. He turned to me and smiled. Would learn to smile a lot; smile when he didn't know what else to say; smile when politeness, fear of hurting – all those things families don't bother with – sat between us.

'Do you think you could talk to them?' I said. 'Just to hear your voice would be enough.'

'Sure,' he said. 'Whatever you want.'

I left him in the room. Caught the odd words like, 'home' and 'doing well' and lots about 'Grace', and I knew it was my mother talking to him, this woman who had read up on so much since his discovery; a woman who was not forcing in her conversation, a woman who could wait that bit longer because she'd already waited and it was enough he was in the world.

He found us in the kitchen. Came down the stairs as if they were fragile. I handed him a glass.

'Here,' I said, and poured out the wine. 'This was your favourite.'

'Right,' he said awkwardly.

We watched him drink.

'It's nice.' He raised the glass to the light. 'Is it expensive?'

'Horribly so,' I said.

'Can I afford it?'

'Think so. You can check your accounts tomorrow, if you want.'

'Am I rich?'

'Not bad.'

'Do I have enough to give away?'

'I don't know,' I said, and shrugged. 'Do you want to give it away?'

'I don't know what I want,' he said, refilling his glass.

He listened to start with, to stories about home life or about my life in London, but would then suddenly take himself off to bed or out of a room, and that was the hardest; the sudden ennui at people he didn't remember, didn't know, had no curiosity in knowing. His interest was held only by stories of Grace or the films he watched in hospital, or Gerry in ICU or the porters, precious stories of his post-accident life, the five weeks of his life that reverberated with the contagion of memory. The life we were not part of.

'What are you writing?' he asked me one day after a hospital checkup.

'A column for a newspaper. It's what I do. My job.'

'What's it about?'

'You, in part. I've called you Max. And Charlie. And Jenny Penny.'

'Who's she?'

'A childhood friend. You knew her once. She's in prison now. Murdered her husband.'

'Nice friend,' he said, laughing. Uncaring.

That threw me. He threw me.

'Yeah, she is,' I said quietly.

We got as close as we could. The smell of burning oil had given way to the stench of the unspeakable. He read the photocopied sheets of paper depicting the Missing, and somewhere I knew he still felt that way. We split up and I watched him work his way past fifty, maybe sixty, smiling faces before he suddenly stopped and touched one of the photos.

'Elly,' he said, and gestured for me to join him. 'It's me.' And there, nestled by the grandmother, with frayed worn edges, was his smiling face; the black and white shimmer of a swimming pool behind him. He took the picture down and folded it; put it into his pocket.

'Let's go home,' I said.

'No. Let's go on.'

I looked back at the empty space. I knew I should have felt happier.

We'd walked too far; he'd overestimated his strength and soon his faced paled beneath exhaustion. We took it slow across the bridge and I told him how he used to love the bridge, and that he'd probably taken it the night of his attack. We headed down to the promenade, to the bench we always sat on; the bench on which he was found by the young man from Illinois, the young man we would later know as Vince.

'Did we come here a lot?' he asked.

'I s'pose so. When we needed to talk, if we had problems. It seemed to work down here, looking over at the city. We'd always talked about this city as kids. Actually, not kids – you know, adolescents – it was our escape; the place we were gonna go to. "New York, New York." You know, everyone's dream. We were going to live it all here. It's where you ran away to, where you flourished.'

'I ran away?'

'Yeah. We both did, in a way. You did it physically, that's all.'

'What was I running from?'

I shrugged. 'You?'

He laughed. 'Didn't get far, then?'

'No, not really.'

He took out the folded sheet of paper and looked at himself.

'Was I a nice person?'

It was strange to hear him refer to himself in the past.

'Yes. You were funny and kind. Generous. Difficult. But so sweet.'

'What problems did I have?'

'Same as everyone else's.'

'Is that why I came here that night, do you think?'

'Maybe.'

'I asked Charlie if I had a boyfriend.'

'And what did he say?'

'He said I never had a boyfriend. I made it hard for people who loved me. Do you know why I did that?'

I shook my head. 'Why does anyone do that?'

He didn't answer.

'I loved you,' I said. 'Still do.'

I looked at the picture still gripped in his hand. Miami. February, nearly eight months before. I'd worried that the holiday was so expensive, so extravagant. How silly, I thought.

'You always looked out for me when we were kids,' I said. 'You protected me.'

He stood up, and knelt down by the bench.

'This is where I was found, right?'

'What are you doing?'

'Looking for blood.'

'I don't think there was much.'

He crouched and leant on the slats.

'Are you waiting for my mind to fully return?'

I took a moment to think how I should answer.

'Yes.'

'What if it doesn't?'

I shrugged.

'Why's it so important for you?'

'Why d'you think? You're my brother.'

'I can still be your brother.'

Not the same, I thought.

'You're the only person who really knows me,' I said. 'It's how we were, how we grew up.'

'That's a bit fucked,' he said. 'No pressure, then?'

And before I could answer he said, 'I think I've found some,' and he leant closer in to the metal foot. 'Do you want to see?'

'No. Not really.'

He got up and came and sat next to me again.

'I feel like sex a lot of the time,' he said.

'Well, I can't help with that.'

He laughed.

'Where did I go?'

'I don't know. Clubs? Saunas? What did Charlie say?'

'Said he'd take me.'

'You need protection these days.'

'I lost my memory – I'm not fucking stupid.'

'Right,' I said.

I lay in bed, restless and overtired, and it was nearly four when I heard the front door. I could have gone out with them but I'd felt like time apart. Wanted to clear my head, rid myself of the bitter clutter piling behind my words, and I'd reached for music instead, music and wine – plenty of both. But now I lay in bed, drowsy and on edge, a vicious thirst replacing the drunkenness that had seen me to sleep.

I heard footsteps on the stairs, just one pair. I waited. There was a gentle tap on my door. I got up and opened it.

'Hey, Ell.'

'Charlie.'

He stumbled forwards, drunk. I guided him to the bed where he fell and rolled over. He looked miserable.

'Where is he?' I asked.

'I dunno. Got picked up and I left 'em to it.'

'You're soaked.'

'Couldn't find a cab.'

No one would take you, more like.

He tried to tell me something about the evening, about a stripper, but the last of his words were barely audible as he buried them in the dent of my still-warm pillow. I took his clothes off and covered him with the duvet, and soon his breath was deep and unlaboured, even.

I pulled back the shutter and looked out. The street looked greasy and reflective; the rain had stopped and the first of the workers – the cleaners, the postal workers – were heading out. I got up and put on a sweater. It smelt of damp wool ever since I'd washed it. Joe told me I could never wear it out, only at home. That was the Joe before.

I crept downstairs to the kitchen and opened the back door to the smell of earth and rain, the smell I associated with Cornwall, and I suddenly longed to go back, longed to grieve in a landscape born of and eroded by grief, where hills fell into the sea in gestures of despair.

I heard the front door just as the coffee came to the boil. He must have noticed the light because he came down the stairs and put his head round the corner and seemed surprisingly sober.

'Hey,' he said. 'Up early or still up late?'

'Not sure. Want a coffee?'

'Coffee would be good,' he said.

We wrapped up and sat outside on the old bistro chairs, the damp slats soon penetrating the skin, but not uncomfortably so. The sound of traffic was slowly climbing over the back wall, a creeping precursor to the hue of sunrise. He looked around at the garden, seemed soothed by it, could have been the light, though, for shadows hide shadows.

'You were a shit gardener who created a beautiful garden,' I said. 'Ginger used to say that you could make a woman pregnant just by looking at her. She loved you.'

He nodded. Sighed deeply.

'Everybody seemed to love me. What am I supposed to do with that?'

I felt the anger creep back into his voice.

'How was your night?' I asked.

'Strange. I got picked up by some kid and went back to his place. And before I got naked, he told me what a cunt I was and that he wouldn't fuck me if I was the last person on earth. Somewhere around that time his flatmate came out to witness the humiliation.'

'I'm sorry,' I said, trying to hide my laughter.

'No, please go ahead. It's doing wonders for me.'

'Refill?'

'Sure.'

I poured out some more coffee.

'So who was he?' I said.

'Face from the past? Someone I treated bad? Someone who *didn't* love me, I dunno. He thought I was taking the piss when I said I couldn't remember him.'

He reached for his cup.

'I went back to the bench,' he said.

'Why?'

'I walked over the bridge because I wanted to feel what it meant to me, the way you said. Feel the person I'm supposed to be. But I couldn't. Something is dislocated; *I'm* dislocated. I sat and I looked at the city and I longed for those last moments again. I thought it might prompt me to remember something, to frighten me, anything. But it was just a bench. I had no sense of peace, no sense of place. I thought it would help. I'm making everyone so miserable. I'm constantly reminded of someone I can't live up to. No one wants the person I am today.'

'Not true,' I said, lacking all conviction.

'Yes it is. I even wish I could go back into hospital; it was a home of some sorts. There's nothing for me out here. I'm lost.'

*

302

Everything changed after that evening. He had no interest after that. I understood now why Charlie had told my parents to let me come instead of them. It was ultimately empty and it hurt. I had to be patient, that's what the doctors said, but my patience would run out at times. He'd reach for a cheese sandwich and I'd say, 'You don't like cheese,' and depending on his mood he'd look at me and quite often say, 'Well, I do now.'

He mentioned that he wanted to live by himself, didn't want us around, so burdened was he by our expectation, and I couldn't tell my parents, waiting as they were for his planned arrival. He would stay out all day, scoff at photographs I tried to show him at night and tried cruelty as a means to alienate us. He said he didn't even like us. The doctors said it was normal.

We hired a car and drove Upstate to Charlie's. We arrived just as the sun was falling below the mountain line. It should have been beautiful; the shifting colours vying for prominence along the horizon, the fire reflected in our faces, but our faces were sad and none of us had said anything in the car. A sombre air muted our friendship; an eventual parting waiting to be heard.

Charlie showed Joe to his bedroom and we didn't see him for the rest of the evening. We didn't feel like eating; too often now meals were replaced by drink. We were unhappy, each daring the other to voice the unspeakable, the malcontent of our lot.

We went outside to the deck, stayed within the confines of light emanating from the large window that framed the towering Mohonk. We saw flickering eyes in the woodland beyond. Deer? A bear cub? Only last month Charlie had seen one as he was clearing the encroaching scrubland. He sat down and lit a cigarette.

'I was sitting out here the night Bobby phoned me, after the phone call from the hospital. Seems a long time since then.'

He stubbed out his cigarette. He was a useless smoker, always had been. 'I'm so tired, Ell.'

I leant down and held him, kissed the back of his neck; gripped hard.

'Don't you walk away from me now,' I said.

I couldn't look at him, as I went back inside. I knew I'd just condemned him.

Joe didn't emerge for two days. Finally stepped out with the sun, as Ginger would have said, and he walked into the kitchen offering to make us toast. We'd already eaten but we said Yes, the gesture was fine and he looked like he was trying. He hadn't shaved in days and a beard was taking hold, and I felt glad. He looked unfamiliar and that made it easier to hate him.

We ate on the deck and dressed against the chill, commented on the sun, all said it was *warm*. The talk was polite. He asked what I'd been doing. 'Writing,' I said.

'Uh-huh,' he said, and ate his toast.

I waited for him to add something critical, something provoking. I didn't have to wait long.

'I think you're one of those people who write instead of live, aren't you?'

'Fuck off,' I said, adding a smile – a composed smile – the way Nancy always did.

'Touched a nerve.'

We stared at each other for a moment; uncomfortable and smiling.

'I'm building shelves in the pilot's hut,' said Charlie. 'I could do with the help.'

'OK,' said Joe.

And as soon as they'd finished their coffees, they headed to the small building on the edge of the runway, striding over clumps of coarse grass, carrying saws and tool boxes, joined in a shared task. Jealousy was what I felt.

I took the car into town and bought supplies for the evening meal, wanted to get steak but ended up with crab – didn't know if I could be bothered with the fiddliness of it all. But he liked crab and so did I, and the fridge would be full so we could last the next few days until decisions were made. He wasn't coming back to England, we were sure of that. Hadn't told my parents. How could I? Nancy was with them now, and that was better. Nancy would be with them when I told them. Nancy, the holder of other people's pain. I suddenly rammed on my brakes. Their eyes stared at me. I nearly hit them. Daydreaming. Had to stop. Just missed the woman and child. The woman was screaming at me, threatening me, the child crying. I pulled into a side street until the shaking had stopped. I was becoming a mess.

They worked not by the clock but until the light ran out, and he seemed revived by the physicalness of the work, the unconscious memory his body felt at working with wood, with the feel of wood. As they walked into the kitchen, with its smells of boiling crab and garlic mayonnaise, they were collaborators in a successful day and my exclusion felt ever more intense. They washed their hands and chatted about the new shelving, the possibility of laying a wood floor, and I listened as I dropped the crabs onto the newspaper, half hoping they would scuttle to the floor and interrupt their rigorous prattling. I placed two bottles of wine on the table and sat down exhausted.

Joe reached across to hold our hands.

'Let us pray,' he said, bowing his head.

I looked at Charlie. *What the fuck is this now?*

He shrugged.

'For what we are about to receive,' said Joe, and then he stopped; looked at us. We lowered our heads and repeated what he'd said.

'I'm only joking,' he said as he reached for a crab and broke off its large front claw. 'Just kidding,' he added, and Charlie laughed. I didn't. Fucker, I thought.

I retreated, said nothing all night, simply drank – we all did; no one was counting – and I felt my rage burn acid hot as I watched him grow in his present, seem happy in his present. I didn't know why I felt like this. *Normal*, the doctor would have said, my feelings were normal. That's what we paid him for, for the diagnosis of normal.

Charlie rubbed my leg under the table, a feeble reassurance; he looked at me and grinned, happy with his day of work, with his reconnection. Joe suddenly stopped chewing, and held his mouth; I thought he was about to be sick. Fucking crab shell, I thought, another fucking tooth.

'Spit it out,' I said.

'I'm fine,' he murmured.

'You used to like crab.'

He held up his hand for me to stop. A palm in front of my face. New gesture. I hated it.

'You used to love it,' I said. 'Oh yeah, I forgot – I'm not supposed to mention what you used to like, am I? Too much pressure.'

'Ell, please,' he said, still not chewing, holding his mouth; eyes closed, thinking maybe, trying not to speak. I got up and went to the sink.

'I can't fucking stand this,' I said, and filled my glass with water.

'Elly, it's OK,' said Charlie.

'It's not OK. I've had enough.'

The sound of his chair grated against the flagstones as he pushed it away and came towards me. He reached for my arm.

'Fuck off, Joe,' I said.

'OK,' and he moved away.

'It's too easy, isn't it? You fight for nothing. You're just not interested in any of it. Not us. None of it. You don't care about what went before. You just fucking mock us.'

'I care.'

'Leave it, Elly,' Charlie said.

'I want to tell you so much but you never ask.'

'I don't know where to start, do I?'

'Just *start*,' I said. 'Just fucking start. Anything. *Something*.'

He stood looking at me, formulating nothing, no words. He held his mouth again, closed his eyes.

'Ell,' he said quietly.

'OK, how about I start? You *like* bananas. And fried eggs well done. You like swimming in the ocean but not in swimming pools and you like avocados but not with mayonnaise, and little gem lettuce and walnuts and sponge cake and date slices and Scotch – blended, surprisingly, not single malt – and you like Ealing comedies and Marmite and lardy cake and churches and blessings, and you even thought about becoming Catholic once, after attending Mass with Elliot Bolt. You like ice cream, but not strawberry, and lamb rare – but not well done – and first-of-the-season chard. You weirdly like boat shoes and collarless shirts, orange round-neck jumpers, Oxford over Cambridge, De Niro over Pacino and—'

I suddenly stopped and looked at him. His eyes were shut and tears were rolling down his face.

'Ask me something,' I said. He shook his head.

'You've had measles and chicken pox. And one girlfriend, Dana Hadley. You've broken three ribs. And a finger. In a door, not playing rugby. You don't like raisins or nuts in chocolate, but you like them in salads. You don't like rudeness. Or ignorance. Or prejudice or intolerance. Ask me something.'

He shook his head.

'You don't like rollerblading, or Starbucks coffee, or their fucking mugs.'

He sat down and held his head. Charlie moved over to the table.

'You can't throw a Frisbee. And you can't dance. You see, that's who you are, Joe. All these things. That's the person I know, and through him is the way you'll know me, because connected to all these things are *moments*, and for so many of them, I was there. And that's the thing that hurts so much.'

'Elly,' whispered Charlie. 'Stop.'

'You see, you were the only person who knew *everything*. Because *you* were there. And you were my witness. And you make sense of the fucked-up mess I become every now and then. And I could at least look at you and think, at least he knows why I am the way I am. There *were* reasons. But I can't do that any more and I feel so lonely. So forgive me. There's not much point any more, is there?'

And for the first time ever, I emerged from his shadow and walked out, unready, into the darkness, and startled the bats at rest.

It was cold, my breath misted, and I realised that autumn had now gone, it was winter once again. I suddenly didn't know where to go, this was not my land, and the darkness here was fierce; strange sounds, a dog bark or coyotes? I should have known the difference but I didn't. This was ancient land, and the further I went towards the shadow of the mountain, I felt its rage and the visions of history.

I sat down in the middle of the old disused runway, a plaything, once, for a rich landowner, now cracked with grass and daisies growing amidst the tarmac. I watched it reach into the night like a frozen river until it disappeared into the black wall of trees, the land boundary of nothingness at the edge of the world.

He came out of the blackness, boldly striding, his blond curls picking up the remnants of moonlight, a white aura surrounding his head. His strange presence had uncovered a loneliness of such devouring longing, one that reached cruelly back into the past, and I knew I could no longer be around him. I would leave the next day; take the bus back to the city, a plane back to London and an explanation back to Cornwall. One day he might return. One day.

He was no longer striding but running towards me and he frightened me. I stood up and started to back away from him, away from his words, away from, 'Ell, wait,' and his outstretched hand, and before long I was running towards the blackness, into oblivion where nothing existed that night except the call of owls and the flight of midges and the ghosts of planes landing, their stuttering engines reaching for land in the bleakest of silence.

'Leave me alone,' I shouted.

'Wait,' he said, and I felt his hand on my shoulder.

'What the fuck do you want?' I said, my fist clenched at my thigh.

'It's just . . . something came back, Ell. In there. Charlie said I needed to ask you.'

'Ask me what?' I said, my voice cold, unrecognisable.

'The word "*Trehaven*". What is it?'

I LOOKED UP AND SAW ALAN WAVING FROM THE BRIDGE. He looked nervous as we approached and when we stood in front of him he spoke clearly and loudly as if it wasn't only memory that my brother had lost, but his hearing too.

'I'm Alan, Joe. I've known you since you were a little boy. Since you were that high,' and he gestured with his hand at a height that would actually have made my brother a midget.

'Since he was *sixteen*,' I said.

'Was he really that old?' Alan said, turning to me.

'Yes. I was eleven.'

'Well, you weren't a big sixteen,' Alan said. 'That's all I can say.'

'Well, that's good to know,' said my brother. 'And Alan, don't worry. I remember you.'

'Ah, you've made my day,' he said, and picked up our bags

and marched ahead of us up the slope towards his new people carrier with electric sun roof and 'nat sav', as he called it, and the hanging air freshener that held the photo of six-year-old Alana.

Joe suddenly stopped halfway up and looked down on the small station, soft and blurred in the light, the hanging baskets rocking gently in the breeze, the contents forlorn and brown and long since passed, like the summer they coloured. He did that often; just suddenly stopped to help a crippled memory as it faltered midway to comprehension.

'What is it?' I said.

'Ginger, I think,' he said. 'Singing down there. "Beyond the Sea"? Evening dress? Could that be real?'

'Turquoise, high cut?'

'Yes.'

'Yep, that's real. Welcome to your family,' and I ushered him up to the car.

Alan dropped us at the top of the track and we waved as he disappeared along the roadway, carving through the desolate hedgerows like a wheeled scythe. I could smell salt in the air; the tide was probably high and a breeze skipping on the surface welcomed us back. We headed down the gravel track, now more leaf covered than ever, until Charlie shouted, 'Race ya!' and we ran towards the wooden gate, the imaginary finishing line at the end of the way. Charlie got there first, Joe second, my heart wasn't in it so I gave up, and they waited panting as I approached, soaking up the smells and sights of the trees naked in the harsh light of an overcast day. I looked up and saw a lone blackbird plume puffed and unmoving on a branch shrunken by the cold. It buried its beak back into its chest. I blew on my hands and ran towards the gatepost.

'This I remember,' said my brother, as he bent down and

trailed his finger down the letters T R E H A V E N, leaving a green stain on his skin. And then something caught his eye, on the outer surface, to the left of the letters. I knew he saw it, knew he saw the JP and the badly carved heart and the letters CH falling beneath, letters over twenty years old, feelings over twenty years old, hidden, though, for weeks. I knew he saw it, but he didn't say anything, not to me, not to Charlie, and we quickly marched down the slope, he momentarily falling behind, watching us, his eyes piercing my back, finally wanting something, as the pieces shifted and sense came back, and the unspoken that hung above their friendship suddenly spoke in letters as raised as Braille.

We turned the corner, and I'd almost forgotten the effect the house had, bone white and stately in the clearing. In that moment it reached into my heart and buried itself there for ever. They were lined up in front of it in what looked like order of height, and as we got closer – as *my brother* got closer – this formality became unbearable for them and it was my father who broke rank first, then my mother, and they ran towards him, arms splayed out wide, adults playing planes, bearing down on him, shouting and smiling, until they took him in their arms and held him and quietly said, 'My boy.'

'I'm your aunt. Nancy,' said Nancy, breathless from the run. 'I expect you remember me, though.'

'Of course I do,' my brother said, and smiled. '*Raining in my Heart*.'*

'Ah,' said Nancy, pretending to be shy.

'Storm in a teacup, more like,' said Arthur, trying hard to rein in an over-excited Nelson.

* Raining in my Heart was a 1983 Australian film set on an outback farm brought to its knees by a desperate drought.

'You were really good in that film, Nance,' my brother said.

'Thanks, honey,' she said, beaming, as if awards season were suddenly approaching.

And then Joe turned to Arthur.

'Hey, Arthur,' he said. 'How are you doing?'

'Everything you need to know about me is in this,' he said, and pulled his autobiography out of his jacket pocket.

I could hear them downstairs, laughing, and I should have got up but the mattress felt good against my back and I wanted to sleep through the afternoon into the night, through the days and weeks that would follow, so heavy were my eyes after the long hours of empty waiting. But I sat up and poured a glass of water, drank half of it, then some more.

I went to the window and saw them wander down the lawn to the jetty, just as the light was losing its battle against thickening cloud cover. My brother bent down and looked at himself in the water. Charlie knelt down next to him. It was an image I thought would be lost to me for ever, lost under the dust and rubble of that other time that haunted the past, nightghoulish and unwelcome, a time that ripped you from the safety of sleep like flesh away from bone.

My mother came up behind me. I'd heard her on the stairs, heard her call my name, but I felt too tired, too quiet to answer. I felt her breath on my neck.

'Thank you for bringing him home.'

I wanted to turn round and say something, but there were no words, just this image of her son, my brother, amidst us once again; the light clinging to him in the frail dusk, the light that said *never go out*.

Things came back to him consistently after that; slowly at first, sometimes erratically, once even in the middle of a weather front that tore through the landscape, uncovering images and moments that placed him firmly at the scene. He re-covered his tracks along moors and cliff tops, secret paths down to beaches, ice-cream cones he hadn't eaten for years, the taste of vanilla – leading to a memory of a bell floating on the water. 'Could that be right?' he asked. I nodded. *Yes.*

We would follow him, this motley crew of a family, redis-covering memories and incidents long lost to the busyness of life, and we lived again through the vividness of his recall. He'd listen to our stories and ask questions and piece together events, mentally linking the participants until a connection was made, a ragged family tree held together by used tape.

And he uncovered in us a curious need: that we each secretly wanted him to remember us the most. It was strange, both vital and flawed, until I realised that maybe the need to be remembered is stronger than the need to remember. But I'd relinquished my claim to such a position a long time ago. He was so often not the person *I* remembered him to be; long gone was the fragile cynicism that kept him away from normal human encounter, now replaced by a bountiful enthusiasm that saw life like a child. Sometimes I'd miss it, the barbed comment, his darkness, dangerous and poetic, that kept me on the edge, those three-o'clock-in-the-morning calls that I somehow doubted would ever happen again, those calls that made me feel whole and well.

And sometimes his memory buckled at discretion and gave way to the revelations of secrets he'd once promised never to disclose, like the moment he turned to me on the path down to Talland and said, 'So how much *did* Andrew Landauer pay you for sex?' to which I replied, 'Not enough,' as I marched off arm in arm with Nancy, away from the shocked faces of my parents, who were trying to put two and two together, and coming up with nothing close to thirty pounds and sixty pence, the price of that mini cab from Slough.

Or like the moment we settled down for dinner and he turned to my parents and said, 'Have you ever forgiven him?'

And they said, 'Who?'

And he said, 'Mr Golan.'

And they said, 'For what?'

And he told them.

I waited for them outside. It was a cold night but I felt nothing as I sat and watched a bat flicker across the French-navy sky. I knew I'd kept them from my life. Certain years I'd closed doors on them, as if it had been about preventing them from knowing that damaged part of me, the part that once, only they could have put right. I knew I'd hurt them with this distance, with this silence, and now they'd understand; but at what price?

I heard the door open behind me. Saw the shaft of light move left to right, then still. My parents appeared in front of me, bereft and inadequate. My mother sat next to me and took my hand.

'Why didn't you tell us?'

I shrugged. Even then I didn't have the definitive answer.

'I don't know,' I said. 'I was shy. And he was my friend. And I didn't really know what to say.'

'But what about after? When you were older?'

'I got on with life. It's what children do. And I became OK.'

'But we never had a chance to look after you,' my father said, 'or to make it right.'

'You've always made it right,' I said. 'Both of you. Things happen. To everyone. No one escapes.'

'But it's been hard,' she said.

'And I've done all right. Please, let's not go back.'

'But you have to let us,' said my mother, and she reached for me under those covers and pulled back the years. And she enveloped me and took me out of that darkness, and for a brief moment in her arms, as time and memory receded, I faltered and we did go back. And it was right.

'CAN I SWIM?' WAS ALL MY BROTHER HAD SAID. A QUESTION of possibility or safety, I couldn't fathom which, but I dropped anchor and harnessed us to the sandy floor, a mere twenty feet below.

It was three weeks before Christmas and we'd been blessed with a day of freak sunshine that felt like the start of summer again, a day when the air was warm and unchallenged, and only the lack of bee sounds and leaves on trees placed us in the grip of a much later season. My brother felt the temperature – still in December's icy grip – and his flesh pimpled as he peeled off the last layer of clothing.

'Coming in?' he said.

'No, thanks,' I said.

'Charlie?' he said, goading him with his eyes.

'Maybe.'

He dived off the stern and we watched him glide just below

the surface like the lone seals that often played along this stretch of coastline. He surfaced spitting sea water and laughter, and it was another first for him. The cold didn't matter as the sensation gripped his body, another reminder of the return of life, a reminder for *us* to live. I hurriedly peeled off my clothes and beat Charlie to entry, and the cold took my breath away as I swam below into the sandy green depth, my eyes adjusting to the quiet lone world below. I remembered the first time I discovered this world – I must have been ten – eleven, maybe – and I wore a wet suit stuffed with rocks to weigh me down. Now as I sat on the rippled seabed, I looked up and was sure I saw their legs entwined above me. But the water could play tricks. Things distorted, things magnified; even hopes. My lungs felt tight – I was out of practice – and I swam eagerly to the shimmering line above my head and surfaced away from the boat. I saw them holding on to the rope that hung from the stern. I saw my brother place his hand over Charlie's hand. I saw him reach towards his mouth and kiss him. I saw their future at last.

We were scattered about that afternoon, embroiled in tasks long kept on hold. My parents were inside creating a new on-line advertisement for their bed and breakfast, now that they felt ready again for guests. Nancy was sitting in a deck chair next to Nelson and me on the lawn, finishing off her screenplay about a Second World War bisexual double agent, which she'd casually entitled 'Playing for Both Sides'. (A film that would actually go into pre-production the following year, but not, thank goodness, with its working title.) Charlie and Joe were at the bottom of the lawn by the water playing an extreme form of catch. They were throwing it as if it was a rugby ball and launched it high into the air, careful not to let it fall in case it should crack.

I didn't know why they'd bought it in the first place, all they'd said was that they were cooking that night, cooking authentic Thai curry or something similar, and they needed it because it would make all the difference to the flavour, and so they bought it – the only one in the shop, of course – and now they were playing with it as if it was a rugby ball. It was Joe who threw it that final time, launched it high into the air, and Charlie knew it had gone too far, way before it had passed over his head, and he ran back just as Arthur unexpectedly came out of his cottage. It would have been all right if Arthur had stopped momentarily to tuck in his shirt as he usually did, or if he'd fumbled just that second longer, positioning his cane in front of him, or even if he'd just kept going. But he didn't. He stopped, sensing something hovering above him, a bird maybe? And as he instinctively looked skywards, a shadow quickly descended upon his head and a smile formed upon his lips, until there was an almighty Crack! and Arthur lay motionless on the floor; a smashed coconut by his side.

Nancy and I got to him first and shouted that he wasn't breathing. I saw Charlie fumble, look for a phone and then he ran inside. I felt for a pulse; nothing.

'Try again!' shouted Joe, running up the slope.

'He's dead,' Nancy whispered to me.

'Impossible. He can't be. It should have happened ages ago.'

'What do you mean?' said Nancy.

'This is all wrong.'

'What are you talking about?'

'The *yogi*,' I said.

'What *yogi*?'

Suddenly Joe ran over to us. 'Count me,' he said. 'Let me know when I've done thirty,' and we watched as he pumped and willed life back into the bony, unresponsive body. At thirty he bent down and breathed into his mouth, twice. Back up to the chest, thirty. Down to the mouth. Twice. No response.

'Come on, Arthur,' I said. 'Don't do this now.'

'Come back to us, Arthur,' said Nancy. 'Fuck the yogi.'

Charlie ran out with my parents and took over as Joe sat down exhausted onto the lawn. I counted for Charlie. Thirty; down to the mouth; no response. The sound of an ambulance racing towards us. Seventeen, eighteen, nineteen, twenty.

'Come on, Arthur,' said my mother. 'Come on, you can do it.'

'Come on, honey,' said Nancy. 'Breathe, damn it!'

And then all of a sudden, on twenty-seven, I think it was, Arthur coughed, or gasped for air; something that forced his body back to breath. He reached for my hand, and squeezed it frailly; but squeezed it. And just as the paramedics were running across the lawn he looked over at Joe and said, 'Wipe those tears away, my boy. I'm not dead yet.'

I bent down towards him and said, 'How did you know he was crying, Arthur?'

And he said, 'I can see again.'

EVERYONE TOLD ME NOT TO BOTHER, BUT TO WAIT. SAID she'd be out sometime in the New Year. Should have been out before Christmas; I knew that, my father knew that, but the Powers That Be refused. And so I turned up that freezing Wednesday, even though I knew she wouldn't see me – she never had, even after all these years. But I had to see it out, the pact we'd invisibly made, the one that said I am always here for you, communicated in letters and a newspaper column limping towards its finishing line, screaming for her return.

There was no warmth at all that afternoon, not even in the cab from the station; the heater had broken.

'Sorry it's a shit car, miss,' the young man had said. 'I can blow on your hands instead, if you like?'

'I'll manage,' I said.

*

I waited in line holding a small bag of presents, unwrapped, of course – I'd learnt my lesson. I looked behind and saw a young man fidgeting with his phone; they'd take that from him soon enough. I could see it was his first time and usually I kept away from such interactions, but that afternoon I offered him a piece of chocolate, which he gratefully accepted, as much for the sustenance as for the relief of finally having company.

'First time?' I said.

'Can you tell?'

'Yeah, I'm afraid.'

'Cold, isn't it?'

'Freezing,' I said and looked at my watch.

'Who are you visiting?' he asked.

'A friend. She'll be out soon.'

'That's great,' he said. 'My sister's in for three years. Just starting.'

'That sucks.'

'It does, just before Christmas an' all,' he said, and started to stamp his feet. 'Is it all right for them? Inside, I mean.'

'Not bad. People tell me there are plenty worse.'

'That's good then,' he said. 'I'd hate her to be in a shitty place.'

'She'll be all right. Most people end up all right.'

The gates opened and the queue moved forwards.

'Good luck, eh?' I said as we started to move forwards.

I passed through security effortlessly, but I knew the routine by now and they often smiled at me, or enquired about my health. I was known here, had a reputation, the one who always turned up but was never seen, the subject of so much speculation: I was the jilted lover. The hated family member. The Christian volunteer eager to spread the Word.

The visitors' hall was warm, for a change. The decorations were the same as last year, faded and dog eared, and they drooped the same way and brought no smile to the Queen as they hung around her frame in a way that verged on treason. I thought about the tree we'd just put up in Cornwall, the one that joined floor to ceiling in a dense mass of green-scented pine. We'd dressed it a couple of days before, and Arthur had climbed the ladder to place the star on top, now that he had one good eye to see out the rest of his days, and to release Nelson to be the simple dog he was.

The women started to come out, and I saw the young man from the queue joined by his sister – she was one of the first to enter – who looked so happy to see him. And then Maggie over to the left; her daughter was wearing a new track suit. They turned to me and waved. I smiled. Maggie reminded me of Grace Mary Goodfield, and I thought again about her wise ways and sensible shoes and the visit she would make to us in February. I thought how well she would have got on with Ginger, Ginger the Brave. I started to write a gift list – a monocle for Arthur, he'd always wanted a monocle – and as I did a shadow fell across my page, a dark looming cloud from outside, or so I thought. I waited a moment for it to pass on but it didn't, it stayed put.

And when I looked up, she was there.

Gone was the plumpness of those early years, the wild hair she hid her shame behind, the clothes she never grew into. All replaced now by a calm beauty. But the eyes, they were her; the eyes and the smile.

'Hello, Elly,' she said.

I stood up and held her. She smelt like she did as a child, she smelt of chips, and suddenly that world opened up once again, a world unlocked by a simple smell, a world we might finally put right; and as I pulled away to look at her again, she handed me a small tissue-wrapped gift.

'Open it,' she said. And I did.

There, sitting in the palm of my hand, was the fossil; the coiled impression of the creature from another time. *Nothing stays forgotten for long.*

'I kept it safe for you.'

The sun was low; orange emanating across the ancient cityscape, burnished by the modern. We were wrapped in blankets, and candles burned on the battered table, emitting strong gusts of tuberose. I watched her looking out over the rooftops, over the meat market and the people below, and I thought of the path that had brought us here, of the strange day of reconnection six years ago, when her card arrived and pulled me onto her journey. She turned round and smiled. Pointed to the horizon.

'Look, Elly, it's almost gone.'

'Ready to say goodbye?' I said.

'Ready,' she said, and sat back down next to me. I handed her the computer and she started to type.

Acknowledgements

This book could not have been written without the love and encouragement of so many people.

I'd like to thank Mum, Simon and Cathy for a lifetime of support and making so much possible, and to my dear friends here and abroad who have helped along the way; especially Sharon Hayman and David Lumsden for the best years shared. Thank you, Sarah Thomson, for being such a trusted and erudite reader.

My gratitude always to Eamonn Bedford for taking a chance on me when few would, and for introducing me to Robert Caskie – literary agent, friend, unsurpassed in both roles. Thank you for your guidance, Mr Caskie.

My thanks to Leah Woodburn, my editor, for making this a better book, and to all at Headline Review for their overwhelming support and enthusiasm.

Thank you, Patsy, for everything.

Read on for an exclusive preview
of Sarah Winman's new novel

A
Year of
Marvellous
Ways

1

SO HERE SHE WAS, OLD NOW, STANDING BY THE ROADSIDE
waiting.

Ever since she had entered her ninetieth year Marvellous
Ways spent a good part of her day waiting, and not for death,
as you might assume, given her age. She wasn't sure what she
was waiting for because the image was incomplete. It was a
sense, that's all, something that had come to her on the tail
feather of a dream – one of Paper Jack's dreams, God rest his
soul – and it had flown over the landscape of sleep just before
light and she hadn't been able to grasp that tail feather and pull
it back before it disappeared over the horizon and disintegrated
in the heat of a rising sun. But she had known its message:
Wait, for it's coming.

She adjusted the elastic on her large glasses and fitted them
close to her face. The thick lenses magnified her eyes tenfold

and showed them to be as blue and as fickle as the sea. She looked up and down the stretch of road once grandly known as the High Road, which was now used as a cut-through by heavy farm vehicles on their way to Truro. The familiar granite cottages – ten in all – built a century ago to house men for the farms and gardens of large estates, were boarded up and derelict, visited only by ghostly skeins of gorse and bramble that had blown in like rumour from afar.

They called it a village, but St Ophere was, technically, a hamlet, since the church that had given its name to the cluster of dwellings was situated in the tidal creek below where old Marvellous lived. There wasn't a schoolhouse either, for that was situated two miles west in the coastal hamlet of Washaway, a place that had lived up to its name earlier that year when the great drifts of snow had turned effortlessly into floods. But what the village did have, however, was a bakehouse.

Back-along, visitors to the area had often called the village 'Bakehouse' instead of its saintly name because Mrs Hard, the owner, had painted BAKEHOUSE in pink lettering across the grey slate roof: an elegant contrast to the once-white stone walls.

Every morning, when the oven was hotten ready, Mrs Hard used to ring her bell and her customers stirred, and unbeknownst to her, so did every drowned sailor from The Lizard to The Scillies as that bell had been scavenged from a salvaged wreck. The village women would take down their uncooked pies and pasties and loaves and load them into the burning embers. Mrs Hard use to call her oven 'Little Hell', and if you got the position of your pie wrong and took someone else's, that's where you would end up. Well, that's what she told the children when they came to collect their mothers' cooked offerings. It was the cause of many a disturbed night, as children burned up under their oft-darned sheets fearing what was to come if they ever chose wrong.

It had been a destination village on account of its bread. Now, in 1947, it was nothing more than a desolate reminder of the cruel passing of time.

The breeze stirred and lifted the old woman's hair. She looked up to the sky. It was lilac-grey and low, rain-packed, but Marvellous doubted that rain would fall. Blow away, she whispered. She crossed the road and stood in front of the bakehouse. She placed her lamp on the step and pressed her palms firmly against the weather-beaten door. Mrs Hard? she whispered softly.

It was Mrs Hard who had once told Marvellous that she was so good at waiting her life would be filled with good things.

Patience, that's what your father should have called you, she said. *Patience*.

But I'm not patient, said Marvellous. I'm *diligent*.

And Mrs Hard had looked down on the barefooted child with fancy words and ragged clothes, and thought how ungodly it was to rear a child in the woods, running wild and free like a Cornish Black pig. The girl needed a mother.

You need a mother, said Mrs Hard.

I had a mother, said Marvellous.

No. You had a *something*, said Mrs Hard. But I could be your mother.

And she waited for an answer but no answer came from the child's horrified mouth. Mrs Hard shook her head and said, Just you remember, though, it is patience that is a virtue and patience that is godly.

Mrs Hard liked the word 'godly'. She liked God, too. When her husband moved out in 1857, lured by the promise of wealth from South African mines, Jesus and the well-loved reverend moved in. The transition was seamless, as was the first gold mine her husband went to, and the poor man was shunted from pit to pit across the Rand until he died scratching in that foreign dark for a glimpse of that golden key: the one that would fit a lock to a better life.

'*Breathe on me, Breath of God, Fill me with life anew*'.

That's what Mrs Hard had written above the bakehouse door when she heard of her husband's death. Later on, someone – and old Marvellous smiled as she could still make out the faint ochre words that had stained her hands – had changed 'breath' to 'bread', but Mrs Hard never knew because she rarely looked up.

Salvation, for me, will come from the dirt, she once told Marvellous.

Like a potato? said the young child.

The weather vane creaked overhead. October dusk fell quickly on the hamlet as crows upon the overnight dead. Must be nearly November, thought Marvellous. Lights flickered in the distant villages, a solemn reminder of the passing of this one. She took out a box of matches and lit her oil lamp. She stood in the middle of the road and raised the lamp to the hills beyond. I'm still here, the gesture said.

A shaft of yellow light fell upon the hedgerow where a granite cross grew out of a bank of flattened primroses. Marvellous had always believed the cross to be an after-thought, hastily erected after the First War, as she could call it now. '1914–1918', it read, with the names of long-gone faces underneath. But there was one name, she knew, that was not on the list. The name of Simeon Rundle had been excluded from the list.

Back in 1914 when the tide of war had rolled upon the

unsuspecting coast, village life had come to a sudden halt. There were no more fairs, no more dances, no more regattas because the men left and life froze in perpetual wait. A village without men dies, said Marvellous, and the village slowly did. The well-loved reverend was sent to a new parish in the City of London and shortly afterwards Mrs Hard received news that he had been killed in a Zeppelin air raid. She lay down on the shores of Little Jordan, as she referred to the creek, and willed her life to end. It obeyed straight away, such was the force of her will, and the bakehouse oven went out and God beat a retreat. Those left behind prayed constantly for peace but prayers came back with Return to Sender stamped all over them. Only the roll call of the dead grew.

But then one mild morning in May, Peace did appear, for that was the name given to a child born six months before the fighting stopped. Overdue, the child was, refusing to enter until the guns ceased, until the madness ceased, as if no amount of pushing or urging could force Peace into a broken world. And even then, when she came, it was reluctantly. As if she knew. Feet first and a head not budging, all mixed up, she was, feet and hands and legs and a cord. Like a calf.

A head weighed down by the burden of a name, said Marvellous as she whispered and twisted and pulled that child free.

Peace. It's just not as simple as that. And of course it wasn't.

Old ways of life don't return when the lives themselves have never returned. Only Simeon Rundle returned, came back to his new sister Peace, carrying a whole heap of horror with him. One morning, the villagers found him down by the creek, up to his neck in river mud and his own shit, waving a white handkerchief at a large hermit crab.

With his swollen tongue flapping out of his mouth like a slipper, he shouted, I thurrender, I thurrender, I thurrender, before raising his father's shotgun and blasting his heart *clean* from his chest. Or so the story goes.

The villagers gasped – two fainted – as it splattered against the church door like an ornate red knocker. The new lay preacher rushed out proclaiming it was the Devil's own work. Unfortunately, such a careless declaration flew swiftly on rumour's eager wings, and it wasn't long before the village of St Ophere acquired a taint that even the welcome addition of electric light in 1936 couldn't completely eradicate.

There was nothing actually wrong with the place. It was rightness that was at a tilt. Tides seemed higher, mists gathered there thicker and vegetation grew faster, as if nature was doing its best to correct the error, or if not to correct it then at least to hide it. But the suspicion of ill luck remained, and that's why the people slowly left: a steady stream of absences like bingo balls pulled from a hat. Migrating to distant villages whose lights still flickered in a low autumn sky.

Marvellous took a last look up and down the High Road, satisfied that whatever she was waiting for hadn't passed her by. The wind had picked up and the clouds were blowing through. She held the lamp high and crossed the road to the memorial and the standpipe, and made her way through the meadow where she had once kept a cow. The temperature was falling and the grass wet underfoot, and she thought the morning would reveal the first crust of frost. She could see the wood ahead, her ankles braced for the gentle incline and the careful march through the sycamores, the hazels and the sweet chestnuts down towards her creek. The tide was out. She could smell the saltmud, her favourite smell, the smell, she believed, of her blood. She would rake up a pan full of cockles and steam them on a fire that would burn a tiny hole in the night. Her mouth began to water. She stumbled and fell next to a blackthorn bush and made use of the mishap by picking two pocketfuls of sloes. She saw the light from her caravan up ahead. Felt, strangely, lonely. Never get old, she whispered to herself.

Late. An owl hooted and the dark eyes of night gazed unblinking towards the horizon. Marvellous couldn't sleep. She stayed awake sitting by the riverbank keeping the moon company, a pile of shucked cockleshells at her feet. She huddled in the warmth of firelight, her yellow oilskin raincoat bright and pungent and hot to touch. The stars looked faint and distant but it may have been her eyes. She once used binoculars, now she used a telescope; soon night would capture day for ever. She felt comforted by the blurred outline of her old crabber rocking gently on the tide; the familiar creak of rope against wood was a good sound in the undulating nocturnal silence.

She had lived in the creek almost her whole life long and had been happy there – almost – her whole life long. Islanded in the middle was the small church that had once been a chapel but was now a ruin. For as long as she could remember the tide had carved around the church until the church had broken away from the people or maybe the people had broken away from the church? It was so long ago now that old Marvellous couldn't remember what had happened first. But the tide had carved its path until church and headstones and faith had all gone adrift. Sunday services used to be held when the tide was at its lowest point, sometimes at daybreak, sometimes at dusk, and once, she remembered, in the dead of night, a lanterned trail of believers sang their way up the riverbed like pilgrims seeking Galilee.

> Yes, we'll gather at the river,
> The beautiful, the beautiful river;
> Gather with the saints at the river
> That flows by the throne of God.

She swigged from a bottle of sloe gin. Saint's nectar, it was, flowing by the throne of God. Amen. Light from the altar candle slinked out of the church, dusting the tops of gravestones that the tide had mercifully spared. It was its own star, thought Marvellous. She lit that candle every night and had done so for years. A lighthouse keeper, that was what she really was. That's what had drawn Whatshisname to her shore during the war years. That, and the music, of course.

Whatshisname. The *American*. She had watched him go into the church as a shadow, and when he had emerged he was still a shadow with deep hues of mauve emanating from his dark skin, and from his mouth the glowing tip of a cigarette pulsed like the heart of a night insect. He walked across the dry riverbed lured by a familiar song, and as he pulled himself up the bank, he saw the wireless, sitting in a battered pram parked beneath the trees.

He said, Louis Armstrong.

And she said, Marvellous Ways, nice to meet you at last.

And he laughed and she had never heard laughter like that, not in all her days, and his eyes flashed as bright as torchlight. He sat with her, and the table rocked and the river rippled as bombers flew over and the air raid sirens sounded and bombs fell over the Great Port, over Truro too, and barrage balloons cast deep shadows across the sky, and Louis Armstrong sang of lips and arms and hearts as anti-aircraft guns pounded against the indigo dark, and two strangers sat quietly under a tree that had seen it all before.

He talked about his grandfather back home in South Carolina in the Low Country, talked about the fishing trips they took along the oozy marshes, how the smell of mud and salt were the smells of home, and Marvellous said, I know what you mean. And he told her of the trestle bridges that glowed pink at dusk and cedars that grew out of the lush wetlands and the heavy scent of tea olive and jasmine, which reminded him of his late mother. He said he missed eating catfish, and Marvellous said, So do I, even though she had only ever eaten dogfish. Together they toasted Life and clinked their mugs and pretended they were somewhere far far away.

He came often after that. Brought her doughnuts from the American doughnut factory in Union Square, and they ate them with strong black tea even though he preferred coffee, and they listened to the radio Rhythm Club and tapped out rhythms with their jitterbug feet. Sometimes he brought tins of Spam, corned beef, too; he never let her go hungry. And once he brought her a poster of a film she had seen a couple of years before. He was thoughtful like that.

But then days before the planned invasion of France, he asked her for a charm.

A charm? she said.

A lucky charm. To bring me back safely, he said.

She looked into his eyes and said, But that's not what I do. I've never made charms.

Oh, but that's what people said you did.

That's what they've always said, and she held his hand instead and the only charm she had was hers and it radiated out.

June 1944 was The Last Goodbye. Those American boys were shipping out. He strutted over whistling, all gabardine trousers and Hawaiian shirt, gosh he looked so smart. He gave her all he had left – chocolate, cigarettes, stockings – and they sat down under the tree and drank tea and listened to Armstrong and Teagarden, Bechet, too, and someone else who would never be as famous. She watched the young man play rhythm upon his knees, watched his mouth turn clarinet. In that moment, either side of him, she saw two futures vying for space. In one he lay still on Omaha Beach. In the other he sat still, head in a book, trying to make something of himself in a country coloured by hate. When he stood up to leave she said, Go left, and he said, What's that? She said, I don't know what it means but you will when the time comes. You must go left.

So long, Marvellous, he waved.

So long, Henry Manfred Gladstone II, she waved. *Henry Manfred Gladstone II*. So *that* was his name.

It's been a pleasure, he said.

The night grew wild with movement. The concrete barges began to depart and thousands of men embarked from piers and beaches, and there was such a kerfuffle, and yet by morning all was quiet. The generators were quiet. The smell of diesel subsiding. The Americans had left and had left behind tales of romance and unborn children, and so much joy, and it was the women who cried because they always did.

So long, Henry Manfred Gladstone II, she whispered. It's been a pleasure.